For *Love* *Alone*

For Love Alone

A Novel

ANITA STANSFIELD

Covenant Communications, Inc.

Cover photography by Grant Heaton Productions

Published by Covenant Communications, Inc.
American Fork, Utah

Printed in the United States of America
First Printing: January 1999

06 05 04 03 02 01 00 99   10 9 8 7 6 5 4 3 2 1

ISBN 1-57734-427-8

To the many friends who have helped me along the way,
and continue to be a source of great support and inspiration.
You know who you are.
I couldn't have done it without you.

And a special thank-you to my readers. . .
Through you, my characters have truly come to life.

CHAPTER ONE
Highland, Utah

*M*allory Taylor collapsed onto the couch and wrapped her arms around her middle. It was the first minute she'd been completely alone since her world had blown apart. She'd cried initially, but then a deep numbness had enveloped her, making her feel as if she might explode from unvented emotion. And now, in the silence of her empty house, with no one close by attempting to console her, Mallory's mind recounted all that had happened. She couldn't believe it. The more she attempted to make sense of this, the more confused she became. All these years, she had believed that everything was fine. She'd had no reason to think that her marriage wasn't good, that her husband wasn't happy. Had she been blind? Was she stupid? Had she done something to bring this on? Could she have said or done something to prevent it from happening?

As the questions struck deeply, Mallory's numbness began to dissipate. The first sob erupted on a painful wave that racked her entire body. She cried until there was nothing left in her. She felt completely drained of energy, as if she'd been struck by some invisible train. The numbness returned, allowing her thoughts to outweigh her emotions, and she attempted to sort through her memories in search of answers—anything to help make sense of this. With her upbringing and background, she'd believed that she knew how to make a marriage work. Had she missed something somewhere? Had she and Brad really been as happy as she'd believed? Or had there been problems that she'd simply not seen? Obviously there had been. But what?

Brad had always seemed so confident and strong. He was successful in every aspect of his life, and loved by everyone who knew him. And now that he was gone, where would she ever begin to pick up the pieces and make a life for herself? How could she start over when she didn't have any idea at all why this had happened? She just didn't understand.

The first time Mallory had laid eyes on Brad Taylor, she felt drawn to him in a way she'd never felt before. She'd always been attracted to the tall, dark, and handsome type. And with his almost black hair and brown eyes, his appearance hinted at dark European ancestry. They met while she was in dental school, and he'd been doing his residency to become a dentist. Everyone in her family loved Brad, especially her brother, Matthew. Several years older than Mallory, Matthew was already married with a couple of kids before she even met Brad. But Matthew and Brad hit it off, and Brad quickly felt like one of the family. His own family lived in Boston, and even though they were close, Brad had fallen in love with Utah, where he'd come to attend college. And then he fell in love with Mallory.

Mallory loved everything about Brad. He was committed to the gospel, had a strong testimony, and treated her with great respect. She felt valued and adored in his presence, and never had cause to wonder if he would be a good husband. In truth, her relationship with Brad seemed so ideal that she often had to stop and ask herself if she was being blinded by love. Mallory had been raised with a very clear awareness of what dysfunction was and how to handle it, if not avoid it altogether. Her parents had struggled through some horrible things, mostly due to her mother's sexual abuse during her early teen years. But Colin and Janna Trevor had risen above the abuse and dysfunction to become strong, confident people. Colin had achieved his goal to become a lawyer, and had taken it further to become a judge. Matthew had followed in his father's footsteps, and was also practicing law. Janna had gone back to school in nursing, although she mostly used her knowledge in doing volunteer work when it was needed. She had also worked occasionally at a local crisis center, passing her knowledge along to those in need. Colin and Janna were completely committed to each other and their children. They knew how to communicate effectively, and how to solve even the biggest problems. And they had conscientiously passed their knowledge on to their children.

Mallory felt well prepared to go into marriage with the skills to handle any problem that might arise. Matthew had also been a good example. He'd married a woman who had risen above an alcoholic family, and the two of them were doing great. Mallory had carefully observed the way Matthew lovingly nurtured Melody out of her dysfunctional upbringing. And together, with the gospel, they were truly happy.

Mallory's sister, Caitlin, who was barely one year older, had been on a mission when Mallory and Brad met. Mallory had felt some desire to serve a mission as well, but through fasting and prayer she knew that being with Brad was more important for her. Brad himself hadn't served a mission, and though he'd been vague on his reasons, she had every reason to believe that he'd overcome whatever problems might have existed in his past. He was strong and confident. And Mallory loved him.

Mallory and Brad were married in the temple the same month that he began his work as a dentist. Mallory worked as one of his assistants for over two years, until she was nearly ready to give birth to their first child. Little Bethany was born with dark hair and strongly resembled her father, but she quickly turned blonde, which was a stark contrast to her parents. Though Mallory's skin was fair, she'd inherited her mother's dark, curly hair and green eyes.

Soon after Bethany was born, they moved into a home in Highland, less than a block away from Matthew and his family. The home had been custom built by friends of the family, and Mallory hoped to live her life out there. Brad declared that it was the ideal place to settle down, and he often said how he loved living in Highland. It was a twenty-minute drive north to his office in Sandy, and the same distance south to Mallory's parents' home in Provo. Mallory loved their home and the life they shared there. They often spent time with Matthew and Melody, doing just about everything together, including barbecuing regularly, even in the winter months. Brad and Matthew often went to games on the weekends, or watched them on television. Matthew's two young sons, Mark and Luke, occasionally tagged along. Mallory and Melody became friends as well as neighbors, helping with each other's children and sharing every new recipe or piece of knowledge.

A few months after Bethany was born, Matthew and Melody had their third child, their first daughter—Elizabeth. The women enjoyed sharing every aspect of their baby girls, and felt certain the little cousins would grow up to be good friends.

Overall, Mallory felt as if her life was almost like a fairy tale. But she didn't take it for granted. She was continually aware of her many blessings, and often told Brad how happy she was. And she had to believe that her knowledge and effort in making a good relationship counted for something. Prior to their marriage, Mallory had made a point of talking through every possible facet of their views on important issues. She had practiced good communication skills right from the start. Still, there were times when she almost expected some difficult point to come up in their marriage. But Brad was always supportive and sensitive, and their rare disagreements were solved quickly and effectively.

When Bethany turned one, Mallory was asked to serve as the Beehive advisor in the ward, and Brad was serving as Cubmaster. When he went for several months without attending the temple, Mallory felt concerned. He was hesitant to open up to her, simply saying that he just had some spiritual struggles and the bishop was working with him. He said he wanted to feel good about himself. When Bethany was nineteen months old, Brad took Mallory back to the temple, and she'd never felt happier. They went together twice a month while Matthew and Melody took care of the baby.

If Mallory found any fault in her husband, it would be that he was guarded with his feelings, and perhaps distant. But she credited that to his quiet personality. He was attentive and sweet, always willing to help with the baby and around the house. And she had no cause to complain.

Mallory knew that her life wasn't perfect, but with the discovery that they were expecting another baby, she felt like it was pretty close. She'd had no reason to believe that the little struggles wouldn't continue to improve through their years together. If she had only known how brief those years would be.

As her memories drew closer to the present, Mallory mentally picked apart every detail of their lives, searching for any piece of evidence that might give her a clue as to why this had happened.

The first week of March had begun like any other week. There was a light snow falling as Brad left for work on Monday morning. Mallory always felt a little uneasy when he had to drive over the point of the mountain in bad weather. But he called as soon as he arrived at the office and put her at ease.

The snow had completely stopped before it was time for Mallory to go to the doctor. She'd had her initial checkup for her pregnancy a few weeks ago, but she was struggling with nausea much more than she had with the last baby, and she needed to talk with the doctor about her options in dealing with the problem safely. She'd been hoping to get some suggestions over the phone, but they had asked her to come in. She hated doctor's visits, and found them to be one of the negative aspects of being pregnant. Then she arrived at the doctor's office to be told that her regular doctor had been called away to deliver a baby.

"Would you like to reschedule?" the receptionist asked. "Or we can squeeze you in with Dr. Alden."

Mallory would have preferred to see her own doctor, but she was here and wanted to have it done. "I'll wait," she said and sat down, grateful to know that Melody didn't have any plans today and Bethany was all right with her for as long as it took.

The wait was not as long as she'd expected, but when Dr. Alden entered the examination room, Mallory was stunned. While she was trying to find the right words to admit that she recognized this man, he grinned at her and said, "Mallory Trevor. I can't believe it. How are you?"

"I'm doing good," she admitted. "Although it's Mallory Taylor now."

"Of course." He chuckled softly, and for ten minutes she reminisced with *Dr.* Alden about high school and their common activities. Darrell Alden had shared several classes with Mallory, and they'd actually gone out together two or three times. It had never come to anything more than that, but Mallory had always thought he was one of the best-looking, most decent young men she'd known in high school. He'd changed very little, and she found the coincidence amusing—although she was grateful that this appointment was only for discussion. If she'd needed anything more personal, she would have insisted on waiting until she could see her regular doctor.

"So, how are you these days?" he asked when the reminiscing ran down.

"Well, other than feeling awfully sick with this pregnancy, I'm doing great."

He answered her questions and gave her some suggestions on how to handle the nausea, finishing with, "But the fact is, for some women, it's just there and has to be dealt with. Some things help, but nothing but time will really take it away. As long as you're keeping your food down and getting the rest you need, there's no reason to be concerned."

Mallory thanked him, then asked, "And how are you doing?"

A subtle severity that she'd noticed in his eyes deepened as he answered, "I've seen better days, I must admit." He took a deep breath and added, "My wife was killed a few months ago."

"Oh, I'm so sorry," Mallory said with sincerity. She couldn't comprehend how anyone could survive such a thing. She wanted to ask how it had happened, but she simply said, "I don't know how you can even cope."

"Well," he chuckled uncomfortably, "you do what you have to do, I guess. I have to support my children. I have to keep living. But it's been tough. What can I say?"

"How many children do you have?"

"Two daughters," he said with pride. "They're staying with my wife's parents most of the time, which I feel is better for them. I see them as often as I can." He wrapped up the conversation and moved on to his next appointment, but Mallory couldn't get what he'd told her out of her head. She tried to imagine Brad being left alone to care for Bethany and still making a living. Her heart ached at the thought. And in the same respect, she couldn't imagine trying to live without Brad. When he came home that evening, she hugged him tightly and wouldn't let go for several minutes.

"What is this?" he asked, looking into her eyes. While she was searching for an explanation, he laughed softly. "Not that I'm complaining. You can hug me all day if you want, but . . ."

"I just needed to feel close," she said. "I don't know what I'd do without you. You're everything to me."

Brad hugged her back but said nothing. The following evening he took her out to dinner at a new restaurant just over the point of the mountain, about halfway between home and his office. He told her the girls at the office had been talking about it, and he couldn't wait to take her there so they could try it.

She read the sign as they pulled up. "Buchanan's." She glanced around the parking lot. "It looks crowded for a Tuesday."

"I hear that on weekends you can hardly get in," he reported. "Apparently it's phenomenal."

On their way home, Mallory had to agree. The meal had been truly exquisite. The prices had been on the expensive side, but she felt certain they'd gotten their money's worth. It was one of the finest meals she'd ever eaten.

"So how was dinner?" Matthew asked when they stopped to pick up Bethany.

"It was incredible," Brad declared dramatically. "In fact, we're going to have to take you and Melody there. Maybe next week."

"Sounds good," Matthew said. "Do you think we can get baby-sitters if we all go out at the same time?"

"I'm sure we'll manage," Mallory said, taking Bethany from her brother. "How did Bethie do?"

"Fine, as always. She just fits in like one of the family."

"Where's Melody?"

"Oh, she had to deliver some papers for Primary. She shouldn't be long."

"I'll just talk to her in the morning," Mallory said. She gave Matthew a hug and thanked him, then they went home and put Bethany to bed.

While Brad was reading his scriptures, Mallory said, "I'd like to go to the temple this week, if it's possible. Is there a time you can go?"

He seemed vaguely uncomfortable as he told her it was a busy week and he didn't know if he could work it in. Mallory felt a little uneasy, wondering if he would digress again into his habit of not going at all. She wanted to talk about it, but felt that this wasn't the right time. She had no valid indication that anything was wrong—at least not wrong enough to press him. She wondered, as she did occasionally, if there was something inside of him that she didn't understand. She suspected from things he'd said that he had some hard feelings toward his father, but he was hesitant to talk about it specifically. In putting pieces together, she wondered if Brad's struggles with spiritual things came from his father's piousness. He was a good man, but he'd been more than a little overbearing when it came to religion. Brad had told her more than once that he wanted to feel good about himself and not be a hypocrite. But she sensed that he was terribly hard on himself concerning spiritual matters. Perhaps one day he would talk about it. And if it continued to be a problem, she would insist that they get some counseling. She wasn't willing to let any problem come between them without taking serious action. She loved Brad too much to risk having difficulty in their marriage.

The rest of the week went along normally. Mallory found that the doctor's suggestions did help her nausea for the most part. She often felt tired, which she knew was normal, but she rested when she could and was able to carry out her usual responsibilities without too much trouble. She went to her Young Women's meeting on Wednesday evening, and Brad had pack meeting on Thursday.

On Friday, Brad took the car to work that Mallory normally drove. His was nearly out of gas and he was running late. Mallory took his car out on some errands, and when she returned home and turned off the ignition, she accidentally dropped her keys on the floor of the car. Reaching down to get them, she felt the edge of a magazine under the seat and pulled it out curiously. Realizing what it was, she stared at the cover in horror. Then she hurried into the house and tossed it into the wood-burning stove before she walked down the street to get Bethany.

At the first opportunity, she called Brad at work. "Is he with a patient?" Mallory asked the receptionist.

"No, he's right here," she said.

"Hello," Brad said cheerfully. "What's up?"

"Who's been driving your car recently?" she asked without preamble.

Brad was silent for a long moment, but Mallory could hear talking in the background and realized he was distracted.

"Brad, are you there?"

"Yes, but . . . listen, honey. Something's just come up. I'll call you back in a few minutes."

Brad called about ten minutes later, saying right off, "Now, I think you were asking me something about the car."

"Yes," she said. "I was just wondering who's been driving it."

"Well, I loaned it to one of the doctors across the plaza the other day. His car was getting the oil changed and he needed to run an errand. Is there a problem?"

"Is he someone you know well?" she asked, knowing that he wouldn't loan his car to just anybody.

"Well enough, I guess. What's wrong, honey? You sound upset."

"I found a magazine under the seat. It was pornographic, Brad. You'd think if somebody was going to borrow a car, they'd be more careful than that."

"You'd think," he echoed.

"Are you okay?"

"Yes," she insisted. "It just kind of shocked me there for a minute, but I'll get over it."

"Are you sure?"

"Yes, of course. Go back to work. I'm sorry to bother you. It's just that—"

"It's okay. I understand," he said gently. "I'll certainly be more careful who I loan my car to."

Brad told Mallory he loved her before he hung up the phone, and she did her best not to think about it. She wanted to talk to someone about it and get it off her chest, but Melody had taken her children to visit her mother, and Mallory's mother had gone to Salt Lake with a friend.

When Brad got home from work, the first thing he said was, "You're still upset."

"Yes, I suppose I am."

"What did you do with it?" he asked. "The magazine, I mean."

"I burned it," she said. "I only saw the front cover, and even that made me ill." Grateful to have someone to unload her thoughts on, she continued vehemently. "I've always known that such things were out there and readily available, but I guess the reality was a little unsettling. Do you think this guy's wife has any idea what he's doing?"

"What?" Brad asked.

"His wife. He's married, isn't he?"

"Yes, I believe he is."

"Do you think his wife knows?"

"It's hard to say."

"Well, I feel sorry for her—whether she knows or not. I've read studies on pornography. The statistics are appalling. It's incredible how much crime and abuse is tied back to pornography. And remember Judith, who lived in our old neighborhood? Her brother had a problem with it. Her brother's wife said it was almost like the devil himself lived in their home because of the awful spirit there at times. She said his problem was like an addiction; it just got worse and worse. And he started getting downright perverse over some things. She finally left him when she found out that he'd sexually abused their children. Can you even imagine?" Mallory shuddered visibly and shook her head. "Like I said, whoever this guy is, I feel sorry for his family. I would hope he gets some help before he hurts anybody else."

Brad made no comment, which was typical of him. But he was always good to listen patiently and let her vent her emotions. With her thoughts in the open, Mallory was able to let them go. She fixed dinner and went through the evening as she usually did, not giving the incident another thought.

On Saturday, Brad went into the office to take care of an emergency appointment. Then he called to say that he was staying a while to get caught up on some paperwork. At dinnertime she was beginning to wonder what could be taking him so long. She'd barely thought it when he called to apologize profusely. "There are some things messed up on the computer here," he said.

He sounded terribly uptight. "Are you okay?" she asked.

"Of course," he said, but his voice sounded even more strained. "I'm still going to be a while. Go ahead and eat without me. I'll get home as soon as I can."

Mallory had gone to bed before he finally got home. He crawled into bed and snuggled up close to her, but he said very little.

On Sunday, Brad hardly said a word. He seemed more distant than usual. Mallory questioned him more than once, but he insisted that everything was fine. Again she told herself not to push too hard, but she resolved that if his behavior continued like this, she would get the two of them to a psychologist—no matter how hard she had to push.

On Sunday evening, after Bethany had gone to sleep, Mallory found Brad standing over her crib, pressing his fingers over her wispy blonde curls. He was singing a little lullaby that he'd often sung to her as he'd rocked her when she was an infant. Knowing he would stop if he was aware of her presence, Mallory hovered in the hallway. She was moved to tears when he finished the song and spoke quietly to his sleeping daughter, telling her of his love for her and for her mother. It helped put her frustrations into perspective. Mallory hurried away as he came toward the door, uttering a silent prayer of gratitude for all she'd been blessed with.

That night as she got into bed, Brad snuggled close to her again. She expected, even wanted, some intimacy. But he seemed tired and content just to hold her, and gradually she relaxed in his embrace, enjoying his nearness.

"I love you, Mallory," he whispered when she was almost asleep.

"I love you, too," she murmured and drifted off.

Mallory awakened with her heart pounding. Through her sleep-blurred mind she attempted to put a name to the sound that had startled her. She reached for Brad, expecting him to explain—or at least to volunteer to investigate. But he wasn't there. Bethany began to cry, obviously startled by the same noise. *Gunshot.* Could it be? Could she possibly have been awakened by a gunshot too close to be anywhere but in her own home? Was there an intruder? Where was Brad?

She pushed her feet into a pair of slippers and tied a robe around her waist. "Please help me, Lord," she whispered aloud as she pulled the baby into her arms and wrapped her in a blanket to ward off the chill of the house. Bethany stopped crying once she was in her mother's arms. Mallory continued praying silently, asking for guidance, not wanting to put herself or her baby in any danger. Should she call the police? She wasn't sure about that, but as she moved with trepidation into the hallway, she felt a definite impression that they were not in any danger. She wondered if Brad had shot an intruder. It made sense. She knew he had a gun, although he kept it locked in the storage room, and all of the ammunition was locked up in his study. As Mallory quickly went from room to room, turning on lights, finding nothing out of the ordinary, the pounding of her heart began to increase. Something was horribly wrong, and she knew it. But what?

The first thing Mallory noticed when she went down the stairs was the light coming from beneath the door of Brad's study. She rushed to the door, paused to study her instincts, then took hold of the doorknob. It was locked.

"Brad, are you in there?" she asked quietly. Then louder, "Brad? Please open the door." She knew he had to be in there. She'd already checked the rest of the house. And why else would the door be locked from the inside? But she hollered and pounded for several minutes with no response. A deep dread rose inside of her, although she didn't stop to analyze it. Realizing the doorknob had a simple spring lock, she went to find something to spring it with. She'd done it more than once when Bethany had accidentally locked herself in one of the bedrooms by pushing the button. She was about to set the baby down in order to get the door open, but a thought appeared in her mind with such strength that she froze. She couldn't explain it. She only knew that the Spirit was telling her *not* to open that door.

"Oh, no," she muttered as an idea occurred to her that she would never have imagined. "Oh, help," she cried, and didn't hesitate even a moment before she flew out of the house, running toward her brother's home. Bethany whimpered in her embrace, as if she sensed her mother's fear.

Mallory was nearly to Matthew's door when it occurred to her that she should have just called him. But it was too late now. Besides, she couldn't have stayed in that house another second—not if her suspicions had any substance at all. If Brad was locked in that room and wouldn't answer the door . . . and she'd been awakened by a gunshot . . . what could that possibly add up to? She couldn't say it. She couldn't even consciously think it.

Mallory rang the doorbell. Then she immediately began pounding on the door, if only to give her something to do. Then she rang the bell again.

"Who is it?" her brother's voice called gruffly from the other side of the door.

"It's me!" she called back.

The door flew open. "What are you doing here? What's wrong?" Matthew ushered her in and closed the door behind her. The fear in his eyes deepened when she began babbling so fast that he couldn't understand her.

"Wait a minute," he insisted, grasping her shoulders with his hands. "Slow down. What happened?"

"I . . . I heard a gunshot," she said, and Matthew's expression tightened. Melody, who had appeared at the bottom of the stairs, put a hand over her mouth. "The door to the study is locked, and . . . I think . . . Brad's in there." Emotion constricted her throat and chest, and she couldn't say any more beyond, "I'm so scared."

Melody put her arm around Mallory, urging her to the couch.

"What are you doing?" Mallory asked when Matthew picked up the phone.

"I'm calling the police. Whatever happened, I'm not going in there alone."

Mallory fought to keep her emotion on a level that wouldn't scare the baby. Tears trailed steadily down her face while her head pounded in time with her heart. Everything inside of her tightened up further as she listened to Matthew repeat the situation over the phone. He gave the address, then said, "And for heaven's sake, don't come in here with sirens blaring and wake the whole neighborhood."

Matthew went upstairs to put on something besides a bathrobe. Melody came to her feet and held her arms out to take the baby. "I'm going to see if I can get Bethany back to sleep," she said. " I won't be far."

Mallory just nodded and continued to cry. Matthew paused on his way out the door only long enough to say to her, "Are you going to be all right?"

Mallory nodded feebly and motioned him out the door. She tried to imagine what he might find at her home, and the thought caused her to cry harder. He hadn't been gone long when Melody returned and sat beside her, saying that Bethany was asleep.

"Thank you," Mallory croaked, feeling a dazed dread replace her emotion.

While Melody held her hand in silence, obviously not knowing what to say, Mallory knew in her heart that something unspeakable had happened. But she just couldn't get her mind to accept it; she *wouldn't* accept it until she heard whatever Matthew had to say. In the meantime, she had to deal with her imagination as it flitted through every possible scenario. She'd never been so afraid in her life.

CHAPTER TWO

*M*atthew watched the police drive away, then he took a minute to gather his senses before he found Mallory's keys and locked up the house. The walk back to his own home seemed far too short as he struggled to find the words to tell his sister what they had discovered. As he stepped through the door and closed it behind him, he noticed the way his wife and sister leaned forward expectantly. Observing Mallory's disheveled appearance and frightened countenance, he was reminded of their mother and the horrors she had gone through when he'd been a young boy. Of course Mallory and the other children wouldn't remember such things. The worst happened before they were ever born, and everything had been better since Caitlin and Mallory grew beyond toddlers. The years since had been good and full of happiness, with only occasional reminders of the nightmares from the past. But this was a whole new nightmare. And it seemed just too much for one family to bear.

Mallory's heart had calmed down to a normal pace as she'd waited in silence for Matthew to return. But it quickly resumed its pounding when she heard him at the door; like the gallop of a race horse, her heart threatened to thud right out of her chest. She swallowed hard as Matthew met her eyes. His face was pale and gaunt, as if he felt physically ill. His eyes looked decades older, as if he'd encountered some unspeakable horror. He pushed a hand over his face, allowing it to linger against his eyes. She noticed that it was trembling as he moved it down to rest on his hip. He glanced at Melody, as if to draw courage from her, then he looked back to Mallory.

"Tell me," Mallory insisted in a voice stronger than she'd believed she could find.

Matthew walked toward her slowly and knelt in front of her, taking her hands into his. Now they were both trembling. "He's dead, Mallory."

Only silence followed, accompanied by a little gasp from Melody before she clamped a hand over her mouth. Mallory felt unexplainably calm—or perhaps just too much in shock to respond. She heard the words. She knew what they meant. But it was as if the signal was moving in slow motion from her head to her heart, and the realization hadn't yet arrived.

She sensed Matthew attempting to gather words to explain, but she became impatient and demanded, "Did someone . . ." She couldn't finish.

Matthew's eyes told her he understood. He shook his head slowly. His chin quivered and he bowed his head, squeezing his eyes closed.

"Oh, help me," Matthew muttered under his breath, wondering how to tell her. But he just had to tell her. There was no way to skirt around it delicately. She had to know. Drawing in a deep breath, he lifted his eyes to meet hers again, saying as gently as he could, "He was all alone, Mallory. There's no other possible explanation." He cleared his throat. "He shot himself in the head."

Mallory watched Matthew's emotion appear on his face then bubble into the open air. He buried his head in Melody's lap and sobbed, while silent tears leaked steadily down her face. Mallory observed their grief as if from a distance, waiting for the inevitable pain to assault her. It reminded her of a time when she had cut her hand and watched it bleed for several seconds before her brain had perceived that it hurt. When the perception finally hit, Mallory pressed both hands over her heart, feeling a tangible, unbearable pain that made her groan and double over.

Mallory had no perception of time as she cried in Matthew's arms, her hand in Melody's. She'd never been so grateful to have family close by. Her neighbors were good people, and she knew they would have helped her. But it just wasn't the same.

Mallory was vaguely aware of Matthew slipping away. But Melody didn't leave her side, even for a moment, allowing Mallory the opportunity to vent her pain.

With Mallory in his wife's care, Matthew slipped upstairs where he sat on the edge of the bed, took a deep breath, and picked up the phone. He punched in his parents' phone number, then glanced at the clock. 4:31 a.m.

"Dad?" he said when Colin Trevor answered.

"Matthew? What is it? What's wrong?"

The words caught in Matthew's throat with a lump of fresh emotion. "Are you sitting down, Dad?" he asked, needing to speak but not wanting to say it aloud again.

"I'm in bed, son. Out with it."

"Mallory woke me." He cleared his throat louder than he'd intended. "The thing is . . . Brad's killed himself."

Only silence followed, except for Matthew's occasional sniffle. Finally Colin said, "I can't believe it."

Matthew made a noise of agreement, then forced his voice. "We need you, Dad; both of you. I can't handle this alone. Mallory's falling apart. Can you and Mom—"

"We'll be there in half an hour. Are you at—"

"My house. Hurry."

Matthew hurried back downstairs, where Mallory was crying harder than when he'd left. He took Melody's place next to her, and he was still there when his parents arrived. Mallory's first reaction to seeing Janna and Colin was immense relief, then she clutched onto her mother and cried harder. A sudden rush of nausea took her off guard, and she hurried to the kitchen sink, knowing she'd never make it to the bathroom. With her stomach empty, she wretched dry heaves until the pain nearly made her pass out. Janna helped her to a kitchen chair, where she continued to cry until the heaves started again. When the routine played through a third time, Janna looked into Mallory's eyes, saying firmly, "You've got to calm down. Do you hear me? I know it hurts. But you're making yourself sick."

Mallory only shook her head and continued to cry. Janna motioned for her husband to come closer. Mallory cried on her father's shoulder while Janna took Matthew and Melody aside. "She needs a priesthood blessing, and perhaps we should call her doctor and get something to calm her down that won't hurt the baby. She's got to sleep."

Melody volunteered to call the doctor, since she knew who it was. Matthew helped his father give Mallory a blessing, even though she never stopped crying through it and seemed oblivious to anything that was said. The doctor called back quickly, and Colin left to pick up a prescription at an all-night pharmacy. By the time he returned Mallory was a little more calm, but still unable to stop crying. And she certainly couldn't relax. Janna urged her to take a pill, then she lay down with her on Matthew and Melody's bed as morning slowly filled the room.

While Janna was upstairs with Mallory, Matthew called their bishop and Relief Society president. When he got off the phone, Melody was cooking breakfast. "You don't have to do that," he said, putting his arms around her from behind. "We can eat toast and cereal if—"

"I have to do this," she said, and he could tell she was crying. "If I don't stay busy I'll . . . I'll . . ."

Matthew turned her toward him, and she cried on his shoulder. He turned off the stove and urged her to the front room, where his father was looking dazed. They were barely seated when Janna came down the stairs to announce, "She's asleep. I hope she sleeps long and hard."

Janna slumped onto the couch next to her husband, putting her head on his shoulder. Then her eyes turned to Matthew. "Now, tell us what happened."

Holding Melody's hand tightly, he repeated everything that had happened from his perspective. He managed to remain emotionless until his father said, "You saw him, then."

Matthew squeezed his eyes shut, but it only enhanced the image in his memory as he nodded his head. "Oh, heaven help me!" he cried, pressing his head into his hands. "He was like a brother to me. I just don't understand."

Janna said tearfully, "None of us do, Matthew. And I would guess that's what will be most difficult for Mallory. We need to stick together and stay close to her."

Melody nodded and came to her feet. "I need to fix breakfast," she said.

"She doesn't have to do that," Colin said, watching her leave.

"I think she does," Matthew said. "She told me she needs to feel busy."

They nodded their understanding. Janna wiped her tears and pointed to the cordless phone. "Will you hand me that?" she said to Matthew. "I need to call your brothers."

Matthew and Colin solemnly stared at the floor as they listened to Janna's conversation. "Hello, Jake. We're at Matthew's house. Will you tell your brother to get on the extension?"

Matthew thought of his two younger brothers. Jake would be graduating from high school in a few months; Dustin was a sophomore at the same school. They both loved Brad as an older brother. His heart ached for them as Janna reported simply, "Brad's been killed. We'll talk about it when you get here. I don't want you to go to school today. We need to be together. There's a great deal that needs to be done. You can help with the little ones. Lock up the house and see that everything's taken care of. Bring what you need to stay overnight, in case you decide you want to." She then consoled their emotion and told them to gather some things for her and Colin and bring them as well.

The children began waking up, and Colin and Janna slipped into their role as grandparents to help with them and ease the strain on Matthew and Melody. Bethany was the last to wake up, but she seemed comfortable and at ease, being in a familiar place with people she knew well. Colin and Matthew both made arrangements to miss work for a few days, then the bishop came by with one of his counselors to find out what they could do to help. It was difficult to know what to tell him, beyond asking for some help in putting a funeral together. But the bishop made them promise to call if they thought of something, and he assured them he would check back regularly.

An hour after he left, the Relief Society presidency came and reported that they would be bringing in meals for the entire family for the next few days, while they prepared the funeral and dealt with their grief. At noon, relish trays and a huge amount of sandwich fixings were delivered by Mallory's visiting teachers. Mallory was still asleep.

Melody sat with Mallory so she wouldn't be alone when she woke up. Colin played with the babies. Jake and Dustin ran some errands. Matthew and his mother walked down to Mallory's house to gather some of her things so she wouldn't have to go back until she was ready. Janna quickly scanned Mallory's bedroom and bathroom, guessing what she might need and putting it into a small suitcase. They also gathered diapers and clothes for Bethany. Then Janna asked Matthew, "Did he leave a note . . . or anything?"

"Not that we could find; nothing obvious, anyway."

Janna held up well as she briefly surveyed the room where the suicide had taken place. They locked up the house and walked back down the street. Then she called the bishop and said calmly, "There's something we need help with, as quickly as possible."

Matthew listened in amazement as his mother discussed having the evidence cleared from Brad's study. She said she would cover the costs, but she would like to have someone make arrangements with a professional cleaning company to take care of the problem, and also to have the carpet replaced. She talked about the importance of seeing that it was dealt with right away, and that every trace of the incident was gone. The bishop kindly assured her that he'd get someone to make some calls and see that it was done. Then Janna called Caitlin, who would just be arriving home from her nursing shift at the hospital. She hung up the phone and reported, "She's pretty upset. She's going to try and rest for a while, then she'll be over."

"You're incredible," Matthew said. "How do you stay so calm?"

She shook her head. "I'm just numb. I hurt so much I feel like I'm going to blow up, but it just won't come out."

"I'm sure it will in time."

"Yes," she said, "that's what scares me. Then I'll need one of Mallory's pills."

"Mother!" Melody called from upstairs with some urgency, and Janna hurried away.

Melody came down the stairs a few minutes later and went straight to the kitchen. "What's wrong?" Matthew asked.

"She's awake. She seems to just be in shock, and she's extremely nauseous. I just wanted Mom to sit with her while I fix her a sandwich."

"Thank you, Mel," he said, touching her face.

"For what?"

"For being a part of my family—even through this."

Melody gave him a sad smile and concentrated on getting food out of the fridge. "You've certainly helped my family through crisis—several times. Besides, being a part of your family is the best thing that ever happened to me."

"And me," he said. Then he hugged her tightly and they both cried a little before she got back to fixing the sandwich.

The police came by a while later to question Mallory. She was grateful to have her father and brother at her side to help her through. But when the police left, she became so upset that Janna insisted she take another pill and go lie down.

For Mallory, the next few days were a blur. After crying helplessly through the first day, she could hardly cry at all most of the time. Occasionally the reality crept in, and she felt as if she'd die. But beyond her bouts of emotion, she remained calm and dazed, as if she was viewing the world through a shroud. She remained at Matthew's house, surrounded continually by her family. Not only were they a continual support, taking care of every little detail, but they also shared her grief. Her parents and younger brothers stayed at her house so they could be close by. But she couldn't go back there—not yet.

The funeral went by in a blur. The casket remained closed, and for Mallory, the entire thing just didn't seem real. It was only her trust in Matthew, who assured her that he had seen Brad, that made her able to believe he was really gone.

The day after the funeral, everyone who had been so busy suddenly had nothing to do, and there was no choice but to try to go on living. Colin and Matthew returned to work; Jake and Dustin went back to school. Janna offered to stay a few more days with Mallory, but she insisted that they had to stay in Mallory's home. "I know it's hard," she said, "but it's your home, and you've got to live there. Matthew and your father blessed the home, and there is no sign of what took place." Janna hesitated before adding, "Everything's been cleaned up in the study, and the carpet has been replaced." Mallory only had to wonder why for a moment before the obvious answer appeared in her head. She wanted to ask how bad it had been, then she realized she didn't want to know.

Mallory knew her mother was right, but walking back into the house was even more difficult than she'd expected. She could tell that some of Brad's obvious belongings had been moved. Everything of his was still in the home, but the things he'd left lying around had been put away.

Mallory was grateful for her mother's company as she attempted to adjust to life without Brad. Caitlin also spent a great deal of time with her sister when she wasn't working, and Matthew and Melody were in and out frequently. It didn't take long to be comfortable in her home again, beyond the reminders of Brad that were in every room. And she just decided to stay out of the study for the time being. Her emotion came in spurts. At times she felt as if she was doing well and she'd be fine; at others she would feel as if she'd die from longing for her husband. The whole thing often seemed like a bad dream; it simply didn't feel real. She was grateful for the knowledge her mother had about the different stages of grief, which helped her understand what she was experiencing and deal with it appropriately. She felt herself fluctuating regularly between denial and anger, and knew that it would take time to find acceptance. At the moment, it was difficult to comprehend ever reaching a point of peace over losing Brad; still, she trusted her mother when she said that it would come. But worse than any level of her grief or longing was the question continually hovering in the back of her mind. *Why?* Why would Brad have done something like that?

Her family had speculated and discussed it until she couldn't bear it any longer. They had talked with people he worked with and every friend and acquaintance that they knew of. No one knew anything about Brad that might give a clue to his suicide. They discovered that statistically by profession, dentists had a higher than average rate of suicide. But Mallory knew that Brad had loved his work and found it very satisfying. Everyone who had worked with him agreed.

Brad's family had come from Boston for the funeral, and they were as baffled as the rest of them. Their grief was obvious, and Mallory ached for them as well. She had no indication that they were blaming her, but she couldn't help thinking that some people might wonder if she had, through some behavior, driven her husband to this. She reminded herself to dismiss such absurd thoughts and deal with her grief realistically.

It was easier to ignore such unsettling thoughts when she was with family. But more than a week after the funeral, she finally had to face being by herself. It was the first time she'd been completely alone since Brad had taken his life. She cried herself into a familiar numbness, then she thought carefully through every aspect of their lives, searching for some piece of evidence. When her thoughts left her only more confused and upset, she forced herself to get up and do something.

Bethany woke up from her nap and Mallory played with her baby, then did a little housework. A late March wind blew outside, making the house feel chilly in spite of the furnace running, so Mallory opened up the wood-burning stove to build a fire. It was practically overflowing with ashes, so she stepped outside to get the ash bucket and shovel. After dumping two scoops into the bucket, it occurred to her that something didn't feel right. A formless panic took hold of her—the same feeling she'd experienced when she'd found the door to the study locked. She left the shovel and bucket as they were and went to the phone, grateful that it was Saturday when Matthew answered.

"Are you okay?" he asked.

"I'm not sure. Could you come over? If you're in the middle of something, it can wait."

"No, I'm not busy. I'll be right over."

When Matthew came in, Mallory pointed to the wood stove and said, "Something's not right."

"What do you mean?"

"The last time we had a fire in there was that evening . . . just before . . ."

"Yes," Matthew spared her from saying it.

"I remember putting wood on it that night, and the ashes had just been cleaned out. But look at it. It's full of ashes—and they're heavy."

Matthew reached a hand into the stove and pulled out a clump of blackened sheets, stuck together. As he carefully peeled them apart, he said, "It's paper; a magazine I believe. But it's too far gone to know what it was."

Mallory thought of the magazine she had burned a few days before Brad's death, but the ashes from that had been cleaned out before the last fire.

Matthew took the shovel and continued cleaning out the ashes, occasionally sifting through them in search of clues. Though Mallory hadn't come right out and said so, he knew she was suspecting—even hoping—for some information that might explain Brad's death.

Matthew's heart actually began to pound as he stuck his hand into the bottom of the stove and felt something strange. He couldn't imagine what it might be until he held it up.

"What is that?" Mallory demanded, hating this persistent panic that wouldn't leave her.

"It's a video tape," he said, turning it over carefully. "Or at least it was."

"What on earth would he . . ." She couldn't even find a thought worth putting to words.

"I don't know, Mallory. But he obviously had some things he wanted destroyed before he left."

"But *what*? Do you think he was some kind of spy in his spare time or something? Did he know something that put his life in danger, or—"

"You've seen too many movies," Matthew interrupted.

"Well, then *you* explain this."

"I can't! But I know he wasn't a spy. That's ridiculous."

Mallory sat on the floor and resisted the urge to cry. Matthew finished cleaning out the ashes and took the bucket out to the trash can. He found another melted video tape before he was done. He washed up and built a fire, then he sat down on the floor close to Mallory.

"What are you thinking, sis?" he asked quietly.

"I just miss him so much. Everywhere I turn, there's something to remind me. He was a part of every single aspect of my life. I wake up at night and think I feel him next to me. When I go out of the house, I expect him to be here when I come back in."

"I can't comprehend what you're going through," Matthew admitted. "As much as I miss him, I can't imagine how you must miss him. If I lost Melody, I don't know if I could bear it."

"I'm not sure I *can* bear it." Mallory hugged her knees to her chest. "And if being without him isn't bad enough, I have to wonder why it had to happen at all. If he had been killed in an accident, it would have been horrible. But I would be able to believe that it was his time to go; that things like that just happen. But this! How do I cope with *this*? How could he do it, Matthew? I just don't understand. Didn't he know what this would do to me?"

"He probably didn't. A person couldn't possibly be thinking clearly to do something like that."

"That's just it. I wonder what he might have been going through, and it just makes my heart ache for him. What was he thinking? What could have been so bad that he had to do something like that?"

"I don't know, Mallory. I've been praying that we could find some peace, that we could understand. We've all been praying."

"I know. Me, too." She shook her head and repeated, "I just don't understand."

Through a minute of silence, Mallory sensed that Matthew was feeling emotional. "What is it?" she asked, taking his hand.

Matthew swallowed hard. "That Sunday . . . the day he . . . well, I had this feeling that I should talk to him. It was just a thought. But the afternoon got busy, then it slipped my mind. I remember when I got in bed that night, thinking that I'd call him when I got home from work Monday, but . . ." His words faltered with emotion. Mallory knew that was the night Brad had ended his life.

"Don't tell me you're blaming yourself," Mallory said, and tears spilled down Matthew's face.

"I know . . . it probably wouldn't have made a difference," he admitted. "If he was determined to do it . . . there's probably nothing I could have said or done . . . but . . . oh, help!" Matthew pressed his face into his hands and cried. "I know we can't change it. I know he's gone, but . . . I just can't believe it!"

Mallory put her arms around her brother and cried with him. If nothing else, it was comforting to know that someone shared her grief, not to mention feelings she hardly dared put a voice to.

The following week, Matthew helped Mallory sort out her finances. With copies of the death certificate, they were able to get the bank accounts changed and collect the life insurance. She was relieved to realize that their policy had a particular clause concerning suicide; if it happened within a year of the purchase of the policy it wasn't valid, but they'd had it much longer than that. Mallory felt immensely blessed and grateful to realize that the policy was excellent. She wondered briefly if Brad had been planning this for a long time, but the policy had been purchased soon after their marriage, and no changes had been made on it since that time. She knew there wasn't a connection. She was simply relieved to know that he had been responsible and prepared. She was also grateful for Matthew's legal assistance in dealing with a glitch in collecting the money from the insurance company. She knew she was being looked out for, and she was grateful.

When all was said and done, Mallory ended up debt-free; even the mortgage was paid off. But the amount left over was minimal. She concluded that it would be necessary for her to work; but at least she would only have to make enough to cover monthly expenses, utilities, and insurance. Matthew and Melody were only too eager to help with Bethany. Jake and Dustin even offered to take turns coming to stay on weekends to help out. And her parents were willing to do all they could. But Mallory wondered what she might do when the baby was born. In five months she would have another child, and leaving it in order to work would be heartbreaking.

Resigning herself to taking it one day at a time, she prayed fervently and knew that she needed to be looking for a job. She still had some time yet, but she certainly had to start trying.

Life settled into a comfortable pattern. Technically everything was fine. Her needs were being met, and she had a great deal of support from ward members and family. But it was difficult to be alone with her thoughts, and she had to continually force herself to stay busy when she didn't have someone to talk to. Caitlin began staying over two or three nights a week, which helped immensely. But she worked four twelve-hour shifts a week at the hospital, and being single, her social life was generally quite full.

Mallory was grateful for all that her family did; she couldn't imagine getting through this without them. Still, she knew in her heart that missing Brad wouldn't go away easily. And the unanswered questions continued to haunt her. But she had to keep going; she had her daughter to think of, as well as the child growing inside her. Thankfully, she was feeling better physically, which was one of many blessings she could see in her life. She never had to think very long to realize how much worse it could be.

A month after Brad's death, Mallory hit a new low. She felt as if she was somehow existing inside of a dark cloud. His absence still seemed dreamlike, as if one day he'd just show up and prove to her that it hadn't been real. The emptiness surrounded her continually, and she was getting just plain weary of the effort it took to be strong and courageous. But a little bright spot appeared when she answered the door one day to see a familiar face behind a bouquet of flowers.

"Darrell," she said, unable to hide her surprise. "What are you doing here?"

"Forgive me if I'm being presumptuous," he said, handing her the flowers. "I was the doctor on call when someone requested a prescription for you; so naturally, I heard about your husband's death. I've been wanting to come by and see how you were doing, but I didn't want to make things more difficult."

"Oh, no," she said, "come in. The flowers are beautiful. Thank you."

"Well, I figured this was about the time all the funeral flowers would be wilted and gone, and the visitors would have slacked off."

"Very perceptive," she said before she recalled that he'd lost his wife not so long ago. "Thankfully, my family is still around a great deal."

"That's nice."

"Sit down," she said, setting the flowers on the coffee table.

Darrell sat on the couch, but she noticed that he seemed a bit nervous. She was wondering what to say when he said, "There's something I want to say to you, but it's . . . not easy. So bear with me."

"Okay."

"I just want you to know that I can truly empathize with what you're going through. I told you that my wife had been killed. What I didn't tell you was that . . . well, she committed suicide."

Mallory stopped breathing for a moment. She felt somehow unsettled and comforted at the same time. The comfort gradually overruled as he talked of his feelings about losing his spouse in a way that she related to so strongly. She felt completely comfortable as they shared thoughts and feelings. And even when she cried, she didn't feel embarrassed. He actually shed a few tears himself.

When a lull came, Mallory had to ask, "Do you know why she did it? I mean . . ."

"I know what you mean," he said, much to her relief. "I don't know exactly what pushed her to the edge. But she had struggled with depression on and off as long as I'd known her. Still, I never expected something so horrible."

They talked a while longer, then he insisted that he needed to leave her in peace. "I've taken far too much of your time," he said, moving toward the door.

"Oh, I've enjoyed it—truly. Thank you."

"Hey," he said, "do you think it would be inappropriate for me to take you to dinner? I know it hasn't been long, but I'm not implying anything romantic at all. It's just been good talking to you, and well . . . I figured maybe you could use a friend and a night out."

Mallory only hesitated a moment before saying, "That sounds great. I'd like that."

Darrell told her he'd pick her up Friday at six, and Mallory found that she was actually looking forward to it. Occasionally certain memories of Brad would tempt her to feel guilty about spending time with a man, but she had a long talk with her mother and felt better. Janna, who had lost her mother at the age of seventeen, assured Mallory that the emptiness would not necessarily ever go away completely. But with time, she would get used to it and find peace. And life had to go on. Just because she missed Brad and ached for him didn't mean she had to sit at home in some abstract honor of his memory.

When Friday evening came, Melody came over to get Bethany and made Mallory promise to relax and enjoy herself. "I'll just put her to bed and you can get her in the morning," she said. "Sleep in tomorrow and make the most of it."

"Thank you," Mallory said. "I could use a sleep-in morning." They hugged and she added, "You're so good to me."

"I love you. You're the sister I never had. Well, I have sisters, but . . . it's just not the same."

"I understand," Mallory said, knowing her sister-in-law had come from a difficult family situation, and she had absolutely nothing in common with her sisters.

Darrell picked Mallory up a few minutes after six. She quickly relaxed once they were on the road, and they visited comfortably. She became so caught up in their conversation that she didn't realize where they were going until he opened the car door for her. "Buchanan's," she said more to herself.

"Is something wrong?" he asked. "We can go somewhere else if—"

"No, it's fine," she insisted, thinking it was likely better to create new memories than to have everything connected exclusively to Brad. "I love this place."

The restaurant was crowded, and they had to wait nearly forty-five minutes to be seated. Thankfully, there was a comfortable lobby where they were able to sit and visit. But Mallory kept recalling how Brad had avoided the crowds by bringing her here on a Tuesday—the Tuesday before he'd died, in fact. When they were finally seated, their server, a tall, good-looking African-American gentleman, apologized for the wait and promptly saw to their every need. Mallory truly enjoyed the meal, and she appreciated the conversation with Darrell. They had a great deal in common, foremost their common grief. He kept her distracted enough that she managed to hold back any emotion related to her thoughts of Brad. And just as the last time she'd eaten here, the food was exquisite—which made her all the more surprised when Darrell called the server to their table and complained about some problem with his steak. Normally, she might not have been embarrassed over such a thing, but she'd felt more vulnerable and sensitive about *everything* since Brad's death. She felt like Darrell's complaint was petty, and when the server offered to get him another steak, Darrell said, just a hint indignantly, "I would prefer to speak with someone in charge."

With calm confidence, the server stated, "I would be happy to solve whatever problem you might have, sir."

"I would prefer to speak to someone in charge," Darrell repeated.

Mallory pressed her face into her hands and wanted to disappear. The server replied in the same calm tone, "I am the highest authority available this evening. I'm afraid you'll have to speak to me."

Darrell sighed as if this was somehow horrible, then he repeated his complaint. After several minutes of pointless conversation, Darrell finally agreed to let them give him another steak. Normally, Mallory might have asserted herself enough to say that she felt Darrell's behavior had been out of line, and to let the server know that *she* appreciated his service. But the formless vulnerability she felt these days prompted her to stay quiet. Their conversation quickly picked back up, and the remainder of the evening went well. Mallory forgot all about the incident with the server until Darrell left such a meager gratuity that she felt embarrassed all over again. On their way out to the car, Darrell spoke vehemently, as if to explain his action. "It's pathetic when such a fine restaurant has such incompetent service."

That did it. Mallory didn't feel *that* vulnerable. "You know, Darrell, I thought he was very kind and handled the situation appropriately."

Darrell looked so stunned that Mallory wondered briefly if she'd ever see him again. But then, if he had such attitudes, perhaps that would be just as well.

In the car he gave her a patronizing explanation about his sensitivity to poor restaurant service because of some bad experience he'd had in the past. Mallory tuned him out, suddenly missing Brad desperately. She thought of how gracious he would have been if he'd had a completely valid complaint, and how generous he was in tipping servers when they ate out. She ached for the comfortable relationship they'd shared and longed just to be home where she could express the grief that was suddenly consuming her.

Mallory turned toward the window when she couldn't hold the tears back. Darrell became silent mid-sentence, then said a minute later, "I'm sorry, Mallory. I got carried away. All of this is terribly petty. Please forgive me."

He took her hand and squeezed it gently. She squeezed back but said nothing. When he took her to the door of her house, he apologized again and asked if he'd said something to upset her.

"No, it's fine," she replied. "I'm just . . . having a hard time. The meal was wonderful, and I enjoyed talking with you. Thank you."

He smiled. "It was my pleasure. I'll keep in touch, okay?"

Mallory nodded and went inside, grateful to be alone. She cried long and hard, then found it impossible to sleep. Knowing that she didn't have to get up and take care of Bethany, she took one of the pills that had been prescribed for her right after Brad's death, and slept deeply until late morning. But her dreams were full of crazy images of her husband that made no sense, and she woke up aching for him all the more.

CHAPTER THREE

*T*he following days were difficult for Mallory as her grief became especially close and intense. She took Bethany to Provo where they stayed with her parents for a few days. It felt good to be out of the house and have company, but in her heart she knew she had to create some structure for her life. She asked for a father's blessing, and in it her feelings were validated. She was told that she needed to get out and do something, for her personal growth as well as her financial situation.

It was difficult going back home, but she spent a lot of time with Melody and occupied herself by going through the want ads in search of a job. She prayed for guidance in finding what would be best for her, but nothing felt right. Then one morning she woke up with a clear memory of walking into Buchanan's where a "Help Wanted" sign had been displayed in the window. As Mallory thought that through, she realized the possibility felt good. It was only a fifteen-minute drive at the most, and she had done some waitressing to work her way through school. Of course there was no guarantee that she would get the job, but she quickly made arrangements for Melody to take the baby so she could drive to the restaurant and get an application. The sign was still in the window, which gave her some hope.

That evening she meticulously filled out the application, praying for guidance in wording everything to her best advantage. Darrell called while she was in the middle of it. At first she resented the reminder of their embarrassing incident at the restaurant; but he apologized profusely, admitting that he'd had a tough week and sometimes he got a little overbearing. They ended up talking for over an hour, and Mallory had to admit that she enjoyed his company. She told herself it wouldn't be right to feel negatively toward him because of that one incident when he'd been so kind and good to her otherwise. She couldn't deny that she really liked him; and even though any romantic interest was the furthest thing from her mind, she couldn't help wondering if something might come together for them in the future. It seemed natural somehow, although at this point she couldn't imagine sharing anything beyond conversation with anyone but Brad. She wondered if that would ever change.

Mallory took the job application in the following day, then forced herself not to think about it. She had no idea how long it might be before they called her—if they called her at all.

But two days later the phone rang, and Buchanan's came up on the caller ID. With her heart pounding, Mallory forced a steady voice and answered.

"Hello," a deep male voice said, "may I speak to Mallory Taylor, please."

"This is she."

"Hi, this is Thomas Buchanan. I'm calling about an application for employment that you submitted at my restaurant."

"Yes."

"I was wondering if you could come in for an interview."

"That would be great. When?"

"Whenever it's convenient."

"Oh, I'm flexible," she stated, fighting to hide her excitement.

"How about ten-thirty tomorrow morning, then?"

"I'll be there. Thank you."

Mallory immediately called Melody and her mother to tell them the good news, and to ask for their prayers on her behalf. She really wanted this job. She found that it was easier to avoid her disturbing thoughts and the full intensity of her grief when she kept busy. And this was the perfect distraction. Buchanan's was a classy establishment, and she liked the caliber of people she'd seen working there.

There was a moment of panic when she found out that Melody had made plans to go to the temple with her mother and wouldn't be able to watch Bethany. In fact, Melody had been hoping that Mallory would watch *her* children. Of course, there were some women in the ward they could call on to tend children occasionally, but Mallory didn't feel nearly as comfortable with them. The problem was solved when Melody called back a while later to say that she'd talked to Janna, who had readily volunteered to come to Highland and watch all of the children.

When Janna arrived, Mallory said, "You really didn't have to do this, Mom. I know how busy you are. We could have made other arrangements."

"I know that. But these are my grandchildren. If I can't spend a day once in a while just being Grandma, what good am I?"

Mallory laughed and hugged her mother. "Well, thank you. I really do appreciate it."

"Are you nervous?" Janna asked.

"Yes." She pressed a hand over her stomach as it quivered in response to the question.

"Just relax and be yourself. Be completely honest and you'll do fine. If this guy is sharp, he'll sense your honesty, and that's the most important thing. If it doesn't work out, then it's not meant to be."

"I know. Just tell me that again when I come back without the job."

"Now, that's being positive," Janna said with light sarcasm. "Just go and get it over with."

Mallory turned the radio up loud through the short drive to the restaurant, hoping to muffle her nerves. She got out of the car and looked down to check her appearance. The cranberry-colored dress looked good on her. She just wished she didn't look quite so pregnant; that alone could deter her chances. But she was determined to be confident and make the most of this.

She approached the hostess at the front desk. "I have an appointment with Thomas Buchanan."

The hostess smiled and pointed to her left. "Down the hall toward the rest rooms and up the stairs on the right."

"Thank you," Mallory said and followed her directions, willing her heart to be calm. She forced thoughts away of the last time she'd gotten a job. It had been to work for Brad. She certainly hadn't been nervous about that interview; in fact, there hadn't been an interview.

At the top of the stairs, she found three doors. But only one said "Thomas Buchanan," and it was slightly ajar. She glanced at her watch. Ten thirty-one. She took a deep breath and knocked lightly.

"Come," a voice replied. She pushed the door open and stepped inside just as the man behind the desk came to his feet. For a moment she was stunned. This was the African-American gentleman who had served their meal the last time she'd eaten here—the one Darrell had argued with. Just her luck; the owner of this restaurant had been filling in to wait on tables that particular evening. She guessed him to be about thirty. He was good-looking, well-dressed, and dignified. She felt embarrassed and intimidated.

"You must be Mallory Taylor," he said, extending a hand across the desk. There was a glimmer of recognition in his eyes, and she felt sure that he knew he'd seen her before.

Mallory shook his hand firmly and replied, "Yes, and you must be Thomas Buchanan."

"That's right. Have a seat."

As Mallory attempted to make herself comfortable in the chair closest to her, she wondered how to handle this. She could hope that he didn't remember and ignore it. But then, she'd always have to wonder if he *did* remember, and it would hang over her. She made a quick decision on advice her mother had often given: It's better to confront something head-on and know where you stand, than to stew about it and let it bother you.

With that foremost in her mind, Mallory hurried to say, "I am really embarrassed, Mr. Buchanan."

"Why?" He chuckled and leaned back in his chair.

"I'm afraid the last time I ate here, my date was a bit obnoxious with you."

"Oh," he said with enlightenment, then he chuckled again. "Don't worry about it. I deal with that sort of thing all the time. And as I recall," he smirked subtly, "you were trying to hide under the table."

"Well," she laughed softly, feeling more at ease, "not literally, but I sure wanted to."

"All in a day's work," he said and leaned forward to look over a paper on his desk, obviously her application.

"So," he said without looking back up, "have you had any experience waiting tables?"

"In college, I worked as a waitress for a couple of years. Oh, I guess the politically correct term now is *server*."

"Yes," he chuckled, "but I'm not too picky about that, personally."

When he said nothing more, Mallory attempted to fill in the silence. "Of course, the place I worked at before wasn't nearly as nice as this, but I can learn."

He nodded and set the application down, leaning back again. "It says here that your education is in dental work. If you have a degree there, why are you applying for something like this?"

Mallory reminded herself of her mother's advice to be completely honest. If she got a job any other way, she could never live with herself. As uncomfortable as it was, she stated firmly, "My work in dentistry was done with my husband. I'm afraid the thought of working in it now would be too difficult."

"Divorced?" he asked with a little raise of his eyebrows.

Mallory cleared her throat. "No, widowed."

Though it was subtle, a compassion rose in his eyes that made her like him. "How long has it been?" he asked, but the tone of his voice made it evident the question was out of concern, rather than having to do with the job.

"Seven weeks," she said.

"Whoa. It's still raw then, I assume."

"Yes," she said, hoping he would change the subject, which he did. He asked her several questions about dealing with unhappy customers, her memorization skills, and the placement of silverware.

Mallory felt good about her answers and believed that he was impressed. Everything was fine until he said, "I can see that you're expecting a baby. When is it due?"

"Less than four months." She quickly added, "Mr. Buchanan, I realize that my pregnancy is a drawback, but—"

"Mrs. Taylor," he interrupted gently, "I've had pregnant employees before, and some reasonable maternity leave is not a problem. I just know it's difficult for a new mother to leave a baby and work. My only concern is in training you and then losing you."

"I need to work, Mr. Buchanan, and I feel good about this job, or I wouldn't have applied. I can't predict the future, but I do know that if you hire me I will be responsible and do my very best. That's all I can say."

"Is this your first pregnancy?" he asked.

"No, I have a daughter who is nearly two."

"I was simply wondering if you had any problems with the last one. You'll be on your feet a lot, and I don't want you to be too uncomfortable."

Mallory's concern over the question was eased by the way he talked as if she already had the job. Reminding herself not to jump to conclusions, she said, "I do better when I walk and stay active. I think I'll be all right. Again, I can't predict the future, but according to the last pregnancy, I should do fine."

Thomas Buchanan leaned back in his chair and looked thoughtful. She was beginning to think that he was contemplating a way to tell her she could leave and he'd get back to her, when he said, "I think we can make this work, Mrs. Taylor. When can you start?"

Mallory didn't breathe until she sputtered, "You're serious."

"Yes." He chuckled. "I like you. I'm certainly willing to give you a chance."

"Oh, thank you. I can start anytime."

"What will you be doing with your daughter?"

"She'll be with my brother's family most of the time. His wife is like a second mother to her."

"That's good, then." He discussed a tentative work schedule with her, saying that it would be fairly consistent so she could plan for childcare and keep her daughter on a regular schedule.

Mallory sat in the car for several minutes, trying to absorb all that had just taken place. Not only did she have the job, but she had every indication that the man who had just hired her was actually concerned about her personal well-being and her daughter. She muttered a quick prayer of gratitude, then wiped away an unexpected surge of tears as it occurred to her that she had just joined the force of single working mothers.

She arrived at Melody's house to find her mother fixing lunch for the children. "How did it go?" Janna asked right off.

Mallory sighed. Then she laughed. "I got the job."

"That's great!" Janna hugged her tightly.

Over lunch, Mallory told her mother every detail of the interview, interjecting the story of her date with Darrell and how embarrassing it had been.

"So, I take it this Darrell isn't anyone you could really be interested in," Janna said.

"Well, I'm not interested in *anyone* at this point, but . . . well, he really is a nice guy. I wouldn't say *never*."

"So," Janna took the subject back to where it had begun, "what will your schedule be? Did you discuss it?"

"Yes, actually. On Mondays and Wednesdays I'll do the lunch shift, so it's from ten-thirty to two-thirty. That way I can be home on Monday evenings, which I'm really glad for because I've been having home evening with Matthew and Melody. I'd really miss that. And I can have Wednesday evening to go to my Young Women's meeting. They haven't been expecting much of me lately, but I really like the calling and I think I need that in my life as well."

"That's good, then."

"Then I work Thursday, Friday, and Saturday evenings from five until closing. On the weekends they don't close until midnight, then there's a lot of cleaning up to do, so it will be late. But the good part about that is Bethany will be asleep most of the time I'm gone. And Jake and Dustin can maybe help some with Bethany so Matthew and Melody aren't tied up every evening on the weekends. They're closed on Sundays, and I have Tuesdays off."

"And you know your father and I are always willing to fill in. We can keep Bethany at our house one night every week or two, or one of us can come and stay here occasionally if we need to."

Mallory squeezed her mother's hand. "Thank you. You don't know how much that means to me. This way, Bethany will feel more like she's going to visit relatives instead of going to some strange baby-sitter day after day. That would be so hard. I truly am being looked out for."

"You're a good woman, Mallory," her mother said. "You deserve to be looked out for."

Mallory hated the thought that appeared in her mind and attempted to force it away. But, as always, her mother's perception was too quick and too keen to miss anything.

"What's wrong?"

"If I say nothing, you'll think I'm lying."

"I'll *know* you're lying."

Mallory sighed. "It's just that . . . I keep wondering if . . . well . . . maybe I'm not such a good woman after all. Maybe I wasn't as good a wife as I thought I was."

"Why? Because he killed himself? Are you implying that you think you did something to drive him to it?"

"I don't know. Maybe I am."

"That's the most ridiculous thing I've ever heard, Mallory. Whatever the reason, Brad made a choice. Even if there was some kind of difficulty between you, you're too caring and conscientious to make a man feel that uncomfortable. But even *if* you were an extremely difficult wife who made life awful for him, he still made a choice to deal with it that way."

"I know all of that . . . at least I think I do. I just . . . wish I knew why. I wish he had left me a letter, or a note . . . anything to give me just a clue as to why he would do this."

"I assume you've checked everywhere."

"I've gone through the whole house—twice. I haven't been in the study, but Matthew searched everywhere."

"What about the computer?" Janna asked.

"Matthew checked that, too. There was nothing on it except a few business records and scouting lists." Mallory shook her head and repeated. "If only I could understand. I've almost wished it had been murder, if only so I could believe it wasn't his choice. If nothing else, I'm glad to know the police ruled that out. They fingerprinted everything and examined all the evidence carefully. Sometimes I just have to tell myself that he really did put a gun to his head and pull the trigger. And I just don't understand how he could do that—or why."

"Well, whatever the reasons, he had to be far from his senses. I don't believe that any person of sound mind could do something like that."

"I'm sure you're right," Mallory said distantly. The thought in itself was disturbing. To try and comprehend how Brad must have been feeling made her so sick at heart that it took great willpower not to curl up and bawl like a baby.

Janna looked at her daughter long and hard. "You're awfully calm to be saying things like that."

"Sometimes I just feel numb to the whole thing. It doesn't seem real, and I can't feel anything at all."

"Well, I can understand that, but . . . do you feel that way all the time?"

Mallory smiled and patted her mother's hand, touched by her concern. "I can assure you I have my minimum daily requirement of tears, Mother." She became more serious. "It's hardest at night. When the house is quiet and I crawl into bed all alone, my thoughts get way out of hand. Sometimes I feel downright scared; scared to be alone with my thoughts and fears. I feel more vulnerable and sensitive to *everything* since he died. And I wonder if I'll ever get over it."

"Just take it one day at a time," Janna said. "I'm sure that eventually you will be able to understand all of this. If not, you'll at least find peace."

"Do you really think so?"

"If you pray fervently and work toward it, I'm absolutely certain of it." She paused and added, "How long since you've been to the temple?"

"I went a couple of weeks ago with Caitlin. I felt numb then, too."

"Well, maybe you should go again. In fact, you're all dressed up. Why don't you go, and I'll stay with Bethany."

"Are you sure?" Mallory asked, actually liking the idea.

"Yes, of course. Now, go."

Mallory enjoyed her time in the temple, although she saw no sign of Melody and her mother. She figured they had probably left before she even got there. She sat in the celestial room for nearly an hour and cried. She didn't feel any closer to understanding Brad's motives. But she did feel some peace, as if the Spirit had let her know that even though there were difficulties ahead, everything would be all right.

The peace hovered with her, but so did a nagging desire to get to the bottom of this. She felt strongly that she needed to find out what had been going on in Brad's head, and she prayed that the Lord would guide her in finding the answers.

Mallory's first day on the job went well, and she found it easier than she'd expected to memorize the menu and learn what everything was. She liked the tasting part the best, and was quick to tell Thomas—since he'd insisted that they work on a first-name basis.

"Well," he said while she was savoring a sample of some chocolate cake with fruit sauce, unlike anything she'd ever eaten before, "if you taste it, then you can describe it to the customer and give an honest opinion."

"I really like this job," she said when he offered her a sample of another dessert, laughing as he did.

After her first week at work, Mallory felt fairly confident and found she really enjoyed it. She liked the people she worked with, and found that even those who had been there the longest really liked and respected Thomas Buchanan. She learned through the other employees that his father had owned a small chain of restaurants in California, and Thomas had grown up following his father around through the process of running the business. He had a degree in business management, and another in culinary arts. Although he rarely cooked himself, he declared the need to know what he was tasting and what made it good or bad.

Mallory wondered what had brought Thomas to Utah, but she didn't want to be too nosy so she didn't ask. She got a clue, however, when he took an afternoon off to go to the temple. She did ask someone if he was married. She got the answer that he was divorced with no children, and he lived alone in a condo nearby. With her curiosity satisfied, Mallory was grateful to be working for such a good man.

All in all, she figured life was going as well as it could be under the circumstances—except for that nagging urge to uncover Brad's motives. Not knowing seemed to somehow magnify her grief, and she felt certain that getting some answers would help her move forward. While a part of her wondered if there was something she would be better off not knowing, she simply believed that she would feel more peace if she knew.

On a Sunday morning while she was getting ready for church, Mallory felt a need to make an appointment with the bishop. He'd been a wonderful support to her through all of this, and he'd kept close track of her. But she'd never completely expressed her concerns about this issue that wouldn't leave her in peace. Only now did it occur to her that Brad had told her he'd been working with the bishop to overcome some personal struggles through those months when he wasn't attending the temple. All through sacrament meeting, Mallory wondered how she could have been so dense as to have forgotten such an obvious clue. She concluded that perhaps the time just hadn't been right; maybe the Lord knew that she could only handle so much at once. That thought in itself was a little unnerving. Did the bishop know something that would be difficult to deal with?

Did she really want to know? Her instincts told her she *needed* to know, but they also told her to take someone along.

Mallory was continually grateful to be in the same ward as her brother's family. And it was especially nice today when she leaned over to Matthew in the middle of their Sunday School class and whispered, "I have an appointment with the bishop at three-thirty. Will you go with me?"

He looked at her in concern, as if to question her motives. "Are you okay?"

"Yes," she whispered. "I just don't want to go alone. I'll explain later. Can you go?"

"Sure. I'll see if Mel can watch Bethany."

"Thank you," she said and squeezed her brother's hand.

When the class ended and they stood up to leave, Matthew kept her hand in his. They were stopped near the door by a woman in her sixties who had recently moved into the ward. Looking a bit sheepish, she said, "Excuse me, Brother Trevor, isn't it?"

"That's right."

"You have to help me out here, so I don't think I'm going crazy. I thought your wife was the woman with long, dark hair who teaches Primary and . . ." She glanced down at Matthew and Mallory's clasped hands. "Well, I'm really confused."

Matthew chuckled. "Don't worry," he said. "I'm not a polygamist or anything. This is my sister, Mallory Taylor. She lives just down the block from me."

"Oh, how nice." The woman laughed with obvious relief, and Mallory found her concern amusing. She also found it endearing that she would come right out and ask rather than speculating behind their backs until someone bothered to straighten her out. She shook Mallory's hand eagerly. "It's a pleasure to meet you, Mallory."

"And you," Mallory said, then they hurried to the nursery to get Elizabeth and Bethany.

"The two little Beths," the nursery leader said. "They're so cute together, and sometimes we can hardly tell them apart. They look more like sisters than cousins."

"That's true," Matthew observed, picking up his daughter as Mallory picked up hers.

Later that day, Mallory was even more nervous than she'd expected as Matthew drove her to the church building for her appointment. They had to wait a few minutes for the bishop to finish up with someone else, then he invited them into his office and they were all seated.

"I see you brought your brother along," Bishop Hansen said. "He's sure good to look out for you."

"Yes, he is," Mallory agreed. "I don't know what I'd do without him."

"So, how are you doing?" the bishop asked Mallory intently. "I assume this isn't to renew your temple recommend, since you didn't come alone."

"No," she said, "I just need to talk. You've been wonderful through all of this, Bishop, but we haven't really *talked*. I guess with all of my family around, I've had the support I've needed that way, but . . . well, there are some aspects of this that I'm having trouble with, that I'm just not able to deal with. I've gone to the temple and prayed, and I just felt like I should come and talk to you."

"Well, then, I hope I can help." While Mallory was gathering her words to go on, he added, "Are you concerned with suicide in general? It can be hard to deal with."

"Well, not really . . . but . . . I mean, I know it's not black and white. I understand that a person would have to be greatly troubled to do something like that, and the Lord understands their frame of mind and is compassionate."

"That's right," the bishop said. "I find that many people have the old-fashioned idea that suicide is the same as cold-blooded murder and the guilty party will go to hell. And that simply isn't true. There is usually some kind of mental illness, addiction, or fear tied up with suicide—things that we can't possibly fully understand from our mortal perspective."

"I understand all of that," Mallory said. "I guess what I'm having trouble with is . . . well . . . Brad was often quiet about his feelings, and guarded about certain things. I know he had some struggles. But he didn't talk about them, and I certainly had no evidence to indicate there was anything serious enough to drive him to suicide." Her voice choked with emotion. "I just don't understand why he did it, Bishop. How could he leave me like this, without giving me any clue at all as to why he would do it? I just don't understand."

"Well," the bishop said thoughtfully, "I would have to assume that this ties into the problem that he discussed with me several times. It makes sense to me that—"

"That's just it, Bishop. *What* problem?"

Mallory's heart quickened at the bishop's expression. He wasn't just mildly concerned. He looked downright upset.

"Oh, dear," he said, and turned to look at the wall as if to think this through. Mallory and Matthew exchanged a hard glance. It seemed like forever before the bishop turned back to look at Mallory, saying gently, "I honestly thought you knew, Mallory. I had no reason to believe otherwise."

Almost wanting to put off hearing something that she knew would upset her, Mallory asked, "Did he tell you I knew?" As she said it, she thought she could live with Brad's neglect in telling her something a lot better than she could live with him lying outright.

"I honestly don't remember. But I don't think he ever said that. Perhaps I just assumed that he had discussed it with you."

"Discussed what?" she finally asked.

"Mallory," the bishop leaned his forearms on the desk and folded his hands, "Brad struggled off and on for years with pornography."

Mallory didn't know what she'd expected, but it wasn't this. It seemed so ridiculous that she almost laughed. "Pornography?" she echoed in a tone that implied this man had no idea what he was talking about. Her mind had heard what he'd said, but her senses refused to accept it. "You're talking about *my* husband? Brad Taylor?"

Bishop Hansen nodded, saying quietly, "I can't believe you didn't know."

Mallory squeezed her eyes shut as her senses began to perceive that she was being told something more horrible than she could ever have comprehended. She understood now the need to have her brother present, and she instinctively reached for his hand. It was cold and sweaty, and he squeezed back so hard that she knew he was as shocked and upset as she. But she wondered how he could manage to appear so calm. Maybe it was his training as a lawyer. Whatever it was, she felt grateful to have him here. If her impulse to fall apart manifested itself, at least he could carry her home.

CHAPTER FOUR

*M*allory said nothing more. She only nodded her head occasionally to indicate that she was listening as the bishop briefly explained her husband's repulsive habit. He'd gotten into it almost accidentally as a teenager. It was the reason he hadn't gone on a mission, and the reason he'd avoided going to the temple for such a long time.

The bishop told Mallory that in spite of Brad's struggle, he didn't see him as being hypocritical. "He tried very hard to get it under control, and would sometimes go for months without any problem. But eventually he was always drawn back to it. Still, he was very careful not to attend the temple or partake of the sacrament when he was struggling.

"Pornography can be an addiction," the bishop continued. "It's like drugs or alcohol or smoking. You lose control and you can't stop. Brad wanted to stop, and he came to me with a great deal of humility. But he refused to get any professional help, and there was only so much I could do."

Following a miserable silence, the bishop said gently, "I know this is a shock to you, Mallory, and it's going to take time for you to digest all of this and adjust. I want you to know that I'm here for you, any time of the day or night, if you need to talk."

She nodded, then felt Matthew help her to her feet as he thanked the bishop and they left the office.

"Are you all right?" he asked when they were in the car.

Mallory only shook her head. Matthew took her home and went inside with her. They sat on the couch in silence for several minutes before he said, "I can't believe it. How can someone have a problem like that and keep it from the people who know him best?"

Mallory finally found her voice. "That's exactly what I've been thinking—over and over. If I didn't know the bishop so well, I'd think he was lying to me."

Matthew turned to Mallory. "Did you have any clue? Anything at all?"

Mallory tried to concentrate, but she was too much in shock to think. "I . . . don't know. If there were clues, I obviously missed them."

"Well, you had no reason to think there was something like that going on." A minute later Matthew added, "At least that explains what we found in the wood-burning stove."

It took Mallory a moment to grasp what he was saying. When she did, the shock began to subside into a sick smoldering in her stomach. Is that what he'd burned? Pornographic magazines and videos? Had those things been in her home all this time? And her husband had been . . .

"Oh, help!" she murmured and doubled over in pain. Matthew held her while she ached to cry, but her emotions were trapped beneath a blanket of absolute shock. While her mind whirled with the reality of what she'd just learned, the sickness she felt turned into a tangible nausea, and she hurried into the bathroom to throw up.

When Mallory left the room, Matthew took the opportunity to call his parents. Janna answered the phone.

"I'm at Mallory's. I think you and Dad had better come over here."

"Is she all right?"

"It's hard to tell."

"Matthew? What is it?"

Matthew sighed. "We just found out why Brad killed himself; or at least we've got a real big clue. She's pretty upset."

"Is it—"

"Please don't make me say it over the phone, Mother. Just come over. And don't bring the boys."

Matthew hung up, then hurried to call Melody and tell her they were having a crisis. "I'll explain later," he said. "Will you be okay with the kids?"

"Of course. Is there anything else I can do?"

"Just pray," he said and got off the phone.

"Who was that?" Mallory asked when she came out of the bathroom.

"It was Mel. She's got the kids under control. I can stay as long as you need me."

"Thank you. I shudder to think what I'd do without my family. Maybe we should call Mom and Dad and—"

"I just did. They're on their way over."

Mallory sighed and sat down hard.

"Are you okay? You seem awfully calm."

"I'm in shock, Matthew. It just seems so detached from Brad; so incomprehensible. I cannot even fathom the Brad I knew being involved with something like that. But he . . ." Mallory stopped as a memory assaulted her.

"What?" Matthew asked when her eyes became distant, then widened in horror.

"Oh, help," she muttered and wrapped her arms around herself as that sick knot tightened inside her again.

"Tell me! What?"

"Oh, Matthew . . . just a few days before he . . . died . . . I found a magazine in the car." She began to breathe sharply as puzzle pieces began falling into place in her mind, and the picture forming was too horrible to believe. She prayed that this numbness would stay with her, knowing that in its absence she would crumble.

"I just assumed that someone had used the car and left it in there. And I . . . I told him so. Apparently he just went along with my story. I made it awfully easy for him to cover it up. I just couldn't possibly imagine him doing something like that." She shook her head. "I still can't imagine it. I just can't."

"Me neither," Matthew said quietly. He was obviously as shocked and horrified as she.

"I have a question," Matthew said a minute later. "How could Brad go through periods of not taking the sacrament without any of us noticing? We all sat together in church. Does that make sense to you?"

Mallory thought about it carefully. "Come to think of it, he spent a lot of time with Bethany out in the foyer after she came along, and . . . well, sometimes he was late for the meeting. But I . . . never really thought about it. Why would I even think something like that was a clue to a problem? Am I so naive?"

"If you're naive, then I am, too. We were awfully close, Mallory. I never would have dreamed."

Mallory groaned and stood up to pace the room. "I thought we were educated, Matthew. Our mother is an abuse survivor who works with victims at crisis centers. She consciously educated us on the things she'd learned."

"Apparently this is something she'd never dealt with. And even if she had, Brad was obviously very skilled at covering up what he was doing. You can't blame yourself for that."

Mallory kept talking about her feelings, saying the same things over and over until an angry momentum built up inside of her. She kept pacing the floor, ranting about the hurt and betrayal she was feeling, not to mention the horror and disgust. Matthew just listened quietly until their parents arrived, then he helped fill in the pieces as Mallory told them what they had learned. As she told her parents the way she felt, her anger grew steadily.

An interruption came when the phone rang. It was Melody, wondering if she should put Bethany to bed.

"No," Mallory said into the phone, needing the comfort of what seemed to be the only good thing that Brad had left her with.

Matthew offered to go get the baby, and Mallory calmed down as she held her little girl and put her to bed. Then the anger set in again, harder and deeper as Mallory contemplated the horror of what this child's father had been doing under their roof. Again her parents and Matthew listened patiently as she raged through every possible thought and emotion. Janna told her more than once that it was good for her to be getting all of this out in the open, but two hours later she was still vacillating between helpless sobs and uncontrollable anger. At that point, Janna said, "Mallory, honey, I wonder if you're not getting worked up a bit much here. You've said the same things several times. Anger reaches a point where it just feeds on itself. Why don't you sit down, and we'll talk. I know you're feeling grief and—"

"How can I possibly feel grief when I feel so *angry*?" Mallory snarled. "I *hate* him. That's all there is to it. I can't believe he would do that to me. How could he possibly do something so horrible?"

"I don't know, Mallory," Janna said calmly while Matthew and Colin just sat at opposite ends of the couch, both looking as if they were about to cry. "But when you get past all of this anger, you're going to have to accept that no matter what he did, you still *do* love him. And you're going to have to forgive him if you ever want to get on with your life."

"*Forgive him?*" she practically shrieked, pacing the room frantically. "How do you forgive something like that? I feel betrayed; double-crossed. It's like he was cheating on me. He might as well have gone out and slept with another woman."

"Mallory," Janna's voice remained steady, "I know that what you're feeling right now is tough, but maybe you need to try and get inside of Brad's head and understand what was behind it. You have no idea how his problem began. He was a good man in many ways, honey. I'm certain it's not black and white. If you can understand what he was going through, then you can work toward coming to terms with it. Let's talk about it and—"

"I don't want to talk about it!" Mallory shouted. "If he was still alive, I'd kill him myself. If—"

"Mallory!" Janna finally raised her voice. Colin and Matthew both looked up. Mallory stopped pacing. "I know you're angry, and I understand how you feel, but you need to—"

"No, you don't!" Mallory actually yelled at her mother. "You have no idea how I feel right now, so don't try to tell me. You have no idea how it feels to find out that your husband, the one person you trusted and loved more than anyone on earth, betrayed you and defiled everything you had together because he—"

"That's enough!" Matthew interrupted firmly, and Mallory turned to him in surprise. She couldn't recall ever hearing him speak to her so brashly. "You have no idea what you're talking about," he said. "So just leave it alone."

Mallory glanced at her mother. Janna's expression betrayed some kind of torment, and huge tears rose into her eyes. At first Mallory thought her mother was simply upset because her anger had been out of line. But a quick glance at her father and brother made it evident that she'd missed something. Letting go of her anger was suddenly easy as a different kind of tension descended over the room. While she was trying to recall what she'd said that had brought this on, her father said firmly, "Sit down, Mallory, and listen to what your mother has to say."

Mallory did as she was told. She saw Janna blink back the tears, and her expression consciously changed to firm and confident, masking whatever heartache had briefly come to the surface. Mallory knew that she'd unwittingly opened a can of worms, but for the life of her she couldn't imagine what. She knew her mother had suffered some horrible things, but she couldn't see how any of it tied into the present situation. And whatever was in that can, Matthew knew about it. In fact, he looked somehow like a wild animal ready to pounce.

"I'm listening," Mallory finally said, if only to break the silence.

Janna cleared her throat and lifted her chin. "I know that what you're feeling right now is unspeakable. You have every right to feel hurt and betrayed, and I understand your anger. It will take time to heal, and even longer to find peace and forgiveness. But anger and bitterness will not bring you any closer to that peace, Mallory. As hard as it is, you've got to concentrate on empathy, and allow the Spirit to help you see the whole picture. We're all willing to help you through this, but we can't do it if you keep screaming and ranting like an angry child. Anger is a step in the grieving process, but it's a step that will end up hurting you if you stay there too long. It's all right to walk through the valley of grief, but you can't camp there."

Mallory stared at her mother in stunned silence, attempting to digest everything she was saying. Matthew spoke in that same brash voice. "Your mother is a very wise woman, Mallory. You'd do well to listen to what she has to say. She's only trying to save you from more misery."

Mallory realized that thoughts of Brad were distant as she read between the lines of all her mother had said. She felt ashamed of her angry outburst and compelled to ask, "What price did you have to pay for your wisdom, Mother?"

Janna didn't answer the question. She just met her husband's eyes, and a tangible energy permeated their gaze. Colin shifted his focus to Mallory and stated with determination, "She paid a higher price than you could ever imagine."

He looked back at Janna as if to imply some secret message. Janna apparently understood when she said, "Don't you dare tell her, Colin. It's in the past. It's done."

"Yes, I know," Colin said to his wife as if they were alone, "but it's a part of what you and I are today. And maybe she *needs* to know, if only to help her get past what she's going through. How could anyone look at you, knowing what you've risen above, and not realize that anything is possible?"

When Janna said nothing, Colin turned to Mallory with such intensity that her heart began to pound. She felt as if he was about to throw something at her that would knock her to the floor.

"Your mother does know how you feel, Mallory. Her losses were different than yours, but she's suffered betrayal of the deepest kind. She's known bitterness and anger, justified as it was, that drove her over the edge."

Mallory felt prone to clarify, "The nervous breakdown. She's told me about it. I was just a baby."

"That's right." Colin spoke now as if Janna wasn't present. "But she didn't tell you why."

Mallory had to protest. "She told me it was all the effects of her abusive past that she hadn't dealt with."

"And that's true. But it's not the whole truth." Colin looked at Janna again, and Mallory knew she'd never forget the gaze they exchanged. Their expressions were far too complex and intense to describe, but something deep and resolute passed between them. Then his eyes shifted back to Mallory. "I haven't said it aloud for over twenty years. Your mother's right when she says it's in the past. It's forgiven and we've found peace. But it's not forgotten; at least not in the sense that you never forget such intense heartache. You're never free of what certain choices do to your life."

Colin leaned his forearms on his thighs, his gaze riveted on Mallory. His voice lowered to a near whisper. "I cheated on her, Mallory. With my children in her care—including you—I went to bed with another woman."

Mallory tried not to appear shocked, but she couldn't help it. "I can't believe it." She gasped and turned to look at Matthew, then at her mother. Their expressions verified that this was no joke.

"Neither can I," Colin said, drawing her attention back to him. "To this day, I cannot believe that I would do something so thoroughly stupid. But it wasn't black and white, Mallory. It was complicated. And sometime when you're beyond this a little more, we can talk about it if you'd like. If it will help you understand and cope with your own struggles, I'm more than willing to share what I've learned. The important thing for you to see right now is that . . . well, look at her. She *hated* me, Mallory—and with good cause. She swore she would never forgive me. But eventually she got past all of that. Look at her!"

Colin motioned toward his wife, and Mallory looked at her mother. There was no malice or bitterness in her eyes at being reminded of this horrible event in her past. Mallory saw nothing but raw compassion for her husband as he talked about something that she knew had to be difficult for him.

"She's incredible, Mallory. If you start adding up all that she's suffered in her life, you wouldn't dare tell her that she doesn't know how you feel. But she's conquered it. She's been to hell and back. But she didn't let it beat her. She's strong, and competent, and she has more to give than any other human being I've ever known."

Colin wiped the tears from his daughter's face, then took her hands into his. "You're strong and competent too, Mallory. And you can get through this. We love you, and we're here for you. Just remember who and what you are. You're a daughter of God, and you are very much like your mother. She's raised you with the skills you need to take on anything and conquer it. If she can do it, you can do it. Don't ever forget that."

Mallory eased into her father's embrace and cried on his shoulder, oblivious to the tears of everyone else in the room. When exhaustion overtook her emotion she drew back, saying, "You're pretty incredible yourself."

Colin wiped the tears from her cheeks, saying sadly, "Only because she forgave me. If she hadn't given me a second chance, I'm not sure I would have amounted to much."

Colin grasped her shoulders and looked at her hard. "I want you to think about that with respect to Brad. His spirit lives on, Mallory. The eternal ramifications of what he's done are complicated and difficult to understand from our perspective. We don't know what brought on his problems, but God knows, and he is merciful and just. Brad obviously felt helpless to fix his problems, but he's gone home now, where he can be helped. I believe he'll have the opportunity to make choices where he is now, and his progress will continue accordingly. I don't think he ever intended to hurt you; he was just caught up in something he couldn't control." He sighed and touched her face again. "You think about that, okay? And we'll talk sometime when you're not so tired."

Mallory nodded, and he hugged her tightly. She *was* tired. But she felt hesitant to leave the comfort of her father's embrace.

Janna offered to stay with Mallory and insisted that Colin and Matthew both return home, since they had to work tomorrow. When the men were gone and the house locked up, Janna sat down next to Mallory on her bed. "You need to get some sleep," she said. "Why don't you get into your pajamas and I'll—"

"I'm not sleepy, Mother. My head is spinning so fast I don't know which way is up."

"Do you need to talk?" Janna offered.

Mallory shuffled through her thoughts, trying to discern where she might start. With the horrible discoveries she'd made today, she was surprised to realize that her most prominent thought concerned her parents. At the risk of making her mother uncomfortable, she just had to ask, "Is it true, Mom? Did he really sleep with another woman?"

Janna sighed and looked down. "Yes, it's true."

"Obviously it still bothers you."

"No, Mallory," Janna looked her straight in the eye, "I forgave your father a long time ago for what he did. He's right when he says it's in the past. The only thing that bothers me now is how you will see it. I'm not against having my children know about our history and our problems, if it will help them to learn and understand life a little better. But your father is a good man, and I don't want you thinking any less of him. It's not black and white."

"He mentioned that earlier. What do you mean?"

Janna sighed again. "I mean that my behavior contributed to the problem. I reached a point where I was so consumed by fear and anguish, as a result of the abuse, that I couldn't even function. I couldn't tolerate letting him touch me because all I could think about was my father's abuse. I treated him horribly. I shut him out completely. Of course, he made the choice to turn to someone else, and he was certainly accountable for that. But it wasn't like he just went out to find another woman because he was bored."

"I still can't believe it."

"Well, I can understand that. But I think you should be more concerned with your own struggles. You have a lot to come to terms with. Your husband had a very serious problem, and he chose to deal with it in a way that's left you with a lot of hurt. I think it's natural for you to feel betrayed and cheated on. I think if it was me, I'd feel…well, perhaps jealous. You've got to wonder where his mind was, and what he was doing with his spare time. You can't think too hard about that, I suppose."

"No, I don't think I can," Mallory said. As her mind shifted gears to the reality of what she'd learned today, an intense heartache enveloped her. She cried as she told her mother how she felt, until exhaustion crept over her again. But she still felt too wound up to sleep.

"Why don't you get ready for bed," Janna said, "and I'll get you one of those pills. I'll listen for Bethie while you get some sleep."

"Thank you, Mother," Mallory said as her mother handed her the pill and a glass of water.

"Today's been rough," Janna said, "but I think you've worked through a lot of emotions. As hard as it may be to see it, you're going in the right direction. I know it doesn't feel that way now, but you're going to be okay."

Mallory was grateful for the drowsiness that overcame her from the drug when her mind wouldn't stop playing through the dramas that had unfolded this day. She slept soundly and woke up feeling groggy. The memories of yesterday came back to her, seeming dreamlike and horrible. She lay in bed for a long time, just trying to comprehend all that had happened, then she glanced at the clock and panicked. She was frantically getting dressed when her mother came through the open bedroom door.

"What are you doing?" Janna asked.

"I'm getting ready for work. I'll be late if I don't hurry. How long have you been up?"

"Since Bethany woke up."

"Can you take her to Mel's for me and—"

"No, I'll just stay with her. Your dad is coming back after his court sessions today. Are you sure you're up to working? I'm certain your boss would understand if you—"

"I *need* to go to work, Mom. It's a lot better than sitting around here thinking."

"Okay, but you have to eat something. Can I fix you some toast and juice for the road?"

"That would be great. Thanks, Mom."

Mallory turned the stereo up loud and tried not to think as she drove over the point of the mountain. But tears came anyway, and she had to quickly retouch her makeup in the rearview mirror before she went in. She quickly got to work, taking care of anything she could see that needed doing. It ended up being a slow day, but she used spare minutes between waiting tables to help in the kitchen, wanting only to stay busy enough to avoid her thoughts.

Thomas startled her when he asked, "What are you doing?"

"I'm scrubbing this pan."

"I can see that, but we have people who are hired to do that kind of thing—people who need to earn their keep."

Mallory kept scrubbing. "Jamie's got the dining room covered. She was reading last I noticed. I needed something to do."

Thomas removed the pan from her hands and gave her a towel. "From the looks of you, I'd say you probably need to go home."

"I'm fine."

"You're lying. You've been upset since you got here. The lunch crowd is gone. Go home."

Mallory looked at Thomas, feeling somehow dazed by his perceptiveness. Then with no warning, tears bubbled out in a large quantity. She turned away and pressed the towel over her eyes, grateful that no one else was in this end of the kitchen at the moment.

"Thanks a lot." She attempted some light sarcasm, if only to ward off her embarrassment. "I was doing just fine until you had to go and tell me I wasn't." She sobbed against her will and suddenly wanted to be home, but she wondered how she would drive in this condition.

As if he'd read her mind, Thomas said, "I think maybe you could use a good cry before you go. Why don't you—"

"I'm not going to sit in a stall in the ladies room and—"

"I was going to suggest that you go upstairs."

As her emotion intensified, Mallory could do nothing but nod in an attempt to express her gratitude. Then she hurried up the stairs to the office, taking the towel with her. She cried long and hard and felt grateful when her emotion finally settled into a familiar, detached ache. She was just gathering her wits enough to drive home when Thomas knocked at the door then peeked his head in.

"You okay?"

"Better, I think. Thank you."

He came in and closed the door behind him. She stood up to go and gripped the back of the chair, feeling a little light-headed. "You can have your office back now. Thank you for—"

"Are you sure you're okay?" he asked, furrowing his brow in concern. "Have you eaten anything?"

Mallory had to think about it. "No, actually. I'll just go home and—"

"No, you sit down and I'll get you something to eat."

Mallory didn't have a chance to protest before he rushed out of the room. She sat back down and fought the urge to cry again. Thomas returned in less than five minutes with a tray that he set on his desk. Mallory was a little stunned to see a spinach salad, a baked potato, a broiled chicken breast, and a glass of lemonade. "Is this okay?" he asked.

"It looks wonderful, but—"

"Stop arguing and just eat it."

"Thank you," she said and took a bite of the salad. "You make me feel like crying again."

"Why?" he asked with a familiar chuckle.

"I don't know," she admitted. "Maybe you're just one more piece of evidence that God is looking out for me. First you give me a job, pregnant and all. Then you actually *care* about me." She took another bite. "Then you give me food that—"

"It's leftover. I'd rather feed it to you than those guys in the kitchen. They're already overweight."

"Yeah, me too," she said with her mouth full, rubbing her rounded belly.

Mallory ate while Thomas sorted through some papers, then he leaned back in his chair and said, "Forgive me if I'm being nosy, but . . . I know you lost your husband not so long ago. I guess I just want to say that . . . well . . . even though I was very young, I remember when my mother died. Weeks, even months after she was gone, I would catch my dad crying uncontrollably. I think it just comes in spurts, and you have to let it out. It's got to be tough."

Mallory contemplated what he'd said. She knew it was true. But she found herself wishing that her grief could be that uncomplicated.

"Did I say something wrong?" he asked.

"Oh, no. Of course not." She wanted to tell him how she felt, but she wondered if that would be pressing their professional relationship a little too far.

Again, he seemed to almost read her mind. "If you want to talk, Mallory, I'm willing to listen. Do you have anybody to talk to?"

"Oh," she laughed softly, "I have so many people to talk to that it's almost pathetic. My brother and his wife live down the street. In fact, we practically live with each other. We're talking all the time. My sister lives close by. She's a nurse and she's dating a lot, but when she's around we talk and talk and talk. And then there are my parents. My mother's practically a psychologist—minus the formal education in that area. She's worked in crisis centers and helped more people than I could count."

"Wow," Thomas said. "Maybe you don't need to talk."

"Well, my family is wonderful. But sometimes I think they're too close to the situation. They all loved my husband too, and . . ." Mallory hesitated. "I'm really not sure I should get into this."

"I've got all day," he said, and something in his eyes told her he meant it. "Maybe somebody unbiased could listen with a new perspective." He chuckled. "I may not be able to give any good advice, but I'm a great listener."

"Well," she leaned back, "you're right when you say the grief comes in spurts. Some days I hardly feel it. Other times it's so close that I feel like I'm going to blow up. I somehow think God designed us that way, so we wouldn't feel it all at once. How could we bear it?"

"I'm sure you're right."

"If I could simply just miss him and mourn his loss, it would be so much easier. But the truth is, at this point, I think if he was still alive, I might be contemplating a divorce. And somehow that's . . ." Her voice cracked. "It's worse because . . . I love him so much and . . ."

Mallory became lost in thought for a moment, then looked up at Thomas. "You've been through a divorce."

"Yes, I have. I'd say it has its own grief and mourning."

"I'm sure it does."

"So, was his death partly a relief?" he asked when she said nothing more. "I can see why that would be confusing and—"

"Oh, no," she interrupted. "His death was devastating. I thought our marriage was close to perfect. I was truly happy."

"So what happened?" he asked with a sincere interest that actually surprised her.

Mallory forced an emotionless voice. "You get the idea that your marriage was not as good as you thought it was when your husband shoots himself in the head."

Thomas's shock was evident. Mallory laughed uncomfortably in an effort to ease the tension.

"I had no idea," he said gently. "Do you know why?"

"I do now; or at least I've finally got a clue. Until yesterday, I was completely baffled. I had nothing to go on."

"And yesterday?" he asked, but Mallory realized that his questions only came after long spells of silence. He really was a good listener.

Mallory looked at Thomas. She hardly knew him. She thought of the answer to that question and realized that she couldn't say it. She couldn't even say the word out loud without getting sick all over again.

"I can't talk any more," she said, bolting to her feet. "Thank you, Thomas. For lunch. For your time; your understanding. You're wonderful. But I . . . I have to go now."

"Will you be okay?" he asked, following her down the stairs.

"Yes, fine. Thank you."

Mallory hurried out to the car as if she was running from a reality that might smother her. She only wished she could run far enough and fast enough to know that it would never catch up with her again.

That evening Mallory's father returned, and Matthew and his family came over to join them for dinner. As soon as they'd eaten, Colin asked if he could use the computer in the study to type up some notes.

"I avoid that room personally," Mallory said, "but you're welcome to use anything there."

After the kitchen was cleaned up, the adults sat down to visit— minus Colin, who was still in the study. Mallory felt dazed and completely emotionless, but afraid to have her family leave, not wanting to be alone with her thoughts. A distinct uneasiness crept up her back when she noticed her father come up the stairs, looking concerned. He whispered something to Matthew, then the two of them went to the basement.

"Business," Janna said. "They can be so boring when they talk business."

But twenty minutes later they both returned to the front room, looking terribly somber.

"Is something wrong?" Janna asked.

Matthew said to his two older children, "Why don't you boys run upstairs and watch your video in Aunt Mallory's bedroom."

They did as their father asked, while Mallory wondered what they wanted to discuss that was for adult ears only. The two little toddlers playing on the floor were too young to understand.

"Mallory," Colin said, sitting close beside her, "I found something on the computer that you should know about."

Mallory leaned forward. Had they found a letter, or something personal from Brad? She didn't know how to ask, beyond the obvious question to her brother. "Didn't you already check it? I thought you said there was nothing personal there at all."

"That's right," Matthew said. "But . . ." He glanced toward his father.

"I deleted what I was working on when it wasn't going the way I wanted it to," Colin explained, "then I decided I wanted to check that first draft for something. So I went into the recycle bin to retrieve it. There were dozens of files there that had been deleted, but were still on reserve. The computer keeps them there in case you change your mind. Apparently Brad got rid of a great deal, but he forgot to dump them permanently."

"Well, what was there?" Mallory demanded, longing for some last piece of evidence that Brad loved her; to know what he was feeling in those final hours.

Colin and Matthew exchanged a severe glance before Matthew cleared his throat and said, "Mallory, there were literally hundreds of pornographic pictures filed on that computer. Apparently he'd gotten them off the Internet, and—"

"Oh, help," Mallory murmured as the sick reality she'd been fighting to escape suddenly welled up and threatened to smother her.

"It's all completely erased now," Colin said. "I'm thankful you didn't come across them yourself. It didn't take much to realize what was there, but it was enough to make me sick."

"Oh, help," she repeated more vehemently, grateful to feel her mother's arm around her.

Mallory fought with everything she had to keep from getting upset. But betrayal and grief and disgust all whirled together in her mind, resulting in a torrent of confused emotion that refused to be held back. Her parents stayed the night, then Colin went to work and left Janna again to spend the day. On Wednesday Mallory managed to stay alone until it was time to go to work, where Thomas asked if she was doing all right, but said nothing more. She returned from work to spend the evening with Matthew and Melody, not going home until she was too exhausted to do anything but sleep. Matthew carried a sleeping Bethany down the street and laid her in her bed, then he hugged Mallory and left.

As always, Mallory's sleep was filled with strange dreams and horrid images. She woke up three times and cried herself back to sleep, so confused, so filled with raw emotions that she doubted her ability to ever feel anything good again. She kept her mind constantly in prayer, knowing it was the only thing that could save her from the frightening reality of what was going through her head. She wondered how she could have lived with a man for so long and been utterly clueless that something so horrid was going on. Was she so stupid? She tried to comprehend the man she loved actually spending time— finding pleasure—looking at images that were likely more repulsive than anything she could even conjure up in her wildest imagination. She wondered what kind of thoughts had been going through his mind while he'd been so quiet and distant. And perhaps most sickening of all, she had to wonder what might have been in his head during their times of intimacy. Had he truly been with her, or had his mind been caught up in other things he'd seen?

The whole thing was so horrible, so unbearable, that Mallory found it difficult to even get out of bed the next morning. She barely took care of Bethany, praying with everything she had that she could be free of—or at least distracted from—the intensity of this pain she felt. She just didn't know how she was going to cope.

CHAPTER FIVE

*M*allory went to work Thursday evening, determined to stay strong, praying with everything inside her for something—anything—to ease this deep heartache and confusion. Thomas pulled her aside once and asked if she was all right. She assured him that she was, thanked him for his concern, and continued working. If nothing else, she was grateful for her job, and grateful for the distraction it offered.

Even though she went to bed terribly late Thursday after getting home from work, Mallory got up early and worked hard. She cleaned every minute she could between her efforts at keeping an active toddler content and safe. When it was time to go to work, she felt tired and wished instead for a nap.

Before Mallory even arrived at the restaurant, she realized she didn't feel very good, and wondered if she had overdone it today. She debated whether or not she should work at all, but she reasoned that Friday was their busiest night, and she could sleep in tomorrow. Convinced that her body was just drained from all of the emotional struggle and extra work, she forced herself through the evening, attempting to ignore the fact that she wasn't feeling well at all. She didn't bother to even define what was bothering her specifically until she felt a sudden cramp and hurried into the bathroom, grateful that her shift was almost ended and the restaurant was nearly cleared of customers. At the discovery that she was spotting a little blood, Mallory didn't even think twice about telling Thomas that she was leaving—if she could find him. Realizing he was upstairs, she headed up, only to be stopped by another cramp. Then another.

Stranded by pain in the center of the stairs, Mallory prayed aloud for help, then she called Thomas's name, hoping it was loud enough for him to hear, but not so loud as to disturb the few remaining diners. Thomas appeared at the top of the stairs. She sighed with relief and said, "I'm going home now. I'm hurting too much to come up the stairs any farther. I'm sure you'll manage without me."

As the pain relented slightly, Mallory turned to go back down the stairs, praying she could just get home. Another cramp forced her to wait to take another step.

"You really are hurting," Thomas said from behind. "What's wrong?"

"I don't know," she admitted. "But if I can just get home, I'll—"

"I don't think you should drive," he insisted, not hesitating to add, "Come on. I'll take you."

Mallory's desire to protest was squelched by more pain. She was not only hurting, she was scared. "Okay," she said. "I'll let you. I can send my brother up for my car tomorrow or . . . Oh, my gosh." She pressed her hands low on her belly. "It really hurts."

"How far along are you?" Thomas asked, helping her into his car.

"Not far enough," was all she said.

Neither of them had much to say as Thomas drove south over the point of the mountain. Beyond noticing that he was driving extremely fast, Mallory was oblivious to anything but the pain she was feeling, and the fear that she might actually be losing this baby. The symptoms were far too intense to rationalize away. They were nearly to Highland when she said, "I think maybe you should just take me to the hospital."

"I was about to ask where it was."

"Just keep going up this highway, then follow the blue H signs. It's not much farther."

Thomas watched Mallory as carefully as he could while he drove, feeling terribly helpless. Her pain was increasingly evident, and he felt sure that whatever might be happening was serious. He didn't know Mallory Taylor very well, but well enough to know that she didn't need any more trauma in her life. Their relationship had been purely professional beyond that one brief conversation in his office. But then, he'd always been one to encourage a certain level of personal interest in the people he worked with. He was glad he'd been available to help her.

And if he could be the right person in the right place for her, so be it. He only wished he could do something to offer her some comfort.

Thomas actually carried Mallory into the hospital when they arrived, and he stayed with her until some medical personnel actively took over. Once she was left in their care, he felt a little lost. He'd gotten her safely to the hospital, and he knew she had family she could call. But he felt hesitant to leave.

Thomas approached a nurse at the desk and asked about Mallory's condition. She directed him to another area of the hospital to wait, and promised him that he would be notified of her condition. He used a pay phone to call the restaurant and make certain that everything was under control. It was late, but he didn't feel tired. He watched TV in the waiting room and thumbed through some magazines, wondering if he should just go home. But instinctively he felt like he should stay, at least until he knew she was all right and had family with her. He wished he had thought to ask who he could call. He considered looking in the phone book, but there were likely hundreds of Taylors, and that was her married name. She'd talked about her brother and parents, but he wouldn't even begin to know who they were.

Resigned to staying, Thomas reminded himself that he had no reason on earth to leave. There was no one who needed him, nothing to go home to. Being alone in the waiting room, he lay back on one of the couches, but it was only a few minutes later that a nurse approached him, saying that Mallory had been taken to a regular room a few minutes ago. He inquired about what had happened, not wanting to have to ask Mallory. And the nurse asked, "Are you a relative or . . ." She stammered slightly. "Her husband?"

"No, no." He chuckled, knowing her hesitation came from the fact that his skin was a different color from Mallory Taylor's. "I'm just a friend; I'm the one who brought her in. Is it a problem if I see her, or—"

"No, that's fine." The nurse then explained that Mallory had lost the baby, which didn't surprise him, but it made his heart ache on her behalf. "We've just given her something for the pain, so she may be a bit groggy." She then gave him the room number and simple directions to find it.

"Thank you," Thomas said, and realized he was nervous as he approached Mallory's room. The door had been left partly open, and he could see her in the dim light, lying on her side, her eyes closed. With trepidation he stepped into the room and sat in a chair close to the bed.

Mallory sensed movement nearby and opened her eyes. She was surprised, but not disappointed, to see Thomas. Trying very hard to not feel the reality of what had just happened, she was grateful for a distraction. "What are you still doing here?" she asked.

"I didn't want you to be alone, and I didn't know who to call."

"Oh," Mallory's eyes closed, made heavy by the medication they'd given her, "you didn't have to stay, but . . ." She opened them again. "But thank you anyway. I . . . I . . . was just thinking I should ask the nurse to call my parents and—"

"Would you like me to do it? If you'll tell me the number, I'd be glad to—"

Mallory repeated the number and Thomas quickly dialed the phone on the bedside table, glancing at his watch which verified that it was past two in the morning.

"What's their last name?" Thomas asked quickly as it was ringing.

"Trevor," she said, appearing to be asleep otherwise.

Thomas's heart quickened as a woman's voice answered in a panicked tone and he realized that he was the bearer of bad news.

"Mrs. Trevor?" he said.

"Yes?"

"My name is Thomas Buchanan. Your daughter Mallory works for me."

"Yes. What's happened?"

"Well, I brought her to the hospital a couple of hours ago. She's doing fine now, but she wanted me to call you."

"Thank you, but . . . what's wrong?"

Thomas wished he'd gone out of the room to make this call. He didn't want to say it in front of Mallory, but he understood her mother's need to know. As quietly and calmly as he could manage, he said, "She's lost the baby, Mrs. Trevor. We're at American Fork hospital. I'll stay with her until you can get here."

"Thank you," she said. "Thank you so much. We'll be there right away."

Thomas gave her the room number, then he hung up the phone and leaned back in the chair, actually glad that he could stay until

Mallory's parents arrived. He wondered if she had fallen asleep, then he noticed tears leak from beneath her eyelids. She bit her lip and turned her face deeper into the pillow. While it was tempting to just ignore her emotion and pretend he wasn't there, Thomas felt compelled to reach out and wipe those tears away.

Mallory felt fingers on her face, and she didn't have to open her eyes to know who they belonged to. While embarrassment was the least of her concerns, she laughed softly in an effort to ease the tension. "I'm sorry," she said. "You're going to think that all I ever do is cry . . . which is probably true."

"You've got good cause to cry, Mallory. I only wish that . . ."

Mallory opened her eyes when he didn't finish. She saw him lean back in the chair and look away.

"That what?" she asked.

"Well," he turned toward her, "I can't possibly understand how you're feeling, and I know I can't fix what's wrong, but . . . I know how much you must be hurting, and . . . you could probably use a shoulder to cry on. I just wish that . . . that I knew you well enough to give you the comfort you need."

Mallory didn't know how to tell him that his presence and his gentle words really had made a difference. She simply reached out a hand toward him, saying, "You're here, and I'm really glad that you are."

"You want to talk?" he asked.

"No, but . . . I don't want to be alone."

"I'll stay until your parents come."

"Thank you," she said and closed her eyes, crying silent tears into her pillow, occasionally tightening her grip on Thomas's hand as if to reassure herself that he was there.

While she cried, Thomas watched her closely, trying to comprehend the source of her tears. He could well imagine that losing a baby had to be one of the most difficult things a woman could go through. But to have to face that along with losing her husband—to suicide, no less . . . and he knew there had to be complications and emotional repercussions tied into her husband's death that were far beyond his comprehension. In fact, he had to wonder how she was coping at all.

Thomas was startled from his thoughts when he heard someone enter the room. He looked up to see a middle-aged couple, obviously

Mallory's parents. In fact, Mallory's resemblance to her mother was striking. Thomas came to his feet and Mallory's mother rushed to her side, bending over the bed to hold her tightly. Mallory became more emotional now that she had the shoulder she needed to cry on.

"Hello," Mallory's father said, extending a hand. "You must be the young man who called us."

"That's right." Thomas shook his hand firmly. "I'm Thomas Buchanan. I run the restaurant where Mallory works."

"Colin Trevor," her father said. "It's a pleasure to meet you. We're very grateful for your bringing her here, and staying with her."

Thomas glanced toward Mallory and said, "I understand she's been through a lot lately. I'm glad I could help."

Thomas excused himself and slipped out of the room, feeling suddenly more alone than he'd felt in a very long time. Given the circumstances of his life, that was pretty bad.

When Mallory finally calmed down, she told her parents what had happened. They stayed with her until she slept, and they were there to take her home later that day after her doctor had given the okay to release her. She hadn't been home long when Thomas called to see how she was doing. He assured her that everything was covered at work for as long as she needed to recuperate, and that he'd call in a few days. Later that day, flowers arrived with a card that read: *Our thoughts and prayers are with you. Your friends at Buchanan's.*

Through the next few days, someone in the family was with Mallory most of the time. The Relief Society brought meals in, and she had several visits from sisters in the ward, as well as the bishop and home teachers. The evidence of how much people cared was touching, especially when ward members had already given so much after Brad's death. Mallory was grateful for their help and compassion, just as she was grateful to have family members surrounding her, willing to give so much. But nothing or no one could take away the layers of heartache that refused to relent. Janna assured her that healing took time, and grief had to run its course. But Mallory felt at times that she would never survive that long. Consolation came only in the fact that losing her baby had made her less preoccupied with Brad's pornography habit. *Some consolation*, she thought wryly.

Mallory had always felt like she had a great deal of faith. She'd never had trouble trusting in the Lord and believing that as long as she did her best to do what was right, whatever happened in life was according to his will. But now she found herself asking questions without answers, and she felt certain that her faith had only come easy because it had never been truly tested.

Looking back at Brad's death, it all seemed dreamlike and unreal. She felt more like he had just left her and decided not to come back. She missed him dreadfully, and at the same time she resented his absence. Thinking through the reasons for his death—or at least the problems he'd had—she felt as if she'd been living in some kind of bubble since the day of their marriage, oblivious to harsh realities that had been taking place right under her nose. She felt incompetent and just plain stupid to have lived with something so horrible for so long without ever having a clue.

And now, as if life wasn't difficult enough, she had to have this child taken from her. She'd felt it moving and thriving inside of her, all the while thinking that it was a gift Brad had left to help compensate for his absence. Now that it was gone, she felt empty. Achingly empty.

Janna urged her to talk regularly, but more and more, Mallory found it difficult to talk. It was difficult to cry. Difficult to feel anything at all.

A week after the loss of the baby, Janna and Mallory talked late into one evening. It was the third night this week that Janna had stayed over so Mallory wouldn't have to be alone. Even though tomorrow was Saturday and Colin didn't have to work, he'd stayed at home to be certain the boys came home from their dates when they were supposed to.

"You know," Janna said, "I lost a few babies myself."

"You did?" Mallory was surprised.

"I thought I'd told you."

"Maybe you did, but I'd forgotten. How far along were you?"

"Well, three of them were pretty early on, but one was probably about the same as you were with this one. I remember feeling it move a great deal, and becoming very attached to it. There's no describing that kind of loss."

"You lost *four* babies?" Mallory couldn't comprehend what she was hearing. "Was there something wrong?" she asked, at the same time realizing that Janna had given birth to five healthy children.

"There was something wrong, all right," Janna said. "My husband was knocking me around."

Mallory squeezed her eyes shut, reminding herself that it could always be worse. A minute later Janna said, "I know you're really struggling right now, Mallory. But what's bothering you most?"

"It's hard to tell," Mallory said.

"Well, what are you thinking about the most?"

Mallory thought about it a minute. "I keep thinking how that baby was the only good thing—except for Bethany, of course—that Brad left with me. And now it's gone."

"Brad left you a great deal that's good, Mallory. You have a lot of good memories, don't you?"

"Yes, but . . . now they're all . . . tainted. I have to wonder what was going on in his head, what he was doing when we weren't together. And it just repulses me. I've heard just enough about pornography habits to make me sick to my stomach when I think about it. And I don't want to know any more than I already do. Maybe if he was here, and we were trying to work it out, it might be worth knowing the details of what he was dealing with, so I could help him. But he's gone. And I don't want to know."

"There's no reason for you to get into that. You just need to heal. It's only a suggestion, but perhaps you should do your best to simply force those negative images away; disconnect them from your memories, and just keep your memories the way they are."

"I don't know if I can," Mallory admitted. "I can't hardly close my eyes without imagining horrible things. And if I force my thoughts away from that, I realize that my baby's gone and . . ."

"Maybe you should have a priesthood blessing, honey. Perhaps that would help free you of these negative thoughts and feelings, and help you find some peace."

"It couldn't hurt, I guess," Mallory said, but in her heart she wondered if she would ever feel peace again.

"Well, I'll get your father and brother over here tomorrow to take care of it. In the meantime, you get some sleep."

Mallory fell asleep quickly, but her dreams were disturbing as they often were, and she woke up before dawn and couldn't go back to sleep. Her memories wandered through the final week of Brad's life, as clearly as if she was watching it on a video tape. Then a thought so horrible struck her that she sat straight up in bed, finding it difficult to breathe.

The house was barely light with morning when she rushed down the hall to the room where her mother was staying. She thanked God that she was not alone as Janna looked up, startled from the book she'd been reading. "What is it?" she asked as Mallory rushed to her side, too consumed with fear to cry and too upset to speak. "What, Mallory?" Janna repeated. "Take a deep breath and tell me what's wrong."

"I . . . I . . . I did it. I did it."

"Did what, Mallory? What did you do?"

"I did it to him, Mom. I did."

"Honey, I'm sorry, but I'm lost. Now settle down. Breathe slowly, and tell me what you think you did."

"I did it to him," she said, nearly hyperventilating. "I killed him." Hearing the thought come back to her aloud, Mallory doubled over with tangible pain and cried, "I did it. I killed him." Over and over she repeated it. "I killed him. Oh, heaven help me," she murmured, "I killed him."

* * * * *

Matthew reached for the phone on the bedside table just as he was coming awake.

"Matthew," his mother's voice sounded alarmed, "I know it's early for a Saturday, but . . . we're having another crisis over here. I need some help, and your father can't get here fast enough."

"I'll be right over," Matthew said and hung up the phone. Then to Melody, "Something's wrong with Mallory. Do you think you can live without me for a while?"

"Sure," she said. "What is it?"

"I don't know."

"That poor girl," Melody sighed and gave her husband a quick kiss. "I pray she can get beyond all of this."

"Yeah, me too."

Matthew used a hidden key and went into the house without knocking.

"We're up here," his mother hollered. He followed her voice

upstairs to the spare bedroom, where Mallory and his mother were both sitting on the edge of the bed.

"What's wrong?" he asked, sitting on the other side of his sister.

"Tell him, Mallory," Janna said.

"I did it. I killed him."

"That's the most ridiculous thing I've ever heard," Matthew said. "What on earth makes you think that—"

"I did it, Matthew," she muttered. "If it weren't for me, he'd still be alive."

"Now you listen to me, Mallory, Brad made a choice."

"But I . . ."

"What?" Janna encouraged. "Come on, Mallory. We've got to talk about this."

After Janna and Matthew both pressed her for several minutes, Mallory finally said, "I remembered how . . . when I found that magazine, and he told me it belonged to some doctor who had borrowed his car, and I . . . I . . ." Emotion finally bubbled out. "I told him how sorry I felt for that guy's wife. I told him about all of the horrible things that resulted from pornography; the crime and abuse, and . . . I went on and on about it. And that was just . . . two days before . . ." She pressed her head into her hands and wailed. "Oh, heaven help me. I killed him."

Matthew had always looked to his mother to be level-headed and know the right thing to say. But she looked helpless—or perhaps just weary of having dealt with so much on her daughter's behalf. She wouldn't have called him if she hadn't needed some help. He took a deep breath and lifted Mallory's chin so that she had no choice but to look at him.

"Listen to me, Mallory," he said. "Brad had a problem. And Brad made a choice. He may not have been thinking clearly, but he still loaded that gun. He put it to his head. And he pulled the trigger."

Mallory winced, and fresh tears surged out. But she continued to look at him, as if she was aching to have him say something that might give her peace.

"If you had known he had a problem, you might not have spoken so boldly about it. But you didn't know because he didn't tell you. He *chose* to keep you ignorant. You can't fix something you can't see,

Mallory. He was a good man in many ways. He treated you well. He was responsible. And we all loved him. But he *deceived* you. Do you hear me? He led you to believe that everything was perfect, when—"

"That's just it, Matthew. I always told him how grateful I was that our relationship was so good; that our lives were so close to perfect. Maybe he didn't tell me because I was so adamant that I didn't want problems between us. Maybe he—"

"Listen to me." Matthew took hold of her shoulders and looked at her deeply. "You didn't do anything wrong. We all make mistakes in ignorance. A lot of times we make mistakes knowing full well that we are. But you have done nothing—*nothing*—to warrant feeling this way. Do you hear me? He was committing a sin. He was allowing something horrible to go on, and he willfully kept you ignorant of it."

"But the bishop said he knew he had a problem, and he was fighting to overcome it, and—"

"Yes, but how hard can we be fighting for something while we keep a spouse in the dark about it? He was being unfair to you, Mallory. Do you remember when you said that sometimes you felt like there was a bad spirit in your home, and you had to work very hard to keep from feeling dark and discouraged?"

Mallory's eyes widened. "Yes."

"You mentioned it to me many times, saying that you thought it was just your imagination, or you wondered if you were just not spiritually strong enough to keep such things away." Matthew's voice deepened. "You were blaming yourself for a problem that he was creating. And when you talked to him about it, he brushed it off and allowed you to go on feeling that way. Is that not true?"

"Yes," she said after a moment's thought.

"Now, I don't think you need to be shattering all of your good memories of Brad by concentrating on the negative. On the other hand, don't go making him some heroic martyr by rationalizing away the things he was doing that were *wrong*. Any time through the course of his struggles he could have come to you with some humility and told you that he had a problem and he needed some help. If he knew you at all, he should have known that you were committed enough to help see him through anything to the best of your ability. But he chose the coward's way out. Counseling is tough. Admitting to your wife that you've got serious problems is tough. In some ways, suicide is the easy way out, Mallory."

Mallory thought about that for several minutes while Matthew and her mother each held one of her hands. Then she looked at her brother and said, "But you told me he couldn't have been thinking clearly to do what he did. You told me God would be merciful and understand what was going on inside of his head."

"And that's all true, Mallory. It's not black and white. We don't know why or how he got started in such a disgusting habit. We don't know the desires of his heart. But God does. And Brad will be given a fair chance to right the wrongs that were beyond his control in this life. That's not our concern. Our concern here and now is that you come to terms with it and find peace. You have a daughter to raise, and a long life ahead of you."

Mallory leaned her head on Matthew's shoulder, and he put his arm around her. "I just feel so lost and confused."

"That's understandable," Janna said. "And you mustn't be too hard on yourself. Healing takes a long time. You're not only grieving the loss of your husband, but the loss of what you believed your marriage was. And on top of that, you've lost a baby. Take it one day at a time. Time truly will help you heal."

Nothing more was said for several minutes, and Janna told Matthew, "I suggested to Mallory last night that she should have a priesthood blessing. I think it would help."

"Yes, I'm sure you're right. Do you think Dad can come over or—"

"He's helping with a service project this morning, but he can come by this evening."

"Well," he glanced at Mallory, "maybe I can call one of her home teachers or something. But first, maybe we should get her something to eat."

Bethany woke up a few minutes later and was quickly running around the house creating havoc. If not for Mallory's organization and a baby-proof home, Matthew thought the child would surely push her over the edge. Of course, his own toddler was equally difficult. But combined with everything else in Mallory's life, Bethany was definitely a challenge.

Janna urged Mallory to take a shower, insisting she'd feel better if she got cleaned up. Then Janna went to the kitchen to start some breakfast while Matthew changed Bethany's diaper and got her dressed. He was barely finished when the doorbell rang.

"Maybe that's the Relief Society with breakfast," Matthew said lightly. "Then you won't have to cook it."

"I'm doing just fine," Janna said with a little laugh. It had become a family joke since the Relief Society had taken such good care of Mallory through her struggles.

Matthew opened the door and was a little surprised to see a man he'd never met before. He was about the same height as Matthew, dressed in a suit. And he was African-American. Wondering if this guy was trying to sell something, Matthew asked, "May I help you?"

"I'm looking for Mallory Taylor. Do I have the right house, or—"

"Yes," Matthew said. "She's busy at the moment. May I tell her who—"

"Mr. Buchanan," Janna said, appearing at Matthew's side. "Come in."

"Thank you," Thomas said, stepping into the entryway and closing the door.

"Matthew, this is Mr. Buchanan. He's the one who took Mallory to the hospital."

"Oh, of course." Matthew shook his hand eagerly. "Mallory works for you. She speaks very highly of you."

Thomas said lightly, "She hasn't known me long enough to know better. And please, call me Thomas."

Matthew chuckled. "I'm Matthew Trevor, Mallory's brother."

"Oh, of course. She tells me how well you take care of her. It's a pleasure to finally meet you."

"Come and sit down," Janna said, motioning toward the front room.

"Oh, I don't need to stay," Thomas said. "I was just on my way back from the temple and thought I'd stop by and see if Mallory needed anything. But she's obviously being looked out for." He paused and added, "How is she doing? I can't imagine having to go through everything she's gone through, and in so short a time."

"Oh, some days are better than others," Janna explained. "I'm afraid today's already been a rough one, but . . . we're doing our best to help her through."

"Well, if there's anything I can do," Thomas said, "anything at all, just call the restaurant. If I'm not there, they can get a message to me anytime."

"Thank you," Matthew said. "Actually," he drawled, feeling compelled to add, "we were just going to hunt down someone to help me give her a blessing. If you're on your way back from the temple, I assume you could help me with that."

Thomas was momentarily taken aback, but he had to admit, "I'd be honored, but . . . perhaps Mallory's not comfortable with that. She really doesn't know me very well."

"Why don't we just ask her?" Janna said.

"As long as you make it clear that I won't be offended if she would prefer someone else."

"Why don't you sit down," Janna said to Thomas, "and I'll go talk to her. I think she's out of the shower now."

Thomas sat down on the couch while Matthew gathered Bethany's dirty clothes off the floor and left to take care of them. He returned to find Bethany attempting to give all of her toys to Thomas. He was setting them one at a time on the couch beside him while she talked in words he couldn't understand, but he did his best to answer.

"This must be Mallory's daughter," Thomas said as Matthew sat back down.

"Yes, this is Bethany," Matthew said. "She's a handful."

Thomas chuckled. "She's certainly adorable."

"Looks like her mother."

"I guess beauty runs in the family," Thomas commented.

Matthew's thoughts were drawn away to Mallory's present heartache, and then back to his childhood when he had observed his mother struggle through so many difficulties. More to himself he said, "That's not all that runs in the family."

CHAPTER SIX

*M*allory was barely dressed when her mother knocked at the bedroom door. "Are you doing okay?" Janna asked while Mallory combed through her wet hair.

"I think so," she said. "It's hard to tell."

"Thomas Buchanan is here. Are you up to seeing him, or—"

"Yes, tell him to wait. I won't be long."

"Matthew asked him if he would help give you a blessing." Mallory stopped combing, feeling more surprised than anything. "He was very gracious. He said he'd be honored, but since you didn't know him well, he wouldn't be offended if you would prefer someone else."

"No," Mallory said, "that's fine. It's all the same priesthood, right?"

"That's right." Janna smiled and gave Mallory a hug. "Everything's going to be all right, you know."

"I'd like to think so."

"You're strong, and you're going to get through this."

Mallory attempted a smile. "You just keep telling me that, Mother. I don't feel very strong right now."

"Those are the times when the Savior will help carry you through. All you have to do is trust him enough to let him do it."

"Maybe that's the hard part," Mallory said.

Janna looked concerned as she left the room, adding, "I'll tell him you'll be down in a few minutes."

Thomas was still visiting with Matthew and helping entertain Bethany when Mallory came into the room. "Hello," she said.

Thomas came to his feet. "How are you?" he asked, holding out a hand.

Mallory took it and said, "I'm okay. How about you?"

"I'm fine. It's you I'm worried about."

"Physically, I've recovered well. As for the rest, I'm just taking it one day at a time," she said as they sat down.

Janna broke the tension by suggesting they give Mallory a blessing, then they could all have some breakfast together. Mallory felt tense as the blessing began, but she was quickly filled with warmth. If nothing else, she felt better to know that her spirit was not completely dulled.

In the blessing Mallory was told that Brad was where he needed to be, and that all was well with him. She was also told that the heartache of losing her husband and baby would be compensated for as long as she remained faithful and was striving to live the gospel. She was promised more children in the future, and told that the Lord was mindful of her suffering, and he would not allow her to suffer any more than she could endure. Although her healing would take time, and would often be difficult, she was promised that in time she would find complete peace and understanding.

When the blessing was finished, Matthew gave Mallory a hug, telling her that he loved her. Thomas held out a hand, but impulsively she hugged him too, thanking him for coming. He graciously accepted Janna's breakfast invitation and they all visited casually around the table, while Bethany kept interrupting with her antics. Mallory said little, but she always felt better when there were people around to distract her from the reality.

Mallory didn't feel any miraculous, immediate changes from having a priesthood blessing. But over the following days she felt more calm, less afraid, and she was able to return to work and do all she needed to do without feeling prone to crying all the time.

A couple of weeks after Mallory lost the baby, a huge bouquet of flowers was delivered from Darrell Alden. Mallory was touched by his sentiment, and she almost called to thank him. But she just didn't have the fortitude to initiate anything beyond the bare necessities of her life. Darrell called the following day, and she found that she was truly glad to hear from him.

"I heard about your loss," he said gently. "I just wanted you to know that I was thinking of you. Are you doing all right?"

"As well as could be expected," she said.

"I would have called sooner, but I figured it would be better to give you a little time. Is there anything I can do?"

"No, not really," she admitted. "But it's good to hear from you."

"Well, it's good to talk to you," he said, and the tone of his voice was eager. "The truth is, Mallory, I've thought about you a great deal. But I thought it might be better if I kept my distance until you were able to put Brad's death behind you a little more."

Mallory's heart quickened as she grasped the underlying message of what he'd just said. Was he implying a romantic interest in her? For some reason, the thought spurred a tingling that made her heart go even faster. Wondering if she'd misunderstood, Mallory felt the need to ask, "What are you saying, Darrell?"

"I'm saying that when you're ready, I would like to see more of you—much more. I think we understand each other. I don't know whether or not it could ever come to anything permanent; only time will tell, I suppose. And the last thing I want to do is make you feel pressured. Healing from grief is a very individual thing, but . . . well, I was wondering if perhaps in the meantime, we could . . . well, would you like to go out this weekend? Are you up to it?"

"I wouldn't mind going out," she admitted, suddenly liking the idea very much. "But actually, I work evenings on the weekends."

"Oh, you're working?"

"Yes."

"Where?"

"Buchanan's. That restaurant where—"

"I remember," he said. "Do you like it?"

"Yes, actually. Very much." She wanted to tell him that the man he'd been so rude to was the owner. But that incident was in the past, and she preferred to leave it there.

"How about Sunday evening? There's a fireside here in our stake. Would you like to go to that?"

"Uh . . ." Mallory thought quickly. "That should be fine. I'll see if I can get someone to watch Bethany."

"Great. I'll pick you up at six-thirty."

Mallory looked forward to Sunday, realizing that she was lonely. Of course, she had family she could call anytime. But she was trying very hard not to rely on them so heavily. And in truth, the weeks since Brad's death seemed like an eternity. She longed for some male companionship, and hoped that she wasn't being too hasty. She recalled having a crush on Darrell Alden in high school, and how disappointed she had been when their casual association had not turned into something more. She certainly wasn't ready to think about marrying again. But that didn't mean she couldn't socialize— which, if nothing else, kept her distracted from the emptiness in her life. And she didn't want to wait too terribly long to get married. She prayed that the right man might come along, certain that it might make up for all she'd been through. And maybe, with any luck, Darrell Alden might just be the right man.

Her date with Darrell went well, and she thoroughly enjoyed herself. He took her out again on Tuesday, since it was her only day off, and they talked on the phone every day. And the following week they went out to dinner. He actually suggested going to Buchanan's, but she insisted that she didn't want to eat there. Not only was she exposed to the food each and every day, but she didn't want everyone she worked with gossiping about her social life.

Darrell asked her questions about herself continually, always showing a keen interest in everything she said. And he often made comments that made it clear he was well aware of her.

After a movie one evening, he commented, "I notice you wear dark colors a lot. You must like them."

"I feel like they suit my coloring," she said. "Yes, I suppose I do like dark colors."

"And you don't wear much jewelry, I've noticed."

Mallory glanced down at the simple wedding band she'd worn on her right hand since Brad's death. It was the only jewelry she had on except for a simple pair of little silver loops in her ears.

"No," she said, "I'm not really into jewelry. I collect it more than wear it," she added lightly.

Mallory began seeing Darrell regularly. And even though it wasn't discussed between them, she began to believe they would get married. She asked her mother if she was moving too quickly, but Janna assured her that it was simply up to her, whenever she felt ready. Matthew and Melody agreed with Janna. So, with the validation of those she loved most, Mallory felt eager to get on with her life.

Six months after Brad's death, Mallory's brother, Jake, left on his mission. She had positive memories of the blessings that had come to the family through Matthew's mission, as well as Caitlin's. While it was hard to see him go, it was an exciting time for the entire family. And Mallory was pleased to be able to afford contributing to his monthly financial support. She was so accustomed to relying on others that it felt good to be doing something for somebody else.

Working at Buchanan's became something she enjoyed more and more. Between her wages and the tips, she made enough money to meet the needs of her little family and still have some left over for extras. Thomas continued to be a good friend, showing concern for her and always being fair in whatever came up.

For the most part, Mallory felt numb concerning the losses in her life. Brad's death and all that went along with it simply seemed like a bad dream. She ached from missing him, and the hole he'd left in her life was difficult to work around. But with time, she became more accustomed to his absence and concentrated on hope for the future. The problems she had discovered in his life were still difficult for her to grasp; but she found that, in a way, they helped ease her grief somewhat. There was some relief in knowing that she didn't have to face such problems. She certainly would have been willing to do it had he lived. But he was gone now, and there was nothing she could do about it. If finding something positive about his absence would help, then she was all for it. And one positive aspect was the fact that she didn't have to face up to having a husband with a severe pornography habit. She began to look at his death as something of a sacrifice on her behalf. Looking carefully back over the days before his death, she could almost believe that he had done it to spare her and Bethany any repercussions from his problem. It didn't completely make sense, but it helped ease her own emotions over his death.

In thinking through some memories more closely, Mallory recalled telling Brad, less than a week before his death, that she couldn't live without him; that losing him would be devastating. She realized that he had only heard what he'd wanted to hear, and obviously the circumstances had been distorted according to his state of mind. This understanding helped Mallory believe that in the long run there was nothing she could have said or done to make a difference.

Trying to concentrate on the positive, Mallory took the time to write down some of her good memories with Brad. Her purpose was to record events and reflections that would someday mean something to Bethany, since she would not remember her father. But as she went through the process, Mallory found that it was therapeutic for her; it helped put her life with Brad into perspective. The most difficult memory to write about was the night she'd observed him singing a lullaby to Bethany while she slept. Knowing now that it was only hours before his death, she realized that he'd been telling his daughter good-bye. The thought was chilling and brought on an overflow of emotion, but Mallory felt that the tears were cleansing. She talked to her mother about the progress she'd made, and Janna was pleased. But she cautioned Mallory not to get too comfortable, because grief came in many layers and sometimes in unexpected ways. Janna wanted her daughter to be prepared to handle whatever the future might bring. And Mallory appreciated her mother's insight.

With the coming of fall, Mallory reached a stage of great ambition. She felt motivated to clean her home from top to bottom, and she was able to get rid of most of Brad's things in the process. She harbored some keepsakes and special things, sent a box of things to his parents, and gave the rest to charity. She went through everything of his except for a drawer in the bedroom dresser that was filled with odds and ends of Brad's—mostly junk, she concluded as she rummaged through it. And yet the combination of everything in the drawer somehow illustrated his personality. Mallory decided to leave it for the time being, rationalizing that she wasn't certain what to do with any of it. But a part of her knew she was avoiding it for the sake of clinging to some formless attachment that she hadn't felt for the rest of his belongings. Overall, going through his things was a difficult job, but Matthew and Melody helped her, and once it was finished she felt some renewal.

The only real difficulty that arose through the course of her cleaning project was the occasional pornographic magazine she would find tucked away in an odd place. Each time she would burn it promptly without taking a second glance, forcing away the sick knot that formed in her stomach. She wondered occasionally how she might have felt to come across them if he'd been alive. How would she have confronted him? How would she have felt to realize that he had this problem, and that he'd lied to cover it up? Of course, she loved him and she'd been committed to the marriage. She knew in her heart that she would have done everything in her power to help him overcome his problem and to heal their marriage. And if he had worked with her in overcoming the problem, she believed that eventually everything would have been all right. But no matter how she looked at it, the reality of his death and the reasons for it were difficult.

Mallory urged her mind elsewhere and threw her most recent find into the wood-burning stove. She squirted lighter fluid all over it and struck a match, forcing negative thoughts away as she watched it burn. Then she went into the bathroom to wash her hands, finding herself scrubbing them almost raw, as if she could wash away some kind of filth she might have been exposed to from just touching the magazine. As she dried her hands, a memory surprised her. Brad had been a compulsive hand-washer. He had claimed that it was from his mother's germ consciousness, and she had often teased him about it, never dreaming that it might have deeper implications. But Mallory knew that compulsive behaviors, in some cases, were an effort to cover up something in a person's life that wasn't right. And now she had to wonder if there was a connection.

Needing some feedback, she called her mother. "Did I ever tell you that Brad was a compulsive hand-washer?" Mallory asked.

"You might have. I don't recall."

"Well, think about it for a minute."

"Oh, I see," Janna said.

"And," Mallory added, "remember how fanatic he was about having a clean bathroom?"

"Yes. You often said it was a blessing for you, because you never had to clean it. He always did, even before it needed cleaning."

"That's right. Well, you probably know more about such things than I do. I think you're the one who told me that compulsive cleanliness could be a sign of something amiss. I never dreamed that such a thing might have clued me in to a problem."

"I don't think any of us did, Mallory. He was such a good man in so many ways."

"Yes, he was," Mallory had to agree. "And I miss him, but . . . I found another magazine. I burned it."

"How many is that?"

"I haven't kept track. But I've been through the whole house. There couldn't be any more . . . unless he was really imaginative."

"You never know, I guess, the lengths someone will go to in order to cover something up. It's a lot like drugs or alcoholism. People rationalize that it doesn't hurt anyone else, and they'll do just about anything to keep getting their hands on it, and to keep it hidden from those who would disapprove."

"It's pathetic, isn't it?"

"Yes, Mallory, it is." After a moment's silence, Janna changed the subject. "So, you're going out with Darrell again tonight."

"Yes. Now that Thomas has changed my schedule a little, I can actually go out on a weekend."

"That's nice. Do you know what you're doing?"

"A play and dinner. I've never heard of the play, but the theater has a good reputation. I'm sure it will be nice." Mallory decided now would be a good time to ask her mother something she'd been wondering for weeks. "Mom, do you like Darrell?"

"I've only met him a few times. He seems nice. You like him. Isn't that what counts?"

"Yes, but . . ."

"But what?"

Mallory really wanted to ask if it was normal to feel uncomfortable with little things that didn't really matter. She hadn't felt uneasy about anything with Brad. But then, what difference had that made? He'd outright deceived her. For the most part, she enjoyed being with Darrell. She'd met his daughters and they seemed taken with her, and she believed she could handle taking them on full-time. She just didn't feel one hundred percent good about the situation. But she said nothing more to her mother, and passed her feelings off as being paranoid after the way Brad had misrepresented himself.

On a Saturday in October, Mallory went with Matthew and his family to their parents' home for a big barbecue. Their grandmother—Colin's mother—was there also. Nancy Trevor had been widowed a few years back, but she was in good health and still lived on her own. She took a great interest in her family and declared that she was glad to see Mallory doing so well.

Mallory returned home late evening and put Bethany to bed before she sat down to read from the scriptures. She got up to answer a knock at the door and found Darrell standing on the porch with a large package. "Come in," she said with a little laugh. "How are you?"

"Great. And you?"

"I'm fine."

"I brought you a little something," he said.

"It doesn't look very little." She laughed again. "What's the occasion?"

"Oh, just because," he said.

Mallory sat on the couch and opened the large box to find a beautiful skirt and sweater set.

"Oh, it's very nice," she said, and she meant it. But she didn't bother commenting on the color, which was a pastel pink. She never wore pastels; in fact, she felt like they made her look a little sick. "I've never owned anything pink," she added, wondering if she could find out where he'd purchased it and perhaps exchange it for another color.

"I thought you might like a change," he said as if he was terribly proud of himself. "I saw it and thought you'd just look stunning in it."

"Thank you," she said. "You're very thoughtful."

She wore the outfit the next time they went out, and Darrell raved and raved about it. But Mallory really didn't feel that great in it. She figured that eventually he would learn what she did and didn't like, and it really wasn't that big a deal.

As the holidays approached, Mallory spent more and more time with Darrell and his daughters. She didn't always agree with his methods of disciplining the girls, but she could see that he loved them. More and more, she found herself envisioning a life with him. He often told her that he loved her, and she told him the same, even though she felt that her feelings didn't compare to what she'd felt for Brad. She reasoned that Brad had been her once-in-a-lifetime love, and she couldn't expect to feel that way again. If nothing else, having Darrell in her life made the holidays less difficult.

Mallory spent less time with Matthew and Melody now that her life was so full with Darrell. She spoke to her mother and sister occasionally, but there just never seemed time enough to get into deep conversations. She continued working, and Thomas often asked how and what she was doing, showing a genuine concern. She told him an occasional tidbit about the man she was dating. He teased her some, and she felt a certain closeness to him since he'd helped her through a crisis in her life. But she felt hesitant to open up too much about her feelings, perhaps fearing it might interfere with their professional relationship.

On a particularly busy evening at the restaurant, Thomas asked Mallory to cover the front desk while he waited on tables, since they'd had two different employees call in sick. Mallory was looking over the list of parties waiting to be seated when Thomas appeared at her side, looking at the list over her shoulder. "How are we doing?" he asked.

"Not too bad, actually," she replied quietly. "If we can get this party of eight seated in the next few minutes, we should handle the rest just fine."

When he said nothing more, Mallory glanced up at him in question. She was surprised to find him watching her, his expression intense.

"Is something wrong?" she asked, returning his look firmly. Her mother had taught her long ago the importance of illustrating through body language that you won't allow yourself to be intimidated. Coming from a woman who had been severely abused by two different men in her life, Mallory trusted Janna when she said that people send off subconscious signals that let others know how they will allow themselves to be treated.

"No, Mallory," he said, his gaze deepening, "nothing's wrong."

Mallory's first impulse was to feel frightened, or at the very least concerned, to realize Thomas Buchanan was looking at her that way. But her first impulse quickly receded into something calm and tranquil. She held his gaze, if only for a few seconds, trying to grasp his motive. She felt nothing beyond genuine concern and caring, and she was not the least bit intimidated. Still, something inside of her had to admit she felt powerless. And that's when her heart quickened. She glanced away and took a deep breath, pretending to be unaffected.

"You're doing great," Thomas said and walked away. Mallory glanced after him, hoping to convince herself that what she'd just felt was trite and irrelevant. But simply watching him move through the huge doorway into the dining room made a tingle erupt somewhere inside of her. She turned her attention back to her work, convincing herself that she'd just been alone for too long.

A few days later, Thomas called Mallory to his office to tell her that he was extremely pleased with her work. He asked if she would be interested in being promoted to one of his assistant managers, which would constitute a pay raise. Mallory felt good about his offer, and confident that she could handle the extra responsibility. She felt certain their little exchange the other evening had been nothing more than an appraisal of sorts as he'd considered her for this position. She gladly accepted the job, and over the next few weeks Thomas worked with her a little at a time to teach her the full gamut of the restaurant business. She enjoyed the diversity in her job as she continued serving, but also helped oversee other operations.

Mallory continued seeing Darrell regularly. For Christmas he gave her a necklace and earring set that was obviously expensive and very beautiful. She was gracious about it, reminding herself not to be so petty as to think that this warranted a disagreement. But she simply didn't like jewelry, and recalled telling him so.

Early in January, Darrell asked her out to dinner and told her to wear something nice. Mallory wore the pink sweater and skirt he'd given her, as well as the necklace and earrings. She couldn't be certain, but she suspected he might propose to her. She hoped the evening would go well, but she didn't know whether to feel excited or terrified. Reminding herself that her experience with Brad had made her a little skittish, she resigned herself to be more positive and not let insignificant things bother her so much.

Mallory felt a rush of excitement when she saw Darrell. He truly was an attractive man, and when he kissed her in greeting, she felt warm all over. It was good to have a man in her life again, and the thought of being married and settled was definitely appealing.

"You look so beautiful," he said, looking directly into her eyes. Mallory glanced quickly away, feeling less than confident. She reasoned that if he looked too closely, he might see the fact that she didn't agree with him. She'd never felt less beautiful.

They talked as he drove, and she didn't pay any attention to where they were headed until he pulled into the parking lot of Buchanan's.

"Oh, please don't tell me we're eating here," she said, certain it had to be a joke.

Darrell looked so deflated that she nearly felt embarrassed. "I thought you'd like to go here and feel pampered and waited on for a change, instead of the other way around."

"I *work* here," she said, as if he didn't know. "I eat their leftover food all the time. It's really not that exciting for me anymore."

Darrell looked stunned and disconcerted. "I'm sorry," he said, looking away. "I . . . guess I wasn't thinking. I . . . well, I had reservations, and I . . . made special arrangements."

Mallory sighed. This was going to be a disaster no matter which way it went. If they ate here, she'd be embarrassed and uptight, then she'd have to live with the other employees—especially Thomas—teasing her for weeks to come. If they went elsewhere, Darrell would likely be melancholy and embarrassed, his plans having been foiled. She sighed again. "Okay, fine. But let's be discreet, all right?"

"Of course," he said, beaming like a child as he kissed her hand.

Mallory felt sure the evening would be a disaster when Thomas appeared to show them to their table, since the hostess was taking a break. He did well at behaving as if they were strangers, but she caught a subtle smirk from him as she was seated. Did he remember that this was the man who had embarrassed her here a long time ago? Would he make the connection that this was the man she'd been dating seriously for months now?

Things looked up a little when their server turned out to be a new girl that Mallory had barely met once. The meal actually did taste delicious, and Darrell was delightful company, as he tended to be most of the time. They were halfway through the meal when Mallory realized that the music playing was not the usual repertoire coming through the sound system. Instead, it was a CD that Darrell often played in the car when they were together. He'd commented that many of the songs reminded him of her, even though she wasn't terribly fond of the style of music. When she commented on the music, he proudly told her that he'd made arrangements for them to play it. She wondered who he had talked to, and what he had said.

Darrell complimented her on how beautiful she looked, specifically mentioning her clothes and jewelry. Mallory wondered why she didn't feel beautiful when he seemed so smitten with her.

Her suspicions were correct about him asking her to marry him. And before she had a chance to tell him she needed to think about it, a dessert that she hadn't ordered was delivered to her place, with an elaborate engagement ring situated artistically on the top. Darrell beamed with pride. The server was practically smirking, and Mallory could nearly feel the whispering and curiosity of everyone else in the room, customers and employees alike. She told him the ring was beautiful and took a bite or two of her dessert. Then she told Darrell she would marry him, feeling as if accepting his proposal might somehow free her from the formless strangulation she felt.

Darrell's obvious ecstasy rubbed off on her somewhat as they left the restaurant, being congratulated by several people before they got to the door. In the car he said, "What's wrong? You don't seem very happy for having just become engaged. I hope you weren't just being polite in there. If you don't want to marry me, then—"

"I do want to marry you, Darrell. I think it's the right thing. It's just that . . . well, I'm a little embarrassed, that's all. I'll never hear the end of it when I go to work tomorrow."

Darrell's voice became tight as he said, "I'm sorry. I really thought that once you got in there, you would relax and enjoy yourself."

"I told you a long time ago that I didn't want to eat there."

"I must have forgotten," he said, but she could tell he was angry.

"I'm sorry, Darrell," she said. "It's not that serious. I really appreciate all the trouble you went to, and I'm looking forward to being your wife. Sometimes I just . . . well, ever since Brad died, I just feel more vulnerable and sensitive. I can't explain it, but . . . I'm sure it will get better with time."

"I'm sure it will," he said, kissing her hand.

Mallory felt certain that *everything* would get better with time, and she reminded herself to stay focused on the future with a positive attitude. But being positive was especially difficult when she had to go into work the following day for the lunch shift. She received congratulations from everyone who worked there, but always with a little smirk, as if they had found the incident amusing, or pathetic—or maybe both. Even those who hadn't worked last night seemed to know about it. She managed to avoid Thomas, since he wasn't in when she arrived, then he went straight to his office and stayed there.

She was signing out on her timecard when he appeared behind her, saying, "So, I understand you accepted the grand proposal." He took hold of her left hand to briefly examine the ring, then his eyes met hers. He wasn't smirking. In fact, he looked downright severe.

"Yes, I did," she said, hurrying to finish filling in her hours. She wanted to get away, but Thomas was blocking her. He obviously had something to say, and she prayed it would be work-related.

"That was quite a show he put on last night," Thomas said, his voice even more severe. "I would think you'd be really uncomfortable with that kind of thing—especially having it happen where you work."

"I *was* uncomfortable with it," she said, trying to be polite. "But he really meant well, and he's a very nice man."

"Yes, I remember how nice he was the first time *I* met him."

"Oh, come on," she said, wondering why they were having this conversation. "That was an isolated incident. And what business is it of yours, anyway? I get the impression you're trying to tell me I'm doing something wrong. What I do with my personal life is really up to me. I work for you, Thomas, and that is all."

"That's all?" he asked, lifting his brows. Then his voice lowered as he continued, "I carried you into a hospital, Mallory, and I sat by your bedside. Maybe it's just an *isolated incident*, but I *care* about you. I thought we were friends."

"We are, of course, but—"

"But you don't want anybody interfering with your plans."

"That's right."

"Okay, Mallory. Obviously, what you do is up to you. No one can change your mind—especially not me. But there's something that's been eating at me, and I feel like I have to say it. Beyond that, I'll keep my nose out of it."

"Okay, say it and get it over with."

"You weren't yourself when you walked in here last night, Mallory. Even the way you were dressed—the jewelry. It's like you were wearing some kind of costume. And this . . ." He touched her chin a moment to make her look at him. "This is not the face of a woman in love and ready to be married. You look more like you're going to a funeral."

"You have no idea what I'm feeling, Thomas."

"I've got more of an idea than you think I do." At her indignant glare he softened his voice. "Listen to me. Maybe I'm not seeing the big picture here, but what I do see—and feel—concerns me. Don't think you have to get married just because you don't want to be alone, or because it just seems like the easiest thing to do at the moment. I know I'm being outspoken, and it's not my place. But I care about you, Mallory, and I want you to be happy. Just think about what I said, okay?"

Mallory forced back her anger and reminded herself that he didn't know the full picture, and she had no reason to be defensive. "Thank you," she said. "I'll think about it." She hurried away before he could say anything else, but his words stayed with her far more than she wanted them to.

She reminded herself that everything would likely get better with time, and she quickly became caught up in wedding plans, wanting everything to be simple and uncomplicated, since this was a second marriage for both of them. As weeks passed, moving closer to their March wedding date, Mallory felt herself becoming steadily more stressed. But she knew that planning a wedding could be stressful, and this was a big change in her life. Over and over she just kept telling herself, *Everything will get better with time.*

CHAPTER SEVEN

Contributing to Mallory's stress was an ever-growing tension with members of her family. She felt as if they were suddenly uptight about her getting married, when they had given their full support when she'd started dating Darrell, letting her know that it was okay to get on with her life. When she came right out and asked her mother what the problem was, Janna expressed some concerns about Darrell.

"He seems very nice, Mallory," Janna said, "but . . . he's a little bit *too* nice."

"How can someone be *too* nice?" Mallory retorted.

"You're sounding awfully upset and defensive," Janna said.

"I just want to be able to make my own decisions and live my life."

"That sounds like something a teenager would say. I would think you'd gained a little more maturity and wisdom through your experiences."

Mallory sighed. "Mother, it's just that . . . you really don't know how I feel about Darrell, and—"

"Forgive me, Mallory, but . . ." Janna's voice actually held a trace of anger, which was extremely rare. She was usually so calm and in control. "I certainly can't read your mind and see into your heart. But you *are* my daughter, and like it or not, I can see some striking similarities to your situation and a very bad chapter of my life."

"What are you implying?"

"I'm not implying anything. I'm telling you that Darrell's behavior when I'm around him reminds me a great deal of my first husband. Darrell is perfectly charming, no matter what happens around him. But it has an air of falseness. I sense that something just isn't right."

"Are you trying to tell me that Darrell is some kind of psychotic wife-beater who—"

"I'm not trying to say anything except that you need to study your feelings very closely, Mallory, and look carefully at his every action. A man is on his very best behavior when he's trying to win a woman over. After you marry, masks eventually fall away. And I don't want to see you get hurt again. I'm telling you I'm not comfortable with him. You're going to have to make up your own mind. But bear in mind that by marrying him you are bringing him into your family. Your choice will affect Bethany's life, as well as your unborn children, and the lives of everyone who loves you."

Mallory told her mother she'd think about it, then she did her best to put it out of her head. She actually managed to force it away until Matthew came over a few days later and gave her a nearly identical speech.

"Have you been conspiring with Mother?" Mallory asked.

"I haven't even talked to Mother about this," he insisted, but she didn't believe him.

"Why don't you all just leave me alone and let me live my life!"

"Because I'm concerned about you—and so is everybody else. I don't feel good about this—plain and simple. You certainly didn't want any of us to leave you alone when you were terrified to be alone in the middle of the night, and when you were having one crisis after another. But now you can't trust anyone but your darling Darrell. Well, I pray that you don't regret this, because everyone but you thinks that—"

"Well, you know what, Matthew? This is *my* decision."

"Yes, and you'll go and do it like some dysfunctional teenager out to prove that they're right and the world is wrong. I think you're just determined to get married, as if it will somehow magically exonerate everything else that's gone wrong. And he's the only available scapegoat at the moment. I think you're so numb to feeling anything at all that you have no idea whether you really love him or not, and you have no idea if he really loves you. I think you've trained yourself not to feel, because everything hurt so badly for so long. I can understand that, but for the love of heaven, Mallory, don't screw your life up over this guy. You haven't been yourself since you lost Brad. You used to stick up for yourself and have some spunk. You've admitted that you feel more vulnerable and frightened, and you act like it. How do you know he hasn't picked up on that? How do you really *know* what kind of husband he'll be?"

Matthew stopped in response to Mallory's stunned, angry expression. He sighed and stuffed his hands into his pockets. "Just think about what you're doing, Mallory. Pray about it. Fast about it, and really *listen* to what your feelings are trying to tell you."

Long after Matthew left, Mallory tried to force away the things he'd said—the same way she'd forced away what Thomas and her mother had said. But it just wouldn't relent. She went to the scriptures and didn't read long before she came across the phrase in Ether, chapter five, verse four: *And in the mouth of three witnesses shall these things be established.*

"Oh, help," Mallory muttered and slammed the book closed. Then she wondered about the mouths of *four* witnesses. Her sister was a level-headed woman who wasn't as emotionally involved as her mother and Matthew. And she hadn't seen the worst side of Darrell, as Thomas had. A quick phone call might help balance things out a little.

"Caitlin," she said once the small talk ran down, "what do you think of Darrell? Be honest."

"You really want me to be honest?"

"Yes, of course. But, first of all, have you been talking to Mother or Matthew?"

"Not recently, why?"

"Well, they have some pretty strong feelings about Darrell. I want *your* opinion—not something influenced by them."

"Well, if it makes you feel any better, I haven't heard either of them say anything about him one way or the other. Mother said she was concerned that you seemed awfully stressed out, but she didn't get into details."

"Okay, so answer the question."

"I think Darrell is a self-righteous, controlling jerk."

Mallory was stunned. She finally found her voice enough to retort with sarcasm, "Don't beat around the bush, sis. Just let me have it straight out."

"He's a creep."

"You're serious."

"You'd better believe I'm serious. I've been uncomfortable with him since the first time I met him. But hey, I figured it was your life. There's nothing I can say to make anybody change their mind if they're determined to do something—especially you. I learned that when we were kids."

The phone call was anything but quick. They talked for nearly two hours. Mallory felt more discouraged than ever when she hung up, but at least she was determined to start over with her analysis of this relationship and take it to the Lord with a new perspective.

Over the next few days Mallory avoided Darrell, telling him that she needed some time to think things through. Wanting to be fair with him, she admitted outright that she was having some second thoughts and wondered if she was moving too fast. She traded shifts at work and got Saturday off, so that she could have the weekend to just be alone and ponder. She began a fast on Friday and went to the temple Saturday morning. Then she spent every spare minute in study and prayer, asking her Father in Heaven to help get her back in touch with her feelings so she would know if she was doing the right thing.

Sunday morning she was still feeling numb, and if nothing else, she realized that she was quite accustomed to it. Matthew had been right when he'd said that she'd trained herself not to feel anything at all, because the pain of facing everything she'd lost had been just too unbearable.

During her Young Women's meeting, the numbness began to fade. She was grateful to not be teaching today as the feeling came on slowly, then it gained momentum. Thoughts of Brad's death and the loss of her baby were suddenly foremost in her mind, squelching everything else.

Mallory slipped out of the room, wanting desperately to just get home. She nearly went to get Bethany out of the nursery, but she knew she'd get a protest. The child loved her "church class," as she called it, and always hated to leave. Of course, Matthew's daughter was in there, too. Fighting back her emotions, she peeked into priesthood meeting, hoping to get her brother's attention without too much trouble. The man sitting next to him saw her at the door and elbowed Matthew. He discreetly slipped out of his chair and came to the door. "Is something wrong?" he whispered.

Mallory nodded and barely managed to say, "I'm going home. Just get Bethany for me, will you?"

"Okay, but . . . do you want me to go with you or—"

"No!" she insisted. "Just get the baby."

She hurried out to her car and drove home, then curled up on her bed and cried so hard that it hurt. When the emotion settled, she realized her prayers had been answered. She had asked to get in touch with her feelings again, and with them came a new layer of grief.

Matthew called when he got home from church. "Are you okay?"

"I'm fine. I just need to be alone. We can talk later, okay?"

"All right. Do you want me to keep Bethany? It's not a problem."

"That would be good—especially for her, I think." Her emotion returned as she admitted, "It's a good thing she has you and Mel. I've been a pretty lousy mother."

"You've been going through a great deal since you lost Brad. That doesn't make you a lousy mother. We're more than happy to help out with her. She fits in well, and you know we love her. One day you'll be stronger, and she won't even remember any of this."

"I hope you're right," she said. "I'll call you later."

Mallory had another good, hard cry, then she just lay staring at the ceiling, allowing the silence and solitude to fill her. With her feelings now in place, she searched through the memories of her relationship with Darrell, all the while praying that she would be guided by the Spirit to understand and know what she should do. She could see signs in his behavior that he might have some difficulties. But who didn't? She wanted to be his wife. But she wondered if that was simply a habit she'd acquired. She felt somehow lost and afraid at the thought of being without him. She thought about it until her head ached, which only intensified the pain she felt from crying so long and hard. She finally resigned herself to giving it some more time, praying that she would be able to make a decision with confidence.

Matthew brought Bethany over after she called him, but she had little to say. She told him that she'd prayed to get in touch with her feelings again, and that she'd had a new level of grief assault her. But she said nothing about her efforts to rethink her decision to marry

Darrell. She wasn't going to say anything to anybody until she was absolutely certain one way or the other.

Several days passed while Mallory procrastinated the things she needed to do for the wedding, including taking the information to the printer to have the announcements made. She continued to avoid Darrell, telling him each time he called that she just needed to be alone. And she continued praying, wondering all the time if there was something wrong with her because she couldn't make a decision with any confidence. Knowing that she had married a man with serious problems before didn't help. She wondered if her reasons for marrying now were somehow an attempt to prove that she could catch a *good* husband. But then, if he was the kind of person everyone was telling her he was, wouldn't marrying him prove just the opposite? The thought terrified her, but she still felt somehow afraid of breaking off the engagement and being without him.

When Sunday came again, Mallory knew she had to get on with it one way or another. If she didn't get the announcements ordered in the next couple of days, they would never be done in time. She fasted again and continued to pray, thinking she would go to the temple again tomorrow. Then she remembered that the temples were closed on Mondays. She resigned herself to go on Tuesday and made arrangements for Bethany. But Monday was an especially difficult day. Work seemed longer than usual, and she hated the way Thomas said nothing more to her than casual greetings. It wasn't that they'd shared deep conversations in the past; but he was more distant than usual, and she didn't like it.

After work, Mallory sat on the floor to play with Bethany, grateful for her daughter. Through all she'd struggled with, this child had been her stabilizing influence. She kept Mallory going when nothing else could.

The phone rang and Bethany tried to answer it, then fussed a little when Mallory wouldn't let her. "Hello," Mallory said, distracting Bethany with a picture of a baby in a magazine.

"I'm looking for Mallory Taylor."

"This is she."

"Hi. You don't know me, but . . . I need to talk to you."

The woman on the other end of the phone seemed nervous. Mallory simply said, "Okay."

"Well, it's about my sister. She was married to Darrell Alden."

"Yes," Mallory drawled, feeling her heart begin to pound.

"You are engaged to Darrell Alden, aren't you?"

"Yes," she said again.

"Listen, this may be totally inappropriate, but . . . I just feel like there are some things I need to tell you. What you do with it is up to you. I would prefer to talk to you face to face, but I think it might be better if we just do it over the phone."

"And would you prefer that I not tell Darrell you called?" she asked, almost daring this woman to ask her to lie. In her mind, it would be a definite sign that this was not a good thing.

"I don't care what you tell Darrell. What he says or does is of no consequence to me. I simply don't want him hurting anyone else. That's why I'm calling you."

Mallory swallowed hard and said, "I'm listening."

She heard a heavy sigh. Then the voice on the other end seemed strained. "This is really hard for me. You see, my sister committed suicide. We were very close—at least until she got married."

Mallory listened with growing dread as this woman repeated the incidents that led up to her sister's death. From her perspective, Darrell's first wife had been meek and sweet, somewhat shy, but extremely beautiful and talented. In the years she had been married, she had become withdrawn and depressed, not associating with her family at all. She described attempts made by the family to help her see that something wasn't right, and her refusal to look at it. She described the two little girls her sister had left behind, and the evidence of neglect they had found only a few weeks after the death. The courts actually removed the children from their father, and their mother's parents now had legal custody with only minimal visitation from Darrell.

As Mallory listened, she prayed for discernment. She wanted to be able to discredit what this woman was saying. But instead, everything inside of her responded with compassion and understanding. She knew this woman was telling the truth. And she knew that her phone call was an answer to her prayers. Darrell Alden was controlling, manipulative, and emotionally abusive. And she'd just been too numb to see the signs.

Mallory thanked this woman for her call and offered sincere condolences for the loss of her sister. Then she called her mother and asked, "Mom, tell me how a woman would behave if she was in a relationship with someone who was controlling and manipulative."

"Well, I don't know what you mean specifically, but overall, she would feel incompetent and unable to handle anything on her own. She would be afraid of being without him, because the abuser gives the unspoken message that the woman can't make it without him."

"Somehow I knew you were going to say that."

"Why? What's up?"

"I'm calling off the wedding."

Janna's sigh of relief surged through the phone line, bathing Mallory with new confidence. She'd always known her mother was wise and discerning. Why had she been so stupid as to ignore her advice in this matter?

"I've been fasting and praying a lot, Mother. I've gotten back in touch with my feelings—at least to a point, I think. I began to see reasons for doubting Darrell, but I kept hanging on. I realize now that I was afraid of leaving him."

"I'm proud of you, honey," Janna said. "You've come a long way."

"Have I?" she asked. "Then why do I feel so *stupid?*"

"Stupid? Why?"

Mallory repeated the conversation she'd had with the sister of Darrell's first wife, feeling more strongly as she did that it was truly the answer to her prayers. She concluded by saying, "What's wrong with me that I could be deceived not once, but twice, by a man wearing some mask of decency to cover up such horrible things?"

"Sometimes the only way to learn is by experience, Mallory. And that doesn't make you stupid. You have to remember that these men were out to deceive; and even if their efforts were subconscious, they were still trying to deceive you into believing something that wasn't true. So learn from this and move forward. Your experience in listening to the Spirit will help you find your way from here on."

Mallory wanted to believe her mother, but a part of her felt completely unprepared to face anything. She felt as if her whole life was just plain screwed up. And after attending the temple, she didn't feel much better. She returned home to find that her mother had come to get Bethany from Melody's house, and said she would keep her overnight to give Mallory some time. She was especially grateful when she realized that she couldn't put off telling Darrell.

With a prayer and a studied effort to muster courage, Mallory called his office to leave a message for him to call her. She was taken off guard when the receptionist said, "Oh, he's right here. You have good timing."

Mallory took a deep breath and rehearsed once more what she would say.

"This is a nice surprise," Darrell said into the phone. "What's up?"

"Darrell, I've only got a minute, but . . . I'm calling to tell you that the engagement is off. It doesn't really matter why. I simply can't marry you. I'll be returning the things you've given me. I hope you can find happiness in your future. Good-bye."

She hung up before he could try to question her. She just wasn't up to it. A few minutes later the phone rang, and the caller ID said it was his office. She ignored it. Instead she sat down and wrote him a long letter, explaining how she felt—that he had tried to turn her into someone she wasn't comfortable being, and she'd been too numb with grief to realize it. She expressed her appreciation for his friendship, and said nothing about the phone call from his first wife's sister. Then she put the letter into a box with the clothes and jewelry he'd given her, including the gaudy engagement ring. The absence of it on her finger made her feel like a weight had been lifted from her shoulders.

Knowing he wouldn't be home from work for a while yet, she drove to his home, went inside with a key he'd given her, and left the box on a table with the key on top of it. Then she locked the door and drove away, unable to keep from crying as she did.

Not wanting to go home, Mallory drove around aimlessly, just needing to think. She went to the Mt. Timpanogos Temple and walked around it, ignoring the cold, reviewing every aspect of her life with thoughts that were too sporadic and senseless to do her any good. She sat on the bench behind the temple until the sun had gone down, then she returned to the car and drove up the canyon, then back. After ten o'clock, she still felt hesitant to go home. She started up the freeway and ended up at the Jordan River Temple, marveling that two such beautiful temples could be so close. She sat in her car for a long while, still plagued by senseless thoughts and feelings, the most prominent being her inability to make good choices and make a good life for herself, in spite of all she'd been taught.

Mallory started driving again and ended up at the restaurant just a little after closing time. The only car in the lot was Thomas's, and she knew they must have had a slow evening. Most of the cleanup would have been done before they actually closed, and everyone would have gone right home. The light in an upstairs window told Mallory that Thomas was likely in his office going over the books, and she didn't even bother questioning why she felt drawn here. She simply opened the door with her key, locked it back up again, and slipped inside. She wandered through the quiet restaurant, thinking how at home she'd come to feel here. Most of the lights were out, but the gas fireplace in the corner of the main dining room was still on. The first time she'd seen it, she'd been amazed at how real it looked. And now the flames cast shadows over the room. She sat down on the big hearth and hugged her knees to her chest, watching the fire closely.

Thomas closed up the office and went downstairs, expecting the restaurant to be deserted and locked up.

"Mallory!" he said when he saw her sitting near the fireplace. She looked up, startled, then turned her attention back to the flames. "What are you doing here? I thought you'd be busy with wedding plans."

She said nothing, and he could tell she was upset. He sat beside her, saying with confidence, "Something went wrong."

"Or something went right," she said without looking at him.

"Do you want to talk about it, or did you just come here to be alone?"

"I've been alone most of the day, actually." She turned to look at him. "I called off the wedding."

Thomas watched her for a moment, attempting to gauge her present state of mind. He took her left hand, urging it into his view, fingering the ring's absence.

"Would it be obnoxious of me to say that I'm relieved?"

Mallory shook her head subtly. "It would seem everyone's relieved. Everyone except Darrell, that is."

"Even you?" he asked, his eyes overflowing with concern. She realized then that he had very expressive eyes. In spite of his guarded nature, his eyes often gave away what he was feeling.

"Yes," she admitted, "even me."

"I'm truly sorry, Mallory. Not that you called off the wedding; but I'm sorry for all the heartache you've had to endure. That's why I want you to be happy. You deserve it. And I just don't think he was the man to make you happy."

"Well, you're right about that. I guess I was just too numb to see what everyone else could see. Maybe I just don't have it in me to pick a good man. I feel like I'm playing some kind of demented game. It's called *Pick the Hypocrite*. Well, maybe they're *all* hypocrites."

Thomas looked mildly alarmed, and she had to remind herself that he didn't know the details of her problems with Darrell—or Brad.

"I'm sorry," she said. "I really don't need to plague you with my bad mood. Let's just say that at this point, staying single is looking awfully good."

"Good, or safe?" he asked.

The question struck so deeply that tears pressed into Mallory's eyes. She knew in her heart that she didn't want to stay single the rest of her life. But at the moment, anything else was just too frightening. And somehow, Thomas knew that.

"You want to talk about it?" he asked, wiping a tear from each of her cheeks.

"No," she said, "I really don't. I just didn't want to go home, and . . . well, I guess I needed to tell you privately that you were right. If nothing else, I'm grateful to know that somebody's looking out for me."

"Are you hungry?" Thomas asked.

Mallory had to ponder that. "Actually, I haven't even thought about it, but . . . I haven't eaten since I had lunch at the temple cafeteria."

"You went to the temple. That's nice."

"Yes, although I haven't quite adjusted to going alone."

"Maybe you're not supposed to."

"What?"

"Adjust to going alone."

"Maybe not," she said sadly.

Thomas took her hand and led her to the kitchen, where he opened one of the huge refrigerators. "I didn't get much to eat myself," he said, and together they quickly prepared a reasonable meal. When they sat down to eat it, Thomas offered a blessing, then he began asking her about her family and interests.

Mallory had to admit, "I really don't have many interests beyond my family and church work."

"Well, that's certainly enough," he said.

"I've always liked to sew, and I enjoy cooking when I have the time to do it right. But I haven't done much of either since Brad died."

"You've been busy just coping, haven't you?"

"Yes, I suppose I have," she said. Wanting to change the subject, she asked, "What about you? What do you do when you're not here?"

"Well, the only thing that's really appealed to me the last few years is genealogy."

"Really?" she asked, genuinely interested.

"I've been pretty obsessed with it at times."

"So, have you made much progress? I mean, I've hardly done any myself, but I understand it can be difficult."

"Yes, actually. In fact, I've traced my ancestors on both sides of the family back to slave ship registries."

"Oh, my gosh." Mallory leaned back in her chair, feeling a distinct heartache. "That's so horrible. I mean, it's great that you've traced it that far, but . . . oh, that must be so hard for you to think that . . ." She couldn't finish.

Thomas couldn't recall anyone who wasn't a blood relative to him ever responding so emotionally. Most people were so detached from the reality of slavery that they didn't even pause to consider what it really meant.

"Yes, it is," he said. "There's so much talk of pioneer heritage; of the terrible difficulties and struggles they went through. And it's true; they did. But there is no describing how it feels to try and comprehend what my blood ancestors went through, only two or three generations prior to the pioneer movement west. The research I did revealed unspeakable horrors. On the flip side of that, they are all at peace now. I've done my best to see that their temple work is done."

"Really?" Mallory's face lit up with an enthusiasm as deep and genuine as her compassion had been a minute ago. "That's incredible. What an experience that must have been."

"Yes, it was. I'm the only member of the Church in my family, so it was up to me to do it. I haven't been able to trace anything back to Africa, although I haven't given up yet. Someday I'd like to go there myself. But all of my ancestors, back to and including those who actually came over on the slave ships, have had all of their work done. Of course, the plantations kept very accurate records. The Buchanan name was taken from the owner of a plantation, and from what I can tell, he was actually quite good to his slaves. When they were freed, he helped them relocate to the north where he had relatives, and they would be safer. And fortunately, they became educated and kept records, and I was able to eventually get copies of everything available. My mother's side has a similar story. The family remained in the South until my mother's father came to California as a young man."

"It sounds fascinating," Mallory said. "I'd love to see your records sometime."

"I'd love to show them to someone who is actually interested."

"And you're from California, aren't you?"

"That's right. My parents were both born there."

"So, tell me about your family," she said.

Thomas looked briefly uncomfortable before he glanced at his watch, saying, "I'm afraid that will have to wait until another day. It's way past your bedtime, young lady."

Mallory glanced at her own watch. It was twenty after two. "Oh, my gosh. I can't believe it."

They hurried to clean up after their meal, then Thomas walked her to her car. "You drive carefully now, and I want you to call me at my house when you get home." He wrote his number in the palm of her hand as he said it. "Then I'll know you're safe."

"Thank you," she said. "For everything."

Thomas just smiled and opened the car door for her. "Take care now," he said, "and drive carefully."

"You too," she replied. He stood as he was until she drove away.

CHAPTER EIGHT

*M*allory slept in the following morning, not waking until there was a loud pounding at her door. She looked out the upstairs window and saw Darrell's car parked in the driveway. "Oh, help," she muttered and was tempted to ignore him and go back to bed. But she knew she had to face him sooner or later; and right now, getting it over with seemed like a good option. She threw on her bathrobe and hurried down to answer the door.

"Well," he said with sarcasm, "you are still alive."

"Of course I'm alive."

"Well, I've called a hundred times, last night and this morning. I came by last night at midnight, but you weren't here."

"No, I wasn't. And I turned the phone off."

"Why?"

"Because I needed some peace."

"Well, I need to talk to you." He moved to come inside, but she stood in his way. "May I come in?"

"No. There's nothing to say that can't be said right here. I said everything I needed to in that letter."

"And that's it?"

"Yes, that's it."

"I can't believe you'd call it off over something so petty as—"

"Listen, Darrell, I could give you a long list of reasons why I don't feel good about marrying you. But it's irrelevant, and—"

"Like what?"

"I'm not even going to start."

"Why not? Don't I have a right to—"

"Listen, I know you well enough to know that every reason I might state would just give you information that you could work on discrediting. I'm not going to get into it. I'm not going to marry you. That's all."

"Listen to me, Mallory. I love you, and—"

"If you love me, then why are you shouting at me?"

Darrell lowered his voice and said, "I want to take care of you. Can't you see that?"

"No, I can't. I need to go inside now." She attempted to close the door, but he stopped it with his foot and pushed it back open.

"Listen to me. If you insist on going through with this foolishness, I could make life hell for you. You have no right to—"

"Excuse me," Mallory interrupted as it occurred to her that this man was not expressing any hurt feelings or a broken heart. He was angry. She suspected it was more his pride and ego that hurt, rather than his heart. "If you don't stop threatening me and leave immediately, I'm going to call the police."

"The police?" he echoed with a cynical laugh. "You can't seriously think you can—"

"Leave now, and don't come back. If I ever see you here again, or where I work, I will file a restraining order."

"You wouldn't dare."

"Wouldn't I?" she asked and slammed the door in his face, locking it tightly. Then she called her mother to unload the latest drama of her life and make certain Bethany was all right.

Contemplating the scene with Darrell, Mallory found that his behavior was a stark validation of how messed up he really was. She felt grateful to know that his children were in their grandmother's care. And that she didn't have to deal with him anymore.

Mallory got over Darrell so quickly that it made her wonder what kind of fog she had been living in. She uncovered a new layer of grief for the loss of her marriage to Brad, however, both figuratively and literally. She'd lost him in death, but she'd also lost him long before that through the horrible things he'd been doing, even if she hadn't known about it at the time.

A week after she'd broken her engagement, Mallory got a phone call from Brad's mother. Mallory could tell right off that she was upset, but she simply wasn't prepared to be screamed at and accused of driving Brad to suicide. "I don't know what was going on in that marriage, Mallory, but it must have been pretty horrible to push him to something like that. You will be judged for what you've done to him, and to me," she cried, practically hysterical.

"God knows my heart," Mallory stated, forcing a steady voice, "and my conscience is clear. You have absolutely no idea what you're talking about."

Mallory was tempted to tell Brad's mother about the pornography, but instinctively she knew it wouldn't make any difference. It would only give her something to accuse Mallory of lying about. She attempted several times to interrupt her ranting and say something to counter the accusations, then finally she hung up on her and immediately called her mother.

"Mom, please tell me I'm not accountable for Brad's death."

"Of course you're not, dear."

"And even if I'd had problems that affected my husband, he still made the choice to deal with it that way. Right?"

"Right. Why? What's wrong?"

"Brad's mother just called and accused me of driving him to it."

"She obviously doesn't have the full picture. Are you okay?"

"I think so, but . . . well, it is upsetting."

"Yes, I'm sure it is."

"Why do you suppose she's calling me now, after all this time?"

"If she's not dealing with his death, which she obviously isn't, then she's probably just reached a breaking point. She's probably just trying to find something to blame her pain on. And you're the obvious choice. But remember, what anyone else thinks doesn't matter."

"I know that, but . . . I hate the thought of them thinking I did something wrong, when Brad was so obviously at fault."

"Did you tell her about his problem?"

"No. She wouldn't have listened."

"That's probably true."

"But I think I might call Louise."

"If you think it might help, go ahead. But be careful, and don't expect her to side with you. I know you got along well with her, but she has family ties that are stronger than her ties with you."

"I know. I'll think about it."

Mallory didn't get up the nerve to call Brad's sister that day, which she thought was probably better than calling immediately after his mother had thrown a fit. She prayed and decided that calling Louise was the right thing to do, but she waited a few days to do it. They hadn't seen each other or talked since the funeral, and she doubted they ever would again. She found that to be a point in her favor if the conversation was a disaster.

Louise was kind on the phone, but she basically said that they were all hurting over Brad's death, and she wasn't going to take sides or get involved.

"I wouldn't expect you to," Mallory said. "I don't know what your parents are thinking happened here; your mother was too upset to get into anything specific. Maybe she just has to place the blame for her hurt somewhere, I don't know. But I simply want to tell you that Brad had a very serious problem. He tried to overcome it, but he was too proud to get the help he needed. I believe it was guilt and helplessness that overcame him in the end. If he had lived, I believe we could have worked it out. But I couldn't help him when I didn't know about it."

Louise was silent for a long moment. "Was it drugs?"

"No, Louise. It really doesn't matter. I just want you to know that for the most part our marriage was good, and we loved each other very much. I love him still. I'm every bit as brokenhearted as any of the rest of you. He was the center of my everyday life. But I'm equally troubled by the problem he had. I didn't even know it existed until after his death."

Again Louise was silent until she asked, "Was he drinking?"

"No."

"Gambling?"

"No, Louise. It really doesn't matter. But if you ever get the chance, please tell your parents that I loved him very much, and I would never have done anything to hurt him. I know I wasn't perfect, and maybe some of my attitudes made it harder for him to face his struggles. I don't know. All I know is that losing him has been the hardest thing I've ever faced in my life."

The remainder of the conversation was brief. Mallory sensed that Louise was intently curious, but she felt that it was better left unsaid. She hoped she hadn't said too much already.

Louise did admit that her mother's behavior had been way out of line, but her grief over losing her son had been extremely difficult, and she wasn't doing well.

Mallory's heart went out to Brad's family. She'd thought of them often, but they'd never called or checked on her since his death. And she'd been too caught up in her own grief to call them. She knew, however, that Janna had called and notified them when she'd lost the baby. And she'd heard nothing in return.

She felt disturbed by the entire incident, but she reminded herself of how misunderstood many of the prophets in the scriptures had been. And Jesus Christ, more than anyone who had ever walked the earth, was the most misunderstood of all. The thought made her own struggles seem petty and insignificant. She reminded herself of all she had to be grateful for, and tried not to dwell on the negative aspects of her life.

A few days later, Louise called her back. Mallory hoped she wasn't calling on her mother's behalf to get angry with her again. But Louise started out by saying, "I've been thinking about the things you said, and I just had to call you. I think I know what Brad's problem was."

Mallory didn't say anything. She almost didn't dare. A part of her wanted Louise's validation, while at the same time she didn't even want to acknowledge it aloud.

"It was pornography, wasn't it," she said.

Mallory sighed. "Yes, it was."

"I thought so."

"How did you know?"

"Well, I didn't *know*, but more than once when we were teenagers, I found stuff around the house in weird places. I confronted Brad about it once. He just said it was no big deal, and that Dad had given him the stuff."

Mallory gasped before she could even think of holding it back. "Are you serious?"

"That's what he said. I thought he was lying. I threw the stuff away and figured he'd grow out of it. I was terribly naive. Maybe I still am. But the thing is, I've seen evidence that my father has a problem with it. I think Brad was telling me the truth. He was the only boy in the family. I think Dad's had a problem for years, and he passed it along to his son for reasons I will never understand. It makes me sick to think about it, so I try not to.

"More than once in my adult life I've tried to talk to Mother about Dad's problem, but she just won't see it. In a way, I can't blame her. To acknowledge that such a thing has been going on all these years would be terribly painful."

"I can relate to that."

"They're getting old. They're set in their ways. And I can't fix their problems. I just try to love them the best I can.

"Anyway," Louise went on while Mallory sat with her hand over her mouth, her eyes squeezed shut, "I think that Mother wouldn't look at Brad's problems, any more than she would look at her own husband's. And Dad would certainly never acknowledge that he had a problem. I guess we can be thankful that none of us kids were sexually abused, which often goes along with the problem."

Louise sighed as if she had just let go of a huge burden. "I wondered, when we learned of Brad's suicide, if he was still doing things he shouldn't. But I didn't want to stir anything up. My heart goes out to you, Mallory. I don't think there's anything else either one of us can do, except to learn from this and protect ourselves and our children by teaching them properly."

"Yes, I'm sure you're right," Mallory said, feeling sick inside and at the same time extremely grateful for Louise's call. She told her so, and they promised to keep in touch. But Mallory doubted they would ever talk again.

For days following Louise's phone call, Mallory felt especially melancholy. Thinking through the things she had said, it was difficult not to be angry toward Brad's father. If he hadn't had a problem, if he hadn't passed it along to Brad, none of this would have happened. Brad would still be alive, and they would be happy, and . . . She had to consciously will away the anger—especially when she thought of Brad's mother blaming *her,* when the real problem was right under her own nose. Through a great deal of prayer and intense effort, Mallory was finally able to let go of her negative feelings. But it was still difficult not to feel down.

Technically, Mallory felt like she was doing pretty well. She had a job she enjoyed. Her financial needs were being met. She had a beautiful daughter, and she was grateful for her family. She could look back and understand the things that had led to Brad's death without getting angry or bitter. For the most part she had come to terms with his death, even though she still missed him desperately at times. She had even come to accept the loss of her baby. Even though she still ached for that child from time to time, and the grief was real, she often felt relieved at not having to deal with an infant under the circumstances. She frequently recalled that she had been promised more children in a priesthood blessing. But after her experience with Darrell, the thought of dating and pursuing marriage again was terrifying.

One year after Brad's death, Mallory could see that her life was good for the most part—at least as good as it could be. But she couldn't deny that she was lonely, and more than a little bit scared to do anything about it. She just prayed that time would continue to heal her wounds, and that one day she would find love again—and be able to accept it when she did.

Mallory began doing more things with her sister, now that they were in the same boat. Since they were both unmarried, they went to many single-adult church functions together, and occasionally Caitlin lined Mallory up with someone and they would double-date. But Mallory's dating experiences were making her realize that she felt highly uncomfortable with men in general. She had to admit that the hurt inside her was deep, and she found it difficult to trust a man to be what he appeared to be. Even at church, she often felt as if the people around her were wearing masks, and she shuddered to think what might be beneath them. She tried to add up the men she truly respected and trusted. Beyond her father and brother, she couldn't think of anyone. Oh, the bishop was a nice man, and he'd been good to her. But she didn't know him well enough to know what he might really be like. She had to admit that Thomas was a good man, but even as well as she thought she knew him, he was very private about his personal life, and she didn't know much about the *real* man. All in all, Mallory decided she didn't like dating much, which made her long for Brad, wishing that her life could be as it had been, without the complications of her husband's bad habits tainting what they'd shared.

While Mallory was longing for the past and dreading the future, Caitlin met the man of her dreams and announced that she was getting married. After waiting so long to marry, Caitlin was ecstatic. Kenneth certainly seemed like a nice guy, and the family loved him. But then, they'd loved Brad, too. Mallory was polite and gracious, but she was uncomfortable around him for reasons she didn't want to think about.

With Caitlin busy making wedding plans and spending every spare minute with Kenneth, Mallory lost the friend she'd found in her sister. She still spent time occasionally with Melody, and they helped each other with the children. But Mallory's being a widow put them in different walks of life, and she just felt a little out of place. Of course, Matthew was always available if she needed anything, and her parents were there for her. Still, Mallory was lonely. But loneliness was exactly what had driven her to Darrell and compelled her to think she should marry him. She was determined not to allow her loneliness to taint her emotions and set her up to be hurt again. So she just kept going from day to day, enjoying Bethany and trying to appreciate life as much as possible.

On a Thursday evening in May, business was slow at the restaurant. Thomas approached Mallory while she was rolling silverware into cloth napkins. "Hey," he said, "are you busy tomorrow evening?"

"No, I don't think so. Do you need me to fill in or—"

"No, I've got everything covered here just fine. I was wondering if you'd go out with me."

Mallory looked up in surprise, then closed her mouth when she realized she was gaping. While she was standing there trying to convince herself that his efforts were likely on a friendship basis only, something warm and pleasant erupted inside of her at the thought of spending exclusive time with Thomas Buchanan. "You mean *out*? Like a date?"

"That's what I mean. You know . . . movie and dinner, that sort of thing."

When Mallory couldn't think of one good reason to tell him no, she said, "That would be fine. Are you sure you want to go out with me? My sister tells me I have a really rotten attitude about dating, and men don't like to be around me."

"All you have to do is come and be yourself."

"Okay. Do you want me to meet you here or—"

"No," he chuckled, "of course not. I'll pick you up. Is six-thirty all right?"

"Sure."

"Dress casual."

"Okay," she said, and he hurried off to the kitchen.

Mallory called Matthew from work, knowing she'd be home late and he would leave early for work in the morning. "Hey, what's up?" he asked.

"I was wondering if you and Mel have plans tomorrow, or if I should make other arrangements for Bethie."

"You have to work?"

"No, actually. I have a date."

"I thought you'd given up dating."

"This is different."

"Different?"

"I'm going out with Thomas."

Matthew laughed. "Really?"

"Is it funny?"

"Funny? No! I think it's great."

"You do?"

"Yeah. He's a nice guy, isn't he?"

"As far as I can tell. But it's just a date. Don't go getting any big ideas."

Matthew laughed again. "You never know. You always told me you liked the tall, dark, and handsome type. Maybe it's destiny."

Mallory said nothing. She didn't want to admit to the way her insides had reacted to Matthew's statement.

"Just a minute," Matthew added. "I'll see if Mel's got plans for tomorrow." He came back to the phone a minute later and said, "We'd be happy to take her, if you'll watch our kids Sunday so we can go to a fireside."

"It's a deal. I really appreciate all the times you take Bethie. You watch her three times more than you let me watch your kids."

"We have three times as many kids. It all works out."

"Thanks, Matthew. I'll see you tomorrow."

Mallory found herself speculating over Thomas's motives in taking her out right up until he came to her door. When she couldn't come up with anything, she came right out and asked as they were driving toward Provo. "Thomas, forgive me if I'm being obnoxious, but . . . I can't help wondering why you're doing this."

"Doing what?"

"Taking me on a date."

"I should think it's obvious."

"Apparently it's not."

"Well," he said, "why do men *usually* ask women out?" She said nothing, and he answered his own question. "I like you, Mallory. I enjoy your company, and I wanted to spend some time with you somewhere besides the restaurant. Is that okay?"

"Oh, it's fine. It's just that . . ."

"I'd like to get to know you better."

Mallory appreciated his answer. She believed he was being honest, but it still didn't tell her what she wanted to hear. Knowing she'd never relax without having a certain point clarified, she had to ask, "Are you implying, then, that you have some romantic interest here?"

Thomas looked so surprised that she was almost embarrassed. Then he smiled, and she was glad she'd asked. "I just have to know," she said.

"If I was implying something romantic, would that make a difference? Are you uncomfortable with that?"

"I'm uncomfortable with a lot of things these days, Thomas. I'm having a hard time trusting mankind in general, but it's nothing personal. I'm glad you asked me out; I just have to know where your head is. I don't want you to be expecting something from me that I can't give."

"Listen," he said, taking her hand into his as he drove, "I'll make you a deal. I promise to be completely honest and up front about everything, if you'll do the same."

"Okay."

"The last thing I want to do is cause problems in our professional relationship, Mallory. But the fact is, I really do find you attractive." He pressed her hand to his lips, and Mallory's insides erupted with butterflies. "Yes," he said, giving her a brief, penetrating gaze before he looked back to the road, "I'm implying something romantic."

Mallory said nothing for several minutes, and Thomas had to ask, "Are you okay with that, Mallory, or am I pushing something here that you don't—"

"It's okay, Thomas, really. As long as we can be honest with each other and . . . well, it just might take some getting used to." He smiled, and a minute later she added, "I always did have a thing for tall, dark, and handsome."

Thomas grinned. Then he laughed. Nothing more was said until they were seated at a restaurant where he'd made reservations. After they had ordered he said, "I have to keep tabs on the competition, you know."

"Oh, so this *is* business," she said, and he laughed. But it didn't take away the tension she was feeling.

"What's wrong, Mallory? You look scared to death." Mallory felt cornered but he added, "You agreed to be honest."

"I *am* scared, Thomas. I like you, too. You've been there for me when I've needed a friend, and I've always felt comfortable with you."

"Until now."

She laughed tensely and repeated, "Until now."

"And why is that?"

"I know practically nothing about you. The last two men that I got *romantic* with left some pretty deep scars. So, yes, I'm scared. I'm scared to get close to someone, wondering if they can even begin to comprehend the struggles I've been through. And I'm scared to get too close and have the bottom fall out from under me all over again."

"Okay, so let's back up. Forget about the romantic stuff. Let's get to know each other better. Ask me anything you want."

"Anything?" she asked, while a question hovered on the tip of her tongue that she knew would put this honesty thing to the test.

"Anything," he said.

"Okay, Thomas, do you know what it's like to really suffer? Have you ever experienced any real pain in your life? Because I don't know if I can be completely open with someone who hasn't."

"Wow," Thomas said, "I was expecting something like, 'What's your favorite color?'."

"I already know. It's dark green."

"How do you know that?"

"It's the color of your car, the cloth napkins and carpet at the restaurant, and four of your shirts."

"Very good."

She said nothing more, making it clear that he had a question to answer.

"On to the next question," he said, leaning back with a sigh. "Okay, Mallory, let's just say that . . ."

The server brought their drinks and salads, which Thomas stopped to taste and analyze, then he said, "Where were we?"

"You were answering my question."

"And if I don't answer this one, we might as well just talk business, right?"

Mallory just shrugged her shoulders.

"Okay. Where do I start? Why don't I just give you my life story in a nutshell, and you can decide if there's any pain in there."

Mallory nodded, wondering if she'd opened a can of worms. Still, she felt confident in her request. She wasn't even going to pursue a relationship with him if she didn't know a whole lot more about him.

"I was born in central California. My parents were both born in that area. My father's father ran a little diner his entire life. When my father graduated from college, he took the family business a step further and opened up a nice restaurant, which did fairly well. I have only one sibling, a brother two years younger than me. My father was active in the Baptist church. My mother was passive about it, which was one of many differences between them. When I was four, my parents divorced. Robert—that's my brother—and I lived with my mother, but my father came to get us regularly. My mother remarried in less than a year. And a year after that, my stepfather killed her, then he killed himself."

"Oh, good heavens," Mallory murmured and set her fork down. He'd said it so casually that she could almost believe it hadn't affected him. But his eyes said otherwise. When she said nothing more, he went on.

"Fortunately, it happened while we were with our father. And of course, he took very good care of us. He married three times after that. Two divorces, one death. He ended up alone at the age of thirty-nine and never married again. But I have to say, he was a good father. He taught us integrity and responsibility, and he loved us. He took us to church and showed us by example how to do what's right."

"Wait," she said, "I have a question. You told me that your father grieved over your mother's death for many years, but you said they were divorced."

"Yes," he said, "but he never stopped loving her. I think there was a great deal of regret in his heart."

Mallory nodded and motioned for him to go on.

"Needless to say, Robert and I spent our lives in the restaurant. Dad would pick us up from school and take us there. We'd do our homework in his office, and as we got old enough, he'd assign us more and more to do there, always paying us a fair wage. I loved the business. Robert didn't. But then, we had less in common than our parents had. Gradually Dad opened two more restaurants in the area, and they were all very successful. Eventually he became rather well off."

Their salad plates were taken away and Mallory leaned forward eagerly, enjoying every word of his story.

"When I was sixteen," Thomas continued, "I had a friend who was a Mormon. I started going to seminary with him, and I was baptized just before my seventeenth birthday. My father wasn't terribly happy about it, but he told me I had to follow my heart. And he often said that to see me committed to a Christian religion with such conviction was far better than seeing my brother out drinking and smoking and having casual sex.

"I went on a mission, and my dad supported me completely. He paid my way, and he wrote to me faithfully. When I came back, I worked with him to earn my way through college. He always talked about eventually turning everything over to me, and that was fine by me. I graduated from college and married a girl I'd met at church. Sandi. She was beautiful and could sing like an angel; we were married in the temple. Over the years, I began doing more and more of my father's work as he began to have health problems."

Dinner was brought to the table. Thomas tasted everything and made comments, asking Mallory what she liked and didn't like. She'd always enjoyed his unique interest in food, but she decided then that she could really enjoy dating someone who felt the need to *keep tabs on the competition.*

When they were settled into enjoying their meal, Mallory asked Thomas to continue. She was wondering how he got to Utah if he'd been running his father's business.

"Well, then Robert came back after years of carousing and messing up his life. He'd quit his bad habits and said he was going straight—in everything. My father was thrilled, especially when Robert started going to church with him. But I didn't trust him. He was a weasel and I knew it. He always had been. He started working with Dad, and little by little, I found that I was doing less and less. I only talked to my father about it once, and he kindly suggested that I was jealous of my brother. I told him that I only wanted what I had rightfully earned. I couldn't blame my father, really. He was so glad to have Robert back, and he really was too loving and trusting to comprehend that Robert was manipulating him. In fact, I found out after my father died that Robert had actually manipulated him into rewriting his will."

"Are you serious?" Mallory asked, feeling intensely upset on Thomas's behalf.

"Quite serious. He left the entire restaurant business to Robert. Of course, I was left with a significant amount of money, and now that I am where I am, I'm grateful it turned out this way. I was able to come here and open my own place, and I'm glad I don't have to deal with Robert at all, especially since . . ."

Thomas hesitated, suddenly seeming uncomfortable, when he'd just spouted off a difficult story without showing any emotion at all.

"Since what?" Mallory pressed gently.

Thomas glanced away, cleared his throat quietly, then turned to look at her. "Sandi, uh . . ."

"Your wife?" she clarified, noting by his eyes that he had struck an especially sensitive point. More sensitive than having his mother murdered and his brother stealing the family business?

"Yes, she . . . she got involved with another man. Apparently it was going on for quite some time right under my nose, and then . . . she left me for him."

"Oh, Thomas, that's horrible."

"Yes, it is." He chuckled tensely. "But it worked out nicely for her. She was able to keep the name and the business."

Mallory gasped. Then she consciously closed her mouth as she realized he wasn't kidding. "You mean . . . Robert? She left you for your own brother?"

"That's right. It's the prodigal son story with a little twist."

"It's amazing that you're not bitter over it."

"Who said I'm not bitter? I mean . . . I try not to be. I've prayed every single day to be free of negative feelings toward them, and I've come a long way. But occasionally I stop to think about it and . . . well, it hurts."

"But isn't hurting over it different from being bitter?"

Thomas thought about it. "Maybe you're right. But then, I haven't seen either of them in a couple of years. I honestly hope I never do."

"It's probably just as well. But then . . . that leaves you without family, doesn't it?"

"That's right. Oh, I have distant relatives scattered around. But no one I was ever close to beyond a couple of aunts. We keep in touch, but . . . well, my becoming a Mormon didn't impress most of them."

After a long moment of silence, Thomas leaned back in his chair and said, "So, does that answer your question sufficiently? You know my life story now. Did I fill the pain quota to your satisfaction?"

"I'm sorry, Thomas. I'm sure that wasn't a very nice way to approach—"

"No, it's okay, really. Because I must admit myself that, in a roundabout way, I did the same thing. I never would have asked you out if I hadn't known that you'd been through some struggles. I could never be happy with a woman who believed that having her washer break down on laundry day was a significant trial."

Mallory laughed. "I would consider that a blessing. It would give me a good reason to procrastinate doing the laundry." He laughed with her and she added, "Not really, but . . ."

The server took their plates and asked if they wanted dessert. Mallory was enticed but full. Thomas ordered dessert to go.

"You can have it for breakfast," he said.

Mallory laughed. And she gladly held Thomas's hand as he escorted her out of the restaurant and to the theater. She was enjoying herself and felt completely at ease. And for the moment, that was all she needed.

CHAPTER NINE

*M*allory thoroughly enjoyed the movie, even though the film itself was only mediocre. It was late when Thomas pulled the car into her driveway, but she said, "I think I could handle that dessert now. Want to come in for a few minutes?"

He looked surprised. Then he smiled. "I'd love to."

They sat at the kitchen table, eating out of their Styrofoam containers while they talked and laughed about trivial things. When Thomas finally left, Mallory felt exhausted but reluctant to see him go.

"I'll see you at work tomorrow," she said.

He glanced at his watch. "No, actually, it will be later today. You'd better get some sleep."

Mallory slept better that night than she had in a long time. She really didn't believe that she and Thomas would ever end up getting married, but spending time with him now was a worthy distraction, and one that she felt comfortable with. She only wished this feeling could last.

The restaurant was busy the following day, and she hardly saw Thomas except in passing a few times. But his knowing smile reminded her of the time they'd spent together, and she felt a secret thrill. He left before closing with barely a hurried good-bye, but she returned from church the following day to find his home number on her caller ID. She called him back, and his eagerness to hear from her made her feel warm somehow. She didn't bother to stop and analyze her feelings, fearing that it might make her panic if she did.

"Hey," he said, "I was wondering if you'd go to a fireside with me this evening."

"Oh," Mallory couldn't help her disappointment, "I'd love to, but . . . I'm watching my brother's children so *they* can go to a fireside. It was the trade I worked so I could go out Friday."

"Oh, I see." He was quiet for a moment, then he said, "Feel free to tell me if it's not a good idea, but . . . well, could I come by and help you? I haven't been around kids much, but I'd wager that I could be good at it."

"Oh, that would be great," she said, wishing she hadn't sounded so enthusiastic. In a more subdued voice she added, "But I wouldn't want you to miss the fireside if you—"

"The fireside was an excuse, Mallory."

After his meaning sank in, she simply said, "Oh."

"What time should I come?" he asked.

"Well, I'll be getting the kids about six-thirty, but if you'd like to come by earlier, I'll see if I can scrape up something to feed you."

"You don't have to do that, Mallory. There's no need for you to—"

"You know what, Thomas? I'm sick to death of eating alone—especially on Sundays. It would be a pleasure to cook something that someone beyond a two-year-old can appreciate."

"Okay, you talked me into it. Can I bring anything?"

"Just yourself. That will be good enough."

After Mallory got off the phone, she felt more motivated than she had in a long time. She couldn't recall ever feeling this motivated when she'd been dating Darrell. She was relieved to find the ingredients available to make a nice green salad, and potato cheese soup, since she felt confident with the recipe.

Thomas felt nervous as he approached Mallory's front door. He wondered if he was moving too fast, in view of the hurts and fears that still hovered inside of him. Then he reminded himself that he had already analyzed all of this before he'd ever asked her out. He had prayed fervently to know if this was the right step to take; and for whatever might come of it, he knew that pursuing Mallory was the best thing he could be doing with his life right now. He only hoped it would come to something good for both of them. He didn't particularly like the idea of having this turn into a trial that was meant to make him stronger. He knew that Mallory's hurts ran at least as deep as his own, and he hoped and prayed that she would be able to get beyond all of that and trust him enough to open her heart.

He knocked and she answered the door, looking vibrant and glad to see him. Her daughter was in her arms.

"This must be Bethany," he said. "She's grown a great deal since I saw her last."

"Yes, she tends to do that," Mallory said as she closed the door.

"Hello, Bethany," Thomas said. "How are you?"

She pressed her face to her mother's shoulder, then peeked at him and smiled.

"This is Thomas," Mallory said. "Can you say Thomas?"

"Thomas," she said, her voice barely audible.

"Very good," Thomas chuckled. "Does she always speak so clearly?"

"Actually, she does very well. She's two going on twenty-one. Once she warms up, she'll talk your ear off."

Thomas followed Mallory into the kitchen, where she put Bethany into her high chair and set the soup on the table. They talked comfortably through the meal, and Mallory felt grateful for his friendship. She reasoned that looking at their relationship in such a way made it easier for her to avoid feeling afraid. She pushed away the thought that Thomas had come right out and told her his intentions were romantic. She just wasn't ready for that yet.

They had barely cleared the table when Matthew and Melody came with the children.

"You remember Thomas," Mallory said to her brother.

"Of course." Matthew shook his hand eagerly. "How are you?"

"Good, and you?"

"We're doing great. This is my wife, Melody."

"Hello, Melody." Thomas shook her hand.

"I've heard good things about you."

Thomas chuckled. "They just don't know any better."

Matthew and Melody hurried off to the fireside, since they were running a little late. Mallory introduced the children to Thomas, even though they were too busy playing to give the adults much attention. "Mark is eight, and Luke is five," she said, pointing out the boys.

"That's funny," Thomas said. "Matthew, Mark, and Luke."

"Yes," she chuckled, "Matthew certainly thought it was clever.

And Elizabeth is just a few months younger than Bethany. It's a little confusing sometimes because they both answer to Beth, or Bethie, which we use more commonly."

"They're practically twins," Thomas commented. "They even look very much alike."

"Yes, they do. Which is funny, because I really don't look that much like Matthew, but we obviously have the same genes."

Thomas commented lightly, "If you married me, the rest of your children wouldn't look like their cousins."

"Would that be a problem?" Mallory asked, looking at this conversation as purely hypothetical.

"I guess that's what I'm asking you."

"Are you wondering if I'm prejudiced?"

"Well," Thomas said, "prejudice can come in many degrees. Some people have nothing against blacks, as long as they don't intermarry. Some people have no problem with interracial marriages, as long as it's not their own relatives who do it. You've never shown any negativity toward me; you don't have a problem with being my friend or letting me give you a priesthood blessing. But I have to wonder if you'd ever consider marrying someone like me, and if you could live with having children who would look terribly different from the one you've got."

Keeping her thoughts in generalities, Mallory answered easily. "Personally, I have no problem with either one. If I fell in love with a man, and I knew in my heart he was the right one for me, then I would take it on without a second thought about the color of his skin. I'm sure I would love my children no matter what they looked like. The important thing to me is that we share the same values, and that we both live the gospel. Is that what you wanted to know?"

"Yes, I suppose it was," Thomas said, wishing her answer hadn't been quite so impersonal. He reminded himself to be patient and enjoy the moment for what it was.

"I was going to make dessert," Mallory said, changing the subject, "but I ran out of time. Want to help me make some brownies or something?"

"Sure," he said, motioning elaborately toward the kitchen.

"You help keep an eye on the girls," Mallory said to Mark, who was reading on the couch. "We'll be in the kitchen."

"Okay," he said.

While Mallory was searching for her brownie recipe, she said, "Ooh, it's too bad we don't have some of that delectable chocolate stuff we're always serving at the restaurant."

"We could make some," he said as if it was no big deal.

"Are you serious?"

"Yes. It's made from pretty basic ingredients."

"But the recipe is—"

"In my head," Thomas said with a little smirk.

"Ooh," she said, "this could be fun."

"It's a wee bit more complicated than brownies," he said, grabbing a dishtowel, which he tied around his waist. "Are you sure you're up to it?"

"I could use some adventure. Just tell me what to do."

Mallory watched in amazement as Thomas took ordinary ingredients and implements, and made the kitchen look like some kind of laboratory. He mixed a few things that he heated in a saucepan to just the right temperature, which he determined with the tip of his finger. He whipped other things together until they were exactly the right consistency, which he determined by the way it peaked when he lifted the mixer just so. But even more intriguing was the way she felt watching him. She'd never noticed what nice hands he had, or the way the tip of his tongue occasionally appeared at the corner of his mouth when he was concentrating. She noticed the way his shirt fit over his shoulders, and how the color suited him so well. And she noticed the way his eyes occasionally took her in, implying a hidden message that tempted her to feel afraid.

"Where did you learn this stuff?" she asked, attempting to distract herself.

"I learned a lot in school, but this particular recipe was my father's specialty. I watched him make it hundreds of times. And he actually learned it from his mother, who had worked in the kitchen of some wealthy old woman who had nothing better to do with her money than pay people to please her passion for fine food. Grandma assisted several different chefs through the years, and she learned some interesting things."

"Wow," Mallory said, looking into a bowl as if the contents might jump out and grab her. "I think I'll stick to brownies."

He finally put something into the oven and set the timer, saying, "Now I'm not used to your oven, so we have to watch it very closely. A minute can make a big difference."

"Okay," she drawled, then continued to gather what he needed as he mixed up a creamy sauce.

"I know it's a long shot, but do you have any frozen raspberries? The cake is good with the cream sauce alone, but it's better if you have fruit sauce, too."

"No, but I think I have some strawberries in the freezer that were given to me last summer."

"That'll do," he said, and she went to the basement to dig them out. She returned to find that the pan had been removed from the oven, and he was cooking over the stove again.

"Isn't this a lot of trouble for a dessert?"

"Usually," he said, and winked at her. "But not today."

"But you do this nearly *every* day."

"No, I've trained people to do this."

"It's far more complicated than I ever imagined."

Thomas smiled and raised his brows. "That's why people pay so much to eat it. And that's what pays my bills. There are many secrets to running a good restaurant, but one of the most important is having some exclusive dishes that can't be duplicated elsewhere. If people like them, they'll keep coming back."

When everything was finished, Thomas said, "Now we just need to let this fruit stuff get cold for a while, then we can eat some."

"The best part."

"Amen," he said, sliding a bowl into the fridge.

Mallory went to check on the children and returned to find Thomas filling the sink with soapy water. "Hey," she said, "I can do that. You've already done your share."

"I grew up with a strict rule," he said. "If you dirty a dish, you wash it. So don't go upsetting my deeply ingrained habits."

"Okay," she smiled, "but let me help you."

Thomas watched Mallory as she dried dishes and put them away, chattering about childhood memories of helping her mother in the kitchen. He admired the relationships she had with her family members, and felt almost envious of the strength she found there.

"You and your mother are very close," he observed.

"Yes, we are. She's an incredible woman. I don't know how I ever would have made it without her. She's been through enough herself that she knows what she's talking about when she gives advice. Everyone tells her she'd make a good counselor, except that her education is all from practical experience, and she has no desire to go back to school again. She's already got a nursing degree, which she uses mostly for volunteer work and to help people she knows."

"It's easy to imagine her being the way you describe." His voice softened with sincerity. "And you're very much like her."

"Me?" She laughed softly. "No. I mean, I'm told I look a lot like her, and I suppose I do. But she has strength that I don't think I could ever have. And I wouldn't want to go through what she went through to get it."

"You've been through quite a bit yourself."

"Yes, I know, but . . . I guess it's that thing where as bad as your own problems can be, you wouldn't want to trade them for somebody else's problems."

"Like what?" he asked, then quickly added, "Maybe I shouldn't ask. It's really none of my business."

"Actually, Mother's very open about it. She takes the attitude that if the things she learned from her struggles can help others, so be it. She's worked in crisis centers off and on through the years. So I think she tells people her story all the time."

"Okay, give me the nutshell version."

"All right. She was sexually abused by her father."

"Ouch," Thomas said. "That's certainly enough to screw up somebody's life."

"How true. Her mother died when she was seventeen. She got pregnant and ran away from the father of the baby because she was scared. She had the baby, then married some guy in the temple who turned out to be psychotic, among other things. He beat her up all the time, and she had four miscarriages. She finally got away from him, but he found her again and nearly killed her. He went to prison and she married my father, but her first husband kept coming back every time he got out on parole. He didn't hurt her anymore, but he scared her pretty badly. Then her father showed up again. She had a nervous breakdown when I was a baby, and spent some time in the hospital."

"That's incredible," Thomas said, obviously stunned. "To see her now, I'd never have dreamed it."

Mallory thought about the piece of that story she would never repeat aloud: the fact that Janna's behavior had contributed to her husband's adultery. It was a powerful element in the evidence that her parents' relationship was so strong now, but it was private and in the past. She summed it up by saying, "And there were a few other bits and pieces that were pretty rough, but she came out of it well. And as you can see, she's been a powerful influence and done a great deal of good. She's living evidence of the impact one person can have in the world if they choose to grow from their struggles, rather than becoming bitter."

"And, as I said, you're very much like her."

Mallory shook her head and chuckled uncomfortably. "No, I'm not. I don't feel strong at all. I feel frightened and totally unprepared to face anything beyond today."

"Don't you think she ever felt that way?" Thomas asked, turning toward her and drying his hands. "From what you've told me, the majority of her struggles happened before you were old enough to notice."

"That's true. I only know about it because she's told me."

"So, the woman you know now is not necessarily how she was in the midst of coping with so much. The fact that she had a breakdown is evidence that she must have felt pretty frightened and weak."

"I never really looked at it that way," Mallory said, briefly becoming lost in thought. She was surprised when Thomas touched her chin, tilting her face to his view.

"You have the potential to get beyond this, Mallory, and to face whatever it is that's frightening you, and overcome it."

Mallory almost believed him, but she didn't understand why tears came from nowhere. Momentarily lost in the promise she read in his expressive eyes, she was surprised to feel a tear trickle down one side of her face. Thomas's eyes filled with compassion just before he kissed her cheek, pulling away the tear with his lips.

Thomas heard a little gasp from Mallory and wondered if he was being too bold. He drew back to look into her eyes, and he was more prone to think that he'd get no better chance than this to let her know how he *really* felt. Struggling to feel his instincts between the audible beats of his heart, Thomas found no reason to keep from kissing her.

Mallory saw the intensity of Thomas's eyes deepen, and she knew he was going to kiss her. She felt frightened, mostly because she *wanted* him to kiss her. Her heart was getting involved, and the reality of that was frightening. Still, she found no will to protest as his lips meekly made contact with hers. He looked into her eyes, then he kissed her again, at the same time taking her fully into his arms. She suddenly felt as if the law of gravity had just been broken, and they were floating together with nothing to inhibit them or hold them down. She felt momentarily detached from the world and all its heartache and pain. There was only her and Thomas, and everything else fell neatly into place around the nucleus he had created by holding her this way. Without taking time to analyze her feelings, Mallory knew she felt completely secure. There was nothing forceful or controlling about his embrace, but it clearly expressed that his feelings for her were powerful, and he wasn't afraid to show it. That thought alone made her tingle and hold to him tighter, returning his embrace as if he had just become some kind of life preserver in the midst of a dark, black ocean. She found it an interesting contrast to realize that his embrace was intense, almost desperate, while his kiss remained unassuming and benevolent.

"Oh, Mallory," he murmured against her lips, looking into her eyes, refusing to let go of her. "It's been so long since . . . I've been close to a woman, since I've felt this way." He smiled. "I don't know if I've ever felt this way."

"You're scaring me, Thomas," she said, trying to be honest with herself as well as him.

"Then we're both scared," he insisted. "Whatever we're falling into, we're falling together." She tried to ease away, but he held her tighter. "I know you're frightened, Mallory, and I understand why. But . . . don't pull away from me because of it. Let me help you through it. Let me be there for you."

Mallory couldn't deny finding a degree of comfort in his words, but she was too overwhelmed with emotion to know what to say. Instead, she laid her head against his shoulder and relished feeling him close. If only it could last. If only she could feel this secure and not have to wonder if there was some kind of evil lurking behind a mask of kindness. She felt Thomas press his lips into her hair, and instinctively she nuzzled closer to the sensation, wanting the rest of the world to go away. Just as she thought it, the girls both began to wail, fighting over a toy in the other room.

"Excuse me," she said and hurried away, not wanting to leave the security of his embrace, but at the same time grateful for an excuse to leave.

She returned to find that he had all of the dishes washed, and he was wiping off the counters. "I can do that," she insisted.

"So can I. You put the dishes away. I don't know where they go."

Mallory did so, finishing in time to see him remove the soiled dishtowel from around his waist and set it aside. Their eyes met for a long moment while her mind wandered through the experience of being in his arms a few minutes ago. From his expression, she felt certain that his thoughts were in the same place. She forced herself to look away. "Should we have some dessert now?"

"Anytime you want," he said.

"I'll get the dishes out. You can serve it." She laughed softly. "I wouldn't dare."

He had barely cut into the rich, chocolaty texture when Matthew and Melody returned. Mallory invited them to have some dessert, and they sat around the table marveling at how incredible it tasted. Thomas took the compliments graciously and joked about how he couldn't do anything else.

Thomas left soon after Bethany was put to bed. Mallory hated the quiet loneliness of the house after the activity of the evening. She read in her scriptures and went to bed early, hoping to avoid being alone. But hours later she was still awake, her mind replaying the scene in the kitchen over and over. Each time she recalled Thomas's display of affection, she tingled from the inside out. She found herself comparing it to the affection she'd experienced in the past, wondering why this had affected her so intensely. Darrell had kissed her a number of times, but she could see now that his affection had been controlling and overbearing—just as he had been. She'd loved Brad very much, and she'd always considered their relationship to be complete. He certainly hadn't been overbearing with his affection; perhaps exactly the opposite. But there was something about the way Thomas had kissed her and held her that she'd never experienced before. And she just didn't understand. The thought was frightening, but at the same time exciting.

On Monday Mallory worked as usual, wondering if any of the other employees knew that she and Thomas were dating. Did they sense the meaning in his eyes when he looked at her, or the way she felt different when he was anywhere in sight?

During a slow moment he stopped her in the kitchen, saying in a very businesslike manner, "Could I talk to you in the office when you get a minute?"

"Sure," she said, and went up the stairs a few minutes later to find the door to his office ajar. She stepped in but didn't see him until he appeared from behind the door, laughing as he closed it.

Mallory couldn't help laughing with him as he pulled her into his arms, speaking softly. "I couldn't bear it another minute." He pressed a lingering kiss to the side of her face, then he inhaled deeply, as if he could absorb her presence. Mallory pushed away any fear for the sake of enjoying the moment. She returned his embrace, loving the feel of strong male arms around her, knowing he truly cared for her.

Thomas leaned against the door, putting one foot up behind him. Without relinquishing his hold on her, he looked into her eyes, saying with reverence, "You are so beautiful, Mallory." He touched her face and hair and pressed a kiss to her brow, holding his lips there as if he could somehow absorb her thoughts.

Mallory closed her eyes to more fully appreciate the experience of just having him so near. Blindly she reached a hand up to touch his face, loving the feel of stubbled skin after being alone for so long. She couldn't recall ever touching Darrell this way. Was it possible that she'd simply never wanted to? With little thought, Mallory moved her fingers up to touch his hair. She eased back to look at him as she did, fascinated by the feel of it, unlike anything she'd ever touched before. His expression deepened as he took notice of her attention, and she glanced away.

"Maybe I should get back to work," she said.

"Maybe you should let me take you out again tomorrow."

Mallory looked back at him. "Okay," she said. She didn't even care where they were going.

On Tuesday morning, Thomas took Mallory to the temple, then he bought her lunch at the cafeteria and took her home. He gave her a quick kiss when he left her at the door, saying that he'd see her at work the next day.

On Wednesday, Mallory ended up in bed with cramps that were far worse than normal. She called the restaurant to tell them she wouldn't be coming in, hoping to talk to Thomas. But one of the girls answered the phone and said he was busy inspecting a delivery.

He called back a while later, asking right off, "What's wrong? Are you sick?"

"Not really. I just don't feel good. It's nothing to worry about."

"Well, what's wrong?"

Mallory sighed. "It's a feminine thing, Thomas. Could we leave it at that?"

"Sorry," he said sheepishly. "I thought you might be avoiding me."

"Why would I do that?"

"Because I'm desperately in love with you, and you've made it clear that men frighten you."

Mallory was speechless—literally. She knew that Thomas cared for her very much, and it had even crossed her mind that he might love her. But hearing it put to words in such a way simply threw her off balance with the questions it brought to mind. Did he *really* love her? If so, did he love her enough to be completely honest with her, no matter what? Were there things about him that she didn't know, things that would eventually come to the surface and hurt her? Perhaps most difficult of all, did she feel the same way about him? And if she did, would she be able to admit it?

"Mallory." Thomas's voice came through the phone, startling her. "Did I say something wrong?"

Mallory cleared her throat and struggled to gather her wits. "Not if you really mean it."

"I wouldn't say it if I didn't." A full minute later he said, "You're not talking."

"I don't know what to say."

"Okay, well . . . is there anything you need? Are you going to be all right?"

"Oh, I'll be fine tomorrow. The bad part never lasts long."

"Can I bring some dinner over this evening, or would you prefer that I leave you alone?"

"I . . . I don't know," she admitted. "Call me later."

"Okay. Take care of yourself."

"I will. Thank you."

Mallory lay in bed with her hot-water bottle for over an hour, contemplating what Thomas had said and how it made her feel. Thankfully, Bethany was in a good mood and played contentedly near the bed, occasionally climbing up beside her to look at a storybook.

He loved her—*desperately*, he'd said. He was a wonderful man, and he loved her. So, why couldn't she feel happy about that? Where was the joy that should be a part of newly found love? Perhaps she simply didn't love *him*. Could that be why she felt so numb, so afraid? Thinking that through very carefully, she knew that wasn't the case. The way she felt about Thomas went deeper than anything she'd ever felt for Darrell. She'd been willing to marry him— a fact that made her wonder if she even really knew what love felt like. She'd loved Brad; she knew that. But in retrospect, her feelings were confused and unclear.

"Wead a stowy, Mama," Bethany said, situating herself right up against Mallory's arm. "Wead a stowy. Wead a stowy."

Mallory welcomed the distraction and held her daughter close, praying in her heart that she would be able to get beyond these form-less fears and get on with her life.

CHAPTER TEN

*T*homas called about four o'clock. "Unless you have any strong objections," he said, "I'm bringing dinner over for you and Bethie in about an hour."

Mallory quickly gauged her feelings. She looked awful, but vanity was not going to keep her from doing something she wanted to do. And she had to admit that she really wanted to see him. "Okay," she said. "I look horrible, but if you can live with it, I certainly can."

"I'll look forward to seeing the real you. What sounds good? Are you craving anything?"

"Craving?"

"I've been married before," he said lightly. "If you're down with cramps, I'd wager you're craving *something.*"

"Actually," Mallory said, realizing he was right, "I keep thinking about a good old-fashioned hamburger and french fries—with fry sauce."

"That's easy. What about Bethie?"

"Oh, she loves french fries—with *lots* of fry sauce."

"Done. I'll see you soon."

Mallory got out of bed and brushed her hair and teeth. She put a robe on over her pajamas, refilled her hot-water bottle and moved to the couch, bringing along some toys for Bethie to keep her occupied.

"It's open!" Mallory called when she heard a knock at the door. Thomas appeared with his hands full and kicked the door closed. "Hi," she said. "Can I help?"

"No. You stay put. Do you want to eat in the kitchen, or—"

"The coffee table is fine, if you don't mind grabbing Bethie's high chair and that plastic tablecloth I put under it."

Mallory watched Thomas as he eagerly fixed the chair and put Bethany in it. He asked a blessing on the food at her request, then he put french fries and sauce on the high chair tray, laughing at the way Bethany dipped a fry over and over, sucking the sauce off of it. While they ate, he talked about happenings at the restaurant and asked her how she was feeling. He cleaned up the dinner mess and got a wash-cloth so that Mallory could clean up Bethany. He returned the high chair to the kitchen, then he sat beside Mallory and took her hand.

"How are you doing?" he asked.

"Better than this morning," she said. "If nothing else, it feels awfully nice to be waited on."

"Well, I have some experience with that."

"Not in *my* house, you don't. But you learn quickly."

"I'm just trying to impress you," he said. "I'm just hoping you'll like me enough that you won't be too shocked when you discover the real me."

Mallory looked away abruptly. "That's not funny."

"No, Mallory, it's not. But the truth is, I try very hard to be a good man and do what's right. I'm not perfect, however; far from it. And I am honestly afraid that you are going to find something wrong with me, just to give you an excuse to keep your distance."

Mallory said nothing and he added, "What's the matter? You look upset."

"When we agreed to be completely honest with each other, I wasn't expecting you to be so forthright on issues that are . . ."

"What? Sensitive?"

"I guess that covers it."

"Would you prefer that I keep the real feelings to myself, so we can go merrily along pretending that everything's all right?"

"No," Mallory insisted, realizing he'd just described her marriage to Brad.

"Well, then you're going to have to listen to what I have to say. Because I've got so many thoughts and feelings bubbling around inside of me that I'm going to go nuts if I can't say it. Is that all right with you?"

"You don't need my permission to talk, Thomas."

"No, but I need your assurance that you're not going to get scared and run."

Mallory hated the way he had her pegged so accurately, and the way he'd covered every base to make it impossible for her to back away from facing all of this head-on.

"Literally, or figuratively?" she asked.

"Both."

"I can listen, Thomas. But I can't make any promises about how I'll feel."

"Just give me a fair chance, Mallory. That's all I ask."

She nodded and he took a deep breath, attempting to recall words he'd been trying to memorize for days.

"Mallory, I know that all of this may seem awfully fast, especially with the way you're feeling. But the fact is, from my point of view, it's not fast at all. I've wanted you in my life ever since you started dating that Darrell creep. You can't imagine the relief I felt when you broke the engagement, but I wanted to give you some time to heal and get beyond it."

He took her hand and looked into her eyes. "Mallory, I've fasted and prayed and done my best to listen to what the Lord has to tell me. I can't answer for you, but I have to tell you what's in my heart. I'm not going to take you to a fancy restaurant and put you on the spot. I'm not going to buy you a gaudy ring that you'll hate to wear. I'm simply asking you to marry me, and offering all the time you need to think it through and find out what's best for you."

Mallory felt numb, as if she was hearing all of this through some kind of a fog. She said nothing until Thomas's expectant gaze forced her to. "You have a way of making me speechless," she said.

Thomas shrugged and continued to watch her.

"I think you just proposed to me."

"Yes, I think I did."

"I'm sitting here in my pajamas with a hot-water bottle, and you're proposing to me?"

"I did buy you a hamburger," he said facetiously. "And if you look really close, you'll notice that I'm blushing."

It took Mallory a moment to realize the absurdity of a black man saying something like that. Then she laughed. But at least it alleviated some of the tension—for a moment.

"Talk to me, Mallory," he said. "Just tell me what you're feeling. I've got all the time in the world, as long as you don't shut me out."

"Okay," Mallory said, feeling somehow numb. "I'm . . . flattered, and . . . thrilled. Logically, I think I should be the happiest woman alive. You're everything I could ever want, but . . ."

"But?"

"I'm scared, Thomas."

"I can understand that. But don't you think we can work on getting beyond that and—"

"I don't know. Maybe we can, but . . . at this point it just feels . . . crippling. You know how much Brad hurt me, and—"

"No, I don't," he said. "You've told me that you were afraid of getting hurt again, but you never told me why. You don't have to tell me, but don't go assuming that I understand where you're coming from." She said nothing and he added, "I know he shot himself, and you once told me it was complicated. Obviously he hurt you very deeply."

Mallory felt a knot form in her stomach and move slowly toward her head, growing in size as it did. Tears pressed into her eyes, like a valve releasing pressure.

"And obviously you're still grieving," Thomas added, putting his arm around her. "I'm sorry," he whispered. "Maybe I'm pushing you too hard. We can drop this conversation right here if you want, and start over next week, or next month if you—"

"It's all right," she said, feeling saturated with his comfort as he held her close. "I think maybe I need to talk about it. I'm tired of feeling this way, and I want to get on with my life. It's just that . . . some of it's so horrible. And whenever I think about how good he was to me, and how much I loved him, I can't help but think of how he deceived me. All those years, I believed everything was perfect, and he was . . ."

"It's okay, Mallory."

"It's not okay." She sat up straight and clenched her fists. "He cheated on me. He betrayed me, and—"

"Are you telling me he had an affair?"

"No!" she snapped, hating the anger she was feeling when she'd wanted to believe that she'd gotten past it. "Not literally, at least. But who knows what was going on in his mind? While I was going merrily along, being a faithful wife with images of forever in my mind, he was hiding away with filthy pictures. That's what killed him, Thomas. It was pornography."

Thomas grimaced and felt a hard knot gather in his stomach as she went on. "Apparently he couldn't live with the guilt. But I don't know for sure. He didn't bother leaving me a note; no indication whatsoever of his feelings for me. Beyond a good life insurance policy, all he left me was a daughter and the horror of wondering what was really going on in my home all that time. We found burned magazines and melted video tapes in the wood-burning stove. And magazines popped up all over the place when I started doing some deep cleaning. There were even pictures filed on the computer; hundreds of them. My father found them. He said he didn't see much before he realized what it was and deleted everything. But he said there were pictures of things more horrible than he ever could have imagined."

Mallory shook her head, still disbelieving that it was true. She wiped her tears with her hands and sniffled. "All those years I had no clue. Maybe that's what bothers me most of all. I loved him with all my heart and soul. But then, I turned around and nearly married this guy who was trying to make me believe he was something different than what he really was. I still get sick to my stomach when I stop to wonder what is wrong with me, that I can't see beyond a person's mask and know what's really going on."

"But you did, didn't you?" Thomas said. "You figured Darrell out before it was too late. You learned something from that, didn't you?"

"I'd like to think so, but . . . I just get scared. Sometimes when I'm around other people—even at church—all I can see are masks. I find myself wondering what kind of vices people are hiding. I have no reason to believe that you are anything but what you appear to be, Thomas. The problem is with *me*. But you have to understand that I can't just leap into something while I'm feeling this way."

"Have you talked to your mother about this?"

"Oh, many times."

"And what does she say?"

"She says that the only way to truly learn to trust again is simply to trust. She told me it takes risk; that there's no other way."

"So, I guess that means you're going to have to decide whether you love me enough to take the risk. Is that it?"

Mallory sighed and looked at him, wishing she could just open her heart and take what he was offering. "I suppose it is. But I'm not sure I have the strength to do that."

"Maybe not now. But with time, perhaps you will. I think you're stronger than you believe."

"I don't know, Thomas. I don't feel strong at all."

"Listen to me, Mallory. There is nothing I can say or do to convince you that I am what I say I am. The fact that I don't have a prison record, and my credit rating is good, won't appease your fears. I can't talk you into feeling something you don't feel. All I can do is tell you what's in my heart, and do my best to live what I feel."

Mallory was moved to tears again; not from fear or anger, but from the raw sincerity in his eyes. In that moment, it was easy to admit what she'd known deep inside all along. "I do love you, Thomas. I really do."

He smiled and pressed a kiss to her brow. "Well, that's progress."

"But I need some time."

"I understand. In the meantime, I'd like to spend as much time with you as I can get away with."

"You treat us so well, I don't think that will be a problem."

Thomas stayed until Bethany was put to bed. He kissed Mallory quickly at the door and left her longing to be free of being alone.

The following day at work, Thomas said, "I've got the Friday evening shifts covered. What would you think of coming to my place for dinner?"

Mallory smiled. "Really? I'd like that."

"Do you want to bring Bethany? She can—"

"Uh," Mallory interrupted, "it's sweet of you to offer, but the truth is, I won't be able to relax a minute with her there. After I scout out your place and baby-proof it a little, *then* we can take Bethie there."

"I'll look forward to it," he said.

"So, what time do you want me there?"

"I'll come and get you," he insisted. "About six, if that's okay."

"I'll be ready," she said. Then he quickly glanced both directions to be certain no one was looking before he kissed her.

Mallory felt a jittery excitement about spending the evening at Thomas's place. She felt on the brink of a new adventure, and walking through his front door only intensified the feeling. He lived in a condominium that appeared from the outside like townhouses that would line the streets of London.

"This is nice," she said as he took her sweater and hung it on a rack near the door.

"Well, it's home," he said. "But it's never been nicer than it is right now."

Mallory knew by his expression that he was implying her presence here made the difference.

"Would you like a brief tour?" he asked.

"I'd love it."

Without moving, Thomas pointed one direction, then the other. "Kitchen and dining room are there, bathroom over there. Upstairs is the bedroom and den. Downstairs is mostly storage."

"Gee," she laughed softly, "that was a quick tour."

"Don't want to bore you," he said, moving toward the kitchen. "Listen, I've got some things to finish up for dinner. Just relax, okay?"

"Can't I help?"

"Not this time," he said.

While Mallory could hear Thomas working in the kitchen, she slowly perused the front room, savoring each aspect of it as she attempted to integrate her surroundings into the man she knew. The first thing she noticed was a grouping of three watercolor prints. The artwork was a bit abstract, which added a certain beauty to the set. On the left was a little girl with black skin, looking upward toward the center picture. On the right was a little boy, doing the same. In the center was an abstract representation of Martin Luther King. And above him, the words *I have a dream*. Mallory gazed at it for several minutes, attempting to comprehend what that might mean to Thomas. She had to rub a chill from her arms as she moved her gaze around the room, taking in the overall feel. It had a masculine aura, simple but very classy. There were many bookshelves filled with a wide variety of books, along with various ornamental pieces that were far too classy to ever be called bric-a-brac.

"How you doing?" Thomas asked, putting his arms around her from behind. He had a subtle aroma about him that made her anticipate dinner.

"I'm doing great," she said. "This room has your personality in it."

"I never really looked at it that way exactly," he said. "But everything in this room has some kind of personal significance."

"Tell me," she said.

Thomas picked up the items from his shelves one by one, telling her stories of how he'd acquired them and why he liked them. Mallory's favorite was the little porcelain angel with wings—and black skin.

"I'm not sure if angels having black skin is accurate in terms of our religious beliefs," he said. "But then, neither are angels with wings. It's symbolic, right?"

"Yes."

"Well, this angel reminds me of two things." He took it off the shelf and handed it to Mallory. "First of all, that God is no respecter of persons. No matter the color of our skin, we all have value in his eyes. And secondly, when my mother was killed, my Aunt Emerald always told me that Mama was an angel now, and she would be watching over me even better than she could before she died. This," he took the angel from her and held it reverently, "is very close to the image I've always had of my mother as an angel."

Thomas set it back on the shelf and went to the kitchen for a minute to check on dinner. He came back and pointed to some prints on the wall and told her their significance, then he turned and pointed out the Martin Luther King grouping. "I think that's self-explanatory," he said.

"Yeah, it probably is," Mallory said. "But tell me anyway."

"Well," he said, "I assume you know your history enough to know what Martin Luther King meant when he said *I have a dream.*"

"Basically it represents the overcoming of prejudice in this country, and allowing blacks to have equal rights," she said.

Thomas smiled. "Very good."

"Oh," Mallory felt mildly alarmed, "isn't it more correct to say *African-American?*"

Thomas chuckled, and she noticed that his shoulders moved briefly whenever he did. "I believe 'African-American' is the politically correct term. I certainly don't claim to be up on what's the most current on such things, but in my opinion, the term doesn't always work. I'm black, and I don't have a problem with that. I have a deep love for my race and my heritage, and there is a beauty about it that's difficult to describe."

Mallory glanced around the room. "I can agree with that."

"But the term *African-American* cannot automatically replace the word *black* in referring to our race. Maybe it's not meant to; I don't know. But what about the blacks who come from the islands? What about Australia? New Zealand? How can you walk up to someone black and just assume that they are African-American?"

"That's a good point," she said earnestly.

"Of course, the majority of black Americans probably are of African descent—a fact that can be troubling if you look at the reasons. But personally, I would rather be called black than be called African-American and have to tell everyone I meet that I'm from Haiti—even though I'm not." He chuckled again. "Just an analogy."

"Yes, I know."

"Anyway," he looked back up at the image of Martin Luther King, "I have seen the realization of his dream come to pass in many ways through the course of my lifetime. But there are still many barriers caused by prejudice, so I feel that *I* have to carry that dream. I have to do my part to ensure that life in this country will be better for my children than it was for my parents." He laughed softly. "I often felt close to my ancestors as I did their genealogy and temple work, and I have often imagined them watching over me as I have achieved my goals. Just think of those who lived through the Civil War, seeing me graduate from college and run a successful business in a predominantly white community."

He smiled, and Mallory could almost feel his pleasure in the thoughts he described. A moment later he turned and pointed out a print on the other wall. "This is one of my favorites," he said. "When I saw this, I *had* to have it."

Mallory absorbed the picture of a black baby being held high by many hands. "This looks familiar somehow," she said.

"Did you see *Roots?*" he asked.

"Yes, actually, I did." The memory came back of the depiction in the movie of each baby being blessed this way as the tradition was handed down through the generations.

"There you have it," he said. "This is how they bless African babies, in essence. I look at the many hands holding him as a symbol of the family and ancestors that all contribute to the birth and life of a child."

"It's beautiful," she said. Then she asked lightly, "Will you do that with your children when they're born?"

"Well," he laughed, "I figured I would bless them in sacrament meeting like every other Mormon." He glanced at the picture. "But who knows? Maybe I'll just do it for fun. My ancestors might appreciate it."

Mallory thoroughly enjoyed dinner, as fine a meal as if they were eating at the most exquisite restaurant in the country. And she told him so more than once. She helped him wash the dishes, then they sat together on the couch, holding hands. As they talked, Mallory couldn't help but notice his hands. She turned over the one she was holding and pressed her palm to his, noting how his skin was lighter there. "You have nice hands," she said.

"Really?"

"Oh, yes. I've always noticed men's hands. Brad had nice hands, too. And, well . . . I didn't really like Darrell's hands. Not that I would marry a guy because of his hands, but . . . ," she laughed softly, "you do have nice hands."

"You can at least chalk that up in my favor," he said, and she nodded.

They began talking about his ancestors and the genealogy work he'd done, which fascinated Mallory beyond words. He took her upstairs to his den, where he showed her copies of records he'd found in his search. There were birth, marriage, and death dates copied out of old town record books, which he briefly compared to the names and dates on a huge pedigree chart hanging on the wall. Mallory actually got a knot in her stomach when he showed her copies of plantation records where his ancestors were listed as property, and then the slave ship registries where he'd found seemingly miraculous clues that proved the connection to the plantation slaves he was related to.

Thomas stopped talking when he noticed Mallory put a hand over her mouth. He looked at her and realized there were tears running down her face. "What is it?" he asked, putting his arms tightly around her.

"It's just so awful," she said. "I mean . . . I saw *Roots* years ago, and it left an impression on me, but . . . this is just so . . . personal and . . ." She looked up at him. "I was just thinking that in spite of all they went through, I'm so grateful that you're an American . . . and you're here for me. And then I felt so selfish to think it, and . . ."

"Hey," he said, urging her head to his shoulder, "I've thought the same thing. I'm glad I'm here too, Mallory—the same way you're glad that your ancestors joined the Church and endured persecution, and walked across the plains to make it possible for you to grow up a Mormon here in this beautiful place, with peace and security."

"Yes, but . . . it's different. The pioneers came by choice, and . . ."

"I know, Mallory, but . . . it's in the past. I know in my heart that all those who went before me are at peace now. And I am a free man. I am more free than my father, and he was more free than his father, because the acceptance becomes more profound all the time. And beyond that, I have the freedom the gospel has given me. And that gives me more freedom than my father could have ever comprehended."

"You're an incredible man," Mallory said.

"I don't know about that. I just try to regularly remind myself of all I have to be grateful for. It helps me keep perspective."

They visited a while longer before Thomas took Mallory home, but the experience of the evening left a definite impression on her. She felt a deepening of her feelings for him, and for the culture and heritage that stood behind him. Her fears were the farthest thing from her mind. She could only think of seeing him again.

They worked together the following day, and on Sunday he came to her house after church, where they cooked dinner together. He stayed until Bethany was put to bed; and within a few weeks, he was putting her to bed himself on the few evenings every week that he spent with Mallory and her daughter. Bethany became completely comfortable with Thomas, and he became pretty good at potty training.

Thomas began planning his schedule around Mallory's so they could have the same time off. He was rarely at home beyond his need to sleep, unless Mallory and Bethany were with him. But even with some baby-proofing, Bethany was still harder to keep out of trouble at his place.

He got to know Mallory's family better, and enjoyed the opportunity to join in family gatherings. They had a big family barbecue for Mother's Day at her parents' home, where he met Mallory's grandmother—Colin's mother, Nancy Trevor. Thomas could see right off that she had a great deal of vigor for her age, and like many people did when they met him, she gave him a long gaze.

Thomas felt compelled to say, "No, Sister Trevor, your eyes are not deceiving you. I really am black."

"And handsome at that," she said, taking his hand. "Are you taking good care of my Mallory?" she asked.

"I'm certainly doing my best."

"That's all that matters, then," the old woman said. "And call me Grandma."

Thomas chuckled. "It would be a pleasure. I haven't had a grandma since I was a toddler. I barely remember any of my grandparents."

This opened a long conversation between the two of them, while Mallory kept busy helping her mother. Thomas quickly grew to love Nancy Trevor, along with the rest of Mallory's family. And he appreciated—more than he could ever tell any of them—their unquestioning acceptance of him.

Mallory seemed relaxed and at ease as long as Thomas didn't bring up marriage, and he just did his best to be patient. When Caitlin got married in mid-July, Thomas went to the wedding with Mallory. Sitting in a sealing room, holding her hand while the ceremony was performed, made him ache to have her in his life completely. He tried to be cheerful through the remainder of the day, but the thought hovered with him relentlessly. At the reception, Mallory stood in the line next to her sister, wearing a dark green dress. She looked absolutely stunning. Thomas kept busy trying to keep up with Bethany and hanging around with Matthew, who was trying to keep up with Elizabeth. He got a few dubious glances from friends and relatives—but not as many as he suspected he would get when he married Mallory.

When the happy couple had been sent on their way and the cultural hall was all cleaned up, Thomas picked Bethany up from where she'd been sleeping on his jacket in the corner. He carried her out to the car and managed to buckle her into her car seat without waking her. Then he held the door for Mallory, giving her a quick kiss before she got in.

"It was a nice day, don't you think?" she said as he drove toward Highland.

"Yes, it was," he said. "Everything turned out perfect."

Mallory sighed and began chattering about the day's events, until it became evident that she was having a one-sided conversation. "Is something wrong?" she asked.

"I would assume I have to answer that honestly."

"Yes, you do. What's wrong?"

Thomas glanced at Mallory, then back to the road. "I want to get married, Mallory. I'm tired of living this way."

"You told me you'd give me all the time I needed."

"Yes, but what are you doing with it? I don't see any evidence of progress in what's holding you back. I'm assuming the problem is still the same. You're scared, right?"

"Yes," she said scornfully, "I'm scared."

"Well, you know what, Mallory? You're not the only one."

"What do you mean by that?"

"You think *I'm* not scared?" he countered. "Why do you think I waited so blasted long to even approach you with the way I felt? I've been attracted to you since the first time I saw you. But I was *scared*. Every woman in my life has left me. My mother was killed when I was six. I had three stepmothers. Two of them left; the other one died. My wife left me for my own brother, for crying out loud. Sometimes I get knots in my stomach just thinking of the reality that I have exposed myself to you, heart and soul. Because if you left me too, I don't know if I could bear it. But I *love* you, Mallory. And I'm willing to risk it. That's what love is, you know—a risk. When we grieve, it is in direct proportion to how much we love. I'm certain you know that. Neither of us is perfect. We're bound to make mistakes, and we may, through the course of our lives, hurt each other. But if we're committed to seeing this relationship through and solving the problems that arise, then that's the best we can do. There is no guarantee that you or I will live to our full life expectancy. If we get married and live our lives together, one of us may very well end up grieving before our time here on earth is done. But that's the price we may have to pay. And I'm willing to pay it, Mallory. Because I know with all my heart that being with you is the best thing I could possibly do with my life. I know it's right because the Spirit has let me know. And I'm not going to just turn around and walk away from this because you're *scared*. I'm not giving up that easily. But neither am I going to wait around for the rest of my life while you wallow in some kind of denial. I can't do it."

"It sounds to me like you're contradicting yourself."

"No, I am not. I'm just telling you what I'm willing to do. I could wait a long time if I felt like it had some purpose. But more and more, this just seems like empty waiting to me. Matthew and Melody are expecting another baby. At this rate, Bethany's going to be an only child."

"It's not that bad," she insisted.

"From my perspective it is. She could be ten years older than the next in line. Is that what you want?"

"No."

"Then look at the big picture. Consider how your fears are affecting *her* life. And mine. And especially yours."

Mallory's defensiveness melted into an overwhelming sadness. She knew he was right, and there was absolutely nothing she could say to change the fact that he was.

"I'm sorry, Thomas," she said and felt him take her hand. "I'll work on it, okay?"

"Okay," he said gently. "And I'm going to keep nagging you, okay?"

"Okay," she said, not wanting to think too hard about it. A few minutes later she asked, "You were attracted to me the first time you saw me?"

"That's right. I remember it like it was yesterday."

"You mean when I came in with Darrell, and he embarrassed me so badly, you were *attracted* to me?"

"Well, I was certainly thinking *wow, what a babe.* And I had to wonder what a classy woman was doing with a jerk like him. But that wasn't the first time I saw you."

Mallory looked baffled and he added, "I saw you some weeks before that. You came in with somebody else. And I remember it was a weeknight, because it wasn't very crowded."

"That was Brad," she said sadly. "We ate there together less than a week before he died."

"Well," Thomas said, "I wasn't sitting there thinking I had to have you or anything. I could tell you were married. Let's just say that I was . . . aware of you. I'd never felt any attraction at all for a white woman before. I never thought I would."

"Does that bother you?"

"It doesn't bother *me*," he said lightly. "I'm sure we'll all be the same color in the next life."

Mallory smiled and asked, "Is that why you hired me? You were attracted to me?"

Thomas chuckled. "I hired you because your application and interview impressed me. I felt confident you would make a good employee. And that is the absolute truth."

With Caitlin on her honeymoon and the wedding behind them, Mallory called her mother and asked if they could go out to lunch. She talked with Janna about her continuing fear. As always, she validated Mallory's feelings and listened attentively. But her advice came down to the same old thing.

"Mallory, dear. You, like every other person who has the gift of the Holy Ghost, are entitled to personal revelation. As you do your best to replace the fear with faith, you have to trust in the Lord and press forward."

"But I thought marrying Darrell was right, and I nearly got myself into a big mess all over again."

"Okay, Mallory. But you've got a brain. You can look at Thomas as opposed to Darrell and see a great many differences. When your mind and your heart meet, then you know you've made the right choice. You've got to learn to trust your feelings. I don't think you were feeling much of anything when you started dating Darrell; you were still in shock over Brad's death and losing the baby at that point. But you've come a long way. This is just like anything else you learn in life. When you make a mistake, it gives you a point of reference for avoiding that mistake again. You're not going to repeat the same mistake if you do your best to learn and listen to the Spirit."

"So, do you think I should just marry him?"

"I can't make that decision for you; you're going to have to do it. And the Lord will help you if you ask, but he's not going to hit you over the head with a baseball bat. Part of our experience here is to learn to trust our feelings and learn from our choices. I've said it before, Mallory: the only way you're going to learn to trust is to trust. There isn't any magic potion."

"Okay, I know it's my choice. But just for the sake of it . . . how do you feel about Thomas? He's spent a lot of time with the family. You've been around him."

"I think he's wonderful, Mallory. I'm no fortune teller, but I certainly can't find anything wrong with him."

"Okay, but you thought Brad was wonderful, too."

"Yes, I always liked Brad, but I can honestly say that I felt uneasy at times. I sensed that there was something more to his quiet nature than simple shyness."

"You did? Really?"

"Well, it wasn't overwhelming. It just nagged at me once in a while."

"Why didn't you say something?"

"I would have if I'd felt compelled to. But it never felt right."

Mallory thought for a minute then said, "So, you think Thomas is wonderful."

"Don't you?"

"Oh, yes."

"And how do you *feel* about him?"

Mallory smiled. "I love him, Mother. I really do."

"Are you concerned about having an interracial marriage?"

"Should I be?" Mallory asked.

"It doesn't bother me, and as far as I know, everyone in the family agrees. Some people would say that you should be concerned for your children; that life could be more difficult for them."

"What do you think?"

"I think that as long as your children are raised in a loving home with the gospel, anything else is irrelevant. The color of your husband's skin means nothing to me. If there were strong cultural differences, I would be concerned. For instance, take a man who was born and raised an Arab; even if he joined the Church, I fear there would be too much potential for trouble. His background would be too drastically different. But then, I'm prone to never say never. Only the Lord knows what's best. The only way to know is to go to him. As far as you and Thomas are concerned, his beliefs and upbringing very much coincide with yours. He was raised with Christian values in the same country. Your challenges will be minimized in that respect."

For days Mallory pondered the things her mother had said, trying very hard to get in touch with her real feelings. But rather than feeling more at peace, she began to feel uptight. The more she thought about it, the more her anxiety grew. She wondered if this was the Spirit trying to tell her that marrying Thomas wasn't right. But when she prayed for an answer in that direction, nothing changed.

Mallory did her best to hide her anxiety and go about her business, but after a couple of days, Thomas cornered her in his office. "Okay, what's wrong?" he asked.

"What do you mean?"

"You're acting like a scared little rabbit, avoiding me like the plague. Sit down. We're going to talk about this right now."

Mallory sighed. "I don't know," she muttered. "I'm having a really hard time, Thomas. I just don't know. Maybe I should go work somewhere else and put some distance between us. Maybe—"

"Now wait a minute, Mallory. Let's talk about this. No matter what comes of our relationship, it doesn't change anything between us professionally."

"How can you say that, when *everything* has changed between us?"

"Because this is where you work, and you and I are mature and capable adults. We can communicate and keep things in perspective. If you don't want to marry me, fine. But, for heaven's sake, don't turn and run the other way. You can't run from love all your life, Mallory, or you'll end up with nothing. No matter what happens between us, I will always care for you, and I would prefer that you keep your job."

Mallory pressed her head into her hands.

"Talk to me, Mallory. Tell me what you're feeling."

"I don't know what I'm feeling."

"Then tell me what you want."

"I don't know that, either."

"Do you *want* to work somewhere else?"

"No. I like working here. And I don't want to lose having you in my life, for whatever reason."

"Okay, we're narrowing it down."

"Do you want to marry me?" he asked. She looked up at him skeptically and he clarified, "I didn't ask if you *would* marry me. I just asked if you *wanted* to."

"Okay, yes. I want to marry you, Thomas."

He couldn't help sighing audibly as relief enveloped him. But he had to ask, "Then what's wrong, Mallory?"

"I don't know. I'm just so confused, and . . . I wonder if the Lord isn't trying to tell me that it's just not right."

Thomas felt panic strike him. But a quick search of his feelings gave him comfort and confidence. He knew what was happening. "And tell me, Mallory: if we *are* supposed to be together, who is going to try to convince you that it's wrong?" Her eyes widened as he took both her hands into his. "Mallory, Satan knows more than anyone how vulnerable you are. He's well known for taking fear and using it to his advantage."

Mallory said nothing and he went on, hoping to assuage her fears. "The last thing I want to do is put pressure on you and make it harder. But I know you're the right one for me, Mallory. I know it with all my being."

"Well, *I* don't know that."

"How can you know anything when there is so much hurt and fear damming your feelings?"

"Well, I guess that's the problem, isn't it."

"Okay, so what are you going to do about it?"

"I don't know. If I knew, we wouldn't be arguing."

Thomas quieted his voice. "May I make a suggestion?"

"Sure."

"Take a couple of days off. Go to the temple. Do some studying. And maybe you should ask your brother for a blessing. Do everything you can to get closer to the Spirit. Then see how you feel."

Mallory sighed. She knew he was right. "Why didn't I think of that?" she asked.

"Sometimes the obvious is hard to see when opposition is clouding your vision."

"I love you, Thomas."

He kissed her quickly and touched her face. "I love you, too. You call me in a few days, okay? I'll just let you have some space in the meantime."

Mallory nodded, grateful for his patience and understanding. If she couldn't come to terms with herself and marry him, she had to be the biggest fool that ever lived.

CHAPTER ELEVEN

*T*homas nearly went crazy during the next few days. He felt good about giving Mallory some time and space, but he missed her desperately. And it took great willpower not to call or go see her. He kept hoping she would call him, perhaps wanting to talk something through, or even just to connect with him. But she didn't.

Three days after he'd given the advice that he was coming to regret, he finally broke down and called. "Hi," he said. "How are you?"

"I'm okay. I'll be in to work tomorrow."

"That's not why I called."

She said nothing.

"Are you feeling any better?"

"No, actually."

Thomas's heart began to pound. What would he do if she actually made the decision to leave him the way she'd left Darrell? Could he live with it? Did he have any choice?

"What have you been doing?" he asked, wondering if she'd followed any of his advice.

"Not much. I haven't really had the motivation to do anything."

"Did you get a blessing?"

"No."

"Did you go to the temple?"

"No."

Thomas resisted the urge to get angry. While he had been aching to be with her, she had been lying around depressed, doing nothing to alleviate her struggles.

"Do you want to talk?" he asked.

"There's nothing to talk about. I appreciate your concern, Thomas, but I have to do this on my own."

"Do what? This is making no sense to me, Mallory."

"When it makes sense to me, I'll let you know. I have to go. Bethie needs me."

Thomas hung up the phone and put his head into his hands. "Oh, help," he murmured, praying with everything inside of him that he could somehow reach Mallory and convince her of his love.

An hour later, Thomas was still sitting in the same place, still praying and struggling to come up with an answer, trying to find something *he* could do. He felt so helpless. He kept thinking of how Mallory said she always turned to her mother for help and advice, and he wished he had a mother to turn to. Then it occurred to him that he could call Mallory's mother. Maybe she could help him see a perspective he hadn't seen before. It certainly couldn't hurt, he reasoned as he hurried to look up the number. Dustin answered the phone and informed him that Janna and Colin had gone to a meeting; they would be home about nine.

Thomas debated what to do. Feeling edgy and uptight, he got in the car and headed toward Provo. Even if he missed them, he decided the drive might clear his head.

Thomas arrived at the Trevors' home at ten minutes past nine. He silently asked for some divine guidance and knocked at the front door. Janna opened it, looking surprised, then pleased. "Thomas. Come in. We just got home."

"Thank you," he said and stepped inside.

She closed the door and said, "What can we do for you?"

"Well, I must confess, I'm concerned about Mallory and I'm feeling a little helpless."

Janna motioned Thomas to the couch and they both sat down. "Go on," she said.

"Mallory's always telling me how she can turn to you for help and advice, and I was wishing I had a mother I could call. I don't, but . . . I felt like maybe I could call on you. I hope I'm not out of line or—"

"Heavens, no," Janna said. "I'm glad you came. I don't know if I can help, but I'm sure willing to listen."

"If this is a bad time, I can—"

"No, of course not. There's absolutely nothing I need to be doing. If you—"

"I did hear someone at the door," Colin said, coming down the stairs. "How are you, Thomas?"

"Good, and you?" Thomas said, standing to shake Colin's hand in greeting.

"I'm fine. What's up?"

"He's concerned about Mallory," Janna explained as Colin sat beside her.

"We should start a support group," Colin said lightly. "We're all concerned about Mallory."

Colin and Janna asked questions, and Thomas felt completely comfortable telling them where things stood between him and Mallory, and how frustrated he'd become.

"Is it wrong for me to want to get on with my life? I feel like I'm putting this horrible pressure on her, but at the same time I feel justified in telling her that I can't wait forever."

"And you *are* justified," Janna said. "I think you're right when you say she's basically in denial; not willing to look at the things that are troubling her. That kind of denial can go on indefinitely if we let it."

"So, what can *I* do?" Thomas asked.

Janna glanced at her husband. "I think Colin would be more qualified to answer that question."

"I am?" Colin looked baffled.

"You've been exactly where he is, haven't you? In a manner of speaking."

Colin was thoughtful a moment. "Yes, I suppose I have." He sighed, and Thomas waited while he apparently sorted his thoughts. "Well, it's been a long time," Colin said, "but there was a time when Janna was living in some pretty serious denial about the unresolved fears related to her abuse. She basically cut me off, and our relationship became almost nonexistent."

"Was this before you were married?"

"No," Colin said. "Mallory was a baby at the time. I went on and on in this codependency trap, trying to fix her problems for her, allowing her to go on in her denial. She refused to go to a counselor, so I went myself. He was someone we'd worked with before."

Thomas listened with growing interest, marveling at the way Colin could talk about Janna's problems of the past with her sitting there, not seeming affected in the least. He recalled the things Mallory had told him about her mother's struggles, but it was fascinating to hear about it firsthand.

"And what did he tell you?" Thomas asked.

"Well, when it became clear that I'd done all I could do, and Janna wasn't going to take any steps to get help, he suggested that I give her an ultimatum."

"Which was?"

"Well, it *should* have been, 'Get some help or I'm moving out.'"

"Whoa," Thomas said, taken aback by such drastic measures. "What do you mean by *should have been?*"

"Actually, I didn't give her the ultimatum. I was scared, I think. I just kept hoping it would get better. It didn't." Colin took Janna's hand, and their eyes met as they exchanged a poignant gaze. "It's a miracle that we're still together."

"What happened? I mean, you obviously worked it out."

"Yes, eventually," Colin continued. "We ended up separated, but not by my choice. I did some things that broke the trust between us. She had a nervous breakdown. It was a nightmare."

"So, your point is?" Thomas asked.

"Don't be afraid to give her an ultimatum, Thomas. It takes a lot of courage to love someone enough to put up a strong fence line and not allow them to cross it. Mallory's love for you and her desire to be with you may be the only thing that will force her to face up and get on with her life—but only if you don't allow her to take advantage of your love for her."

"I think I'm getting the idea here, but . . . give me an example that's a little more clear."

Janna took over. "Let's say you tell Mallory, 'I love you very much and I want to marry you. But I don't feel that it's right for us to go on this way. I'm willing to do anything I can to help you through this, but if we can't set a date and get past this in say, two weeks, then you're going to have to make a life without me.'"

"Wow," Thomas said. "I don't know if I can do that."

"That's what *I* thought," Colin said. "It takes courage, and you can't be bluffing. Set a boundary you know you can live with, then hold to it. At the same time, give her unconditional love."

"But what if she . . . decides to make a life without me?"

"You can't make her choices, Thomas. As hard as it is, if she isn't going to get past the feelings that are troubling her enough to come around for you now, she's not going to be able to make a marriage relationship work with you."

They talked for another hour, encouraging Thomas to pray about the things they'd discussed before he did anything. He needed to feel confidence in knowing he was doing the right thing. After their conversation, he felt educated and more prepared to face the problem. He also felt scared at the possibility that this might not work out the way he wanted it to.

As Thomas prayed about the things he'd learned and thought them through more carefully, he felt enlightened and gained new understanding of what Mallory was going through, and why it was important for him to stand up for his position in their relationship. He also felt a great deal of hope in seeing the example of success in Mallory's parents. What they had been through was far more severe in many ways. He reminded himself that it could be worse. He knew in his heart that he was more than willing to help Mallory work through her painful past, and he didn't have any trouble with the reality that she had a great deal of love and life invested in her first marriage. But he knew they needed to move forward. He only hoped they could move forward together.

In the days following his conversation with Colin and Janna, Thomas hardly talked to Mallory. She came to work as usual, but their relationship felt as if they'd never shared anything beyond professional small talk. When he finally came to terms with the advice he'd been given, he asked Mallory if she would come to his office when her shift ended. His heart nearly beat out of his chest when she came in and sat down across the desk from him. Praying for the peace and confidence he had felt in preparing for this moment, he cleared his throat and began.

"Mallory, I know you're having a difficult time. And I feel like I've done everything in my power to help you get beyond whatever keeps holding you back. The fact is, there's nothing more I can do under the circumstances. I love you, Mallory, and I want to be your husband. But I can't go on like this."

"What are you saying?"

"I've thought about this a long time. If we can't set a date by the end of the month, and feel good about getting married, then I've got to find a way to go on without you. It rips me apart, Mallory. But I would rather be on my own than be hanging on like this. If you want me to keep my distance in the meantime, that's fine. The ball is in your hands. I'm here for you if you need me."

Thomas absorbed her shocked expression and hurried out of the office before he had a chance to start stammering and apologizing. He only prayed that this would all come together. He knew in his heart that she was the woman for him, but he'd come to accept the fact that her agency was out of his control.

Mallory was so stunned that it took her several minutes to find the motivation to get up and leave the room. She went out to her car in a daze, not seeing Thomas anywhere. She wanted to talk to him, to somehow convince him that she deserved more time, more of a chance. But by the time she got home, she knew that it wouldn't make any difference. He'd already given her more than a fair chance, and she knew it. She began to wonder if she just wasn't the right woman for him. Or perhaps she just wasn't woman enough to keep a man like that.

Mallory hardly slept at all that night, then she called her mother as soon as she knew her father would be gone to work. They talked for over two hours. Janna told her that it wasn't fair of her to keep Thomas hanging on, and she needed to get on with her life.

"If you're depressed and can't break out of it," Janna said, "then maybe you need some medication. But it takes several weeks for that to make a difference, and even medication isn't going to magically take away the problem. It only evens out the chemicals in your brain so you can solve your problems more effectively. You still have to work to face what's bothering you and deal with it. I've been there, Mallory, and the bottom line was that I had to find the strength inside myself to get beyond it. You have that strength."

"I don't know if I do, Mom."

"If you need to talk to a counselor, I can arrange it for you. And maybe medication would help. But honestly, Mallory, I believe that what you need is already inside of you. I think you should do everything in your power before you turn elsewhere. You have the gospel. You have a brain. And you have a strong spirit."

"Where do I start?"

"Start with your physical body. Are you exercising?"

"Not like I should be."

"Okay, then do it. Exercise opens up the brain and gets things moving. Are you eating well?"

"I could do better."

"Okay, watch your diet and keep it balanced. Then you need to work on feeding your spirit. I get the impression that your spirit is malnourished, Mallory." Janna then went on to give her the exact advice that Thomas had given her last week—advice that she had ignored: go to the temple, get a priesthood blessing, and do some serious studying.

"I just feel so unmotivated," Mallory admitted.

"Okay, I'm bringing your father over this evening so he can help Matthew give you a blessing. And I'm going to take you to the temple in the morning. Then we're going to sit down and write some goals, and I'm going to check on you daily to see if you're doing them; hourly if I have to. This is like the law given to the children of Israel after Moses brought them out of Egypt. It had to be very strict, because they were helpless to think for themselves. So, until you can establish some better habits and get out of this, you've got to force yourself through the motions of doing what you need to do. Am I making sense?"

"I think so. Thanks, Mom. I don't know what I'd do without you."

"Well, maybe if I'd had my mother around, I wouldn't have fallen into such a deep hole myself."

Mallory kept in close touch with her mother through the following days, and did her best to do everything she'd outlined. The priesthood blessing and temple visit helped so much that she wondered why she'd put them off for so long. As she studied the scriptures more than she had in weeks, she began to see that Satan had indeed been taking advantage of her fears and weaknesses. And because she had been neglecting the basic elements of staying close to the Spirit, he had been able to keep her feeling discouraged and depressed.

Mallory went to work as she usually did, and found that Thomas was avoiding her. She thought that was just as well, but the reality of not having him in her life was difficult. With that thought in mind, she kept praying and studying regularly. And she went to the temple again and sat in the celestial room for a long while, praying for the peace and guidance she needed. The following day, she woke up feeling different. It was nothing overwhelming or profound, but it was certainly undeniable. She knew everything would be all right, even if time was still a factor in her healing.

Reviewing the circumstances of Brad's death, she felt a new level of understanding settle into her mind and heart. In thinking of his struggles with pornography, she found that rather than feeling hurt and angry, she felt a great deal of compassion. It was as if the Spirit had helped her see Brad's problem with empathy. He'd been lured into the repulsive habit by his father, who had obviously given Brad confusing messages with his example of hypocrisy. While Brad's father had been sinning privately, he had put up a front of piousness. At least Mallory knew from what the bishop had told her that Brad had worked hard to avoid such hypocrisy.

As Mallory contemplated Brad's struggles from a new perspective, she felt a deep compassion for the helplessness and desperation he must have experienced in feeling that suicide was his only option. But even if a part of her still felt unsettled and upset over Brad's death, she found peace in believing that he was being helped on the other side of the veil, and his love for her remained strong—as hers did for him. Mallory recalled her parents' circumstances—the fact that her father had cheated on her mother and committed a horrible sin. It was in the past, and her mother had forgiven him. Their love was strong and true. And now Mallory could see that she'd crossed that same bridge with Brad. She truly had forgiven him, which somehow made it easier to forge ahead with her life and find happiness. She wasn't certain how Thomas would feel to know that her love for Brad was something that would never die, and in some ways, she would never stop missing him. But she figured they just needed to talk it through and move ahead.

Beyond finding peace concerning Brad's death and the complications surrounding it, Mallory knew without a doubt that marrying

Thomas was the right thing to do. In her heart she felt a complete understanding of what her mother had been trying to teach her. The only way she would ever learn to trust was to open her heart and trust. And if she had difficulty trusting that Thomas would not hurt her, at least she could trust in her Father in Heaven. And right now, she knew that he wanted her to marry this man and make the most of it.

Feeling a happiness and excitement that she'd not felt since before she'd lost Brad, Mallory called Melody to make arrangements for Bethany. She got dressed and hurried to leave, hoping to get to the restaurant before Thomas did. She wondered if she'd ever been so happy in her life.

* * * * *

Thomas arrived at work feeling unmotivated and discouraged. He missed Mallory desperately and wondered over and over if he'd done the right thing. He didn't notice her car in the parking lot as he went inside and trudged up the stairs, praying he could make it through another day. He pushed the door open and stepped into the room, startled when the door closed behind him. He turned and his heart went mad.

"Mallory," he said, hardly daring to hope that she might have come to give him good news.

"Can you get some time off today?" she asked.

"I probably could, why?"

"I thought we could celebrate."

"What are we celebrating?" he asked, wondering if his blood pressure could survive this.

Mallory diverted the subject. "I talked to my dad a couple of days ago. He told me some things that made me realize I have a pretty romantic background." Thomas said nothing. "He said that when he asked my mother to marry him, she was hesitant. She had a hard time because of the hurts and insecurities from her past. Sound familiar? Anyway, when she was ready, she actually had to propose to him." Mallory smiled. "Funny how history repeats itself, isn't it?"

"Is history repeating itself?"

"I certainly hope so. If we can make it as far as they've made it, I'll have no cause for complaint."

"Are you proposing to me, Mallory?"

"Yes, I am. And if you accept, then we can go celebrate."

Thomas looked away and closed his eyes. Mallory wondered for a moment if she'd done something wrong as she noticed tears running down his face. "Thomas," she said gently, touching his cheek with her fingertips, "are you okay?"

He pulled her into his arms and buried his face in her hair, crying helplessly as he murmured, "I love you, Mallory. I love you so much."

"I love you too, Thomas," she said, crying herself now. "Forgive me for making it so difficult. I just—"

"It's okay," he whispered, pressing his fingers over her lips. "Just promise me that no matter what comes up, we'll work it out *together*. I need you in my life. Promise me."

"I promise," she said fervently, and he actually laughed.

Thomas looked into her eyes and wanted to ask so many questions. He wondered what had finally come together for her. But he didn't want to get into it here. Taking her hand, he said, "Let's get out of here."

Mallory laughed as they hurried down the stairs and out to the car. Thomas drove to a nearby mall and led her to a bench, where they sat to watch the indoor carousel.

"Now tell me," he said, his arm around her shoulders, "what miracle has taken place to make me this happy."

Mallory talked about the things her mother had challenged her to do, and how she had felt opposition gradually fall away as she had taken away the opportunities for it to control her. They talked as the mall filled with the lunchtime crowd, flocking to a nearby eatery, then filtering away again. Mallory concluded by saying, "I can't say that all of my fears have magically fled. But I have realized that it's important for me to have faith and trust. I realized that even if I couldn't trust a man—any man—I could trust my Father in Heaven. And if I apply the knowledge I've gained, and put my trust in him, he will guide me. I need to have faith—faith in myself to make a good marriage and not allow myself to be mistreated or unhappy. And faith enough to believe you when you tell me that you'll do your best to take care of me and my children. I believe that even if faith is something I might be struggling with, moving forward in this relationship is an act of faith, and I will be blessed for it. Of course there is still some grief inside of me for the things I've lost; but I've made some progress with that too, and I believe that with time I'll be able to come to terms with it more fully. I know in my heart that marrying you is the right thing to do, Thomas, and I will be forever grateful to have you in my life. What you have given me up to this point has replenished me and given me hope. I cannot comprehend the joy we will share in the years to come."

Thomas resisted the urge to cry again and just held her close. They ate some lunch, then went to pick out matching wedding bands. Thomas took Mallory back to her car at the restaurant. He took care of some business and made certain everything was all right, then he followed her home. They spent the remainder of the day making wedding plans, while Bethany played nearby.

Thomas left that evening after putting Bethany to bed. He felt grateful beyond words that he was being given the opportunity to be a father to this child. "And having her mother around won't be too bad, either," he told Mallory. She laughed and kissed him good night, wondering if she'd ever been so happy.

The following day while Mallory was at work, Thomas gathered everyone together in mid-afternoon, when the place was entirely void of customers. It wasn't unusual for him to call an impromptu meeting in the kitchen to announce some change on the menu or a difficulty to be dealt with. She was surprised when he said loudly, "Okay, here's the thing. Mallory's getting a promotion."

She looked up at him, startled. Everyone else appeared baffled. The Polynesian cook voiced what the others seemed to be thinking. "She's already an assistant manager. Does this mean she's taking your job?"

"Pretty close," Thomas said with a little laugh. "I'm still the boss here, but she's going to be the boss at home." He laughed again and held out his hand toward her. "We're getting married."

Everyone cheered and applauded while Thomas hugged her tightly, whispering, "Did I embarrass you as much as Darrell did?"

"Not even close," she said and kissed him quickly.

"Okay," Thomas called, "back to work. You can pass the news along to the next shift. You treat the boss's fiancée with respect."

"They already do," Mallory said loudly enough for everyone to hear.

"They should," Thomas said and laughed again.

A few minutes later, one of dishwashers called, "Hey boss, where you goin' for your honeymoon?"

Thomas glanced at Mallory and she nearly blushed. "I don't know," he said. "But I can guarantee I'll come back with a tan."

Mallory shook her head and laughed, moving close enough to whisper, "Will I be able to get a tan?"

"Nah," he said, looking into her eyes, "you won't have time."

Mallory sighed as an increasingly familiar tingling flared up inside of her. She loved him so much.

As Mallory plunged into wedding plans full force, she felt her happiness and peace deepen each day. She found the contrast interesting as she compared it to her engagement to Darrell, when she had become steadily more stressed out and confused.

Occasionally, she felt a twinge of fear or sadness. But she now knew how to ward it off by praying for help and consciously replacing her negative thoughts with positive ones. She often wished there had been more of a closure with Brad. She hadn't been able to see him after his death, which made it difficult at times to imagine him being dead. And knowing that he'd taken his own life without leaving her any explanation was something that disturbed her. But she talked to Thomas about it and he reminded her that life was eternal, and things that didn't get resolved here on earth would all come together and make sense on the other side. The thought gave her peace and helped her get through the moments of doubt and wondering. But it also brought to mind some disconcerting feelings in regard to Thomas. If she was sealed to Brad, and she believed that he was progressing and overcoming his problems, then she had good cause to believe that she would be with him again one day. She loved Brad; she had married him forever, and a part of her wanted to see the fulfillment of that promise. But she now loved Thomas, as well. If she had to choose which one she wanted to be with in eternity, she wasn't certain she could make that choice. She stewed over the situation until she came to the conclusion that there was nothing to be done about it. But she feared that Thomas might be hurt by her attitude, so she simply chose to not bring it up, concentrating instead on their upcoming wedding.

Mallory continued working her usual schedule, enjoying the prospect of working by Thomas's side for the rest of their lives. The restaurant was doing well, and they were making plans to expand and build another one in the Orem area. Mallory thought it was a good idea, since those people ought to have the opportunity to taste what Thomas Buchanan could do with food—especially chocolate.

On a Saturday evening Mallory asked him, "Do you think it would be possible for you to go to church with me? I mean, you are moving into this ward."

Thomas shrugged. "If I can get someone to take my class, I could do that."

"Is that possible?"

"I'll find out." He asked for her phone book and made a couple of calls, then announced that he had it covered. But she sensed that he wasn't completely comfortable with the idea.

"What's the matter?" she asked. "You seem . . . nervous."

"I guess I am," he admitted.

"Why?"

"Are there any blacks in your ward?" he asked.

Mallory was surprised by the question. "No," she said. "Do you think that's a problem?"

"Not for me, it's not. But I can almost guarantee it will be a problem for somebody else."

Mallory tried to absorb what he was saying. "You're serious."

"Yes, I'm quite serious, Mallory. Since the day I joined the Church, I have rarely walked into a meeting without getting some double-takes. Most people are just curious, and they're basically kind. But occasionally I still get snubbed by *somebody*. Now I'd like to be able to say that I'm used to it, but it's more accurate to say that I've learned to handle it. There are some things that just don't get easier."

Mallory looked dumbstruck.

"What's the matter with you?" he asked.

"I just . . . didn't think people still acted that way. I thought that kind of prejudice was a thing of the past; especially in the Church."

"Let me clarify something, Mallory. As far as *the Church* goes, there is no prejudice. When the priesthood was given to all worthy males, whatever inequality there had been was taken away. *The Church* regards *all* people equally. But there are *people* in this church who *do* have a problem. And I can live with that."

"But it must be difficult. You would think that, if nowhere else, you could go to church and feel accepted—no matter what."

"Most people *do* accept me no matter what. In my ward I got some long stares at first, but I feel at home there now. I taught the gospel doctrine class for a while. The first time I got up to teach, a gentleman walked out. He actually told the bishop there was nothing he needed to learn from a black man. He never came to that class as long as I taught it. But the fact is, he probably learned prejudice from his parents, and he'll likely pass it along to his children. And even people who aren't necessarily prejudiced often feel uncomfortable with something different. People stare at differences. The guy with cerebral palsy. The woman in a wheelchair. The kid with Down's Syndrome. The black man. But I've learned to just smile, and eventually some of them smile back. And I'm certainly not going to let something like that keep me from going to church. I go to church because I have a testimony of Jesus Christ. If it was a segregated meeting and I was forced to sit on the back row and not allowed to actively participate, I would still go. Because my reasons for being there are between me and my Savior. And it would be awfully petty for me to allow a little minor prejudice to keep me from keeping my covenants with him, when he was the most misunderstood and mistreated man who ever lived."

"I admire your attitude, Thomas. I really do."

He gave that little chuckle he was famous for. "Well, don't go putting me on a pedestal, my dear. I've been known to get angry. There have been times when people's attitudes have really gotten to me. When that happens, it takes time to come to terms with it."

"Tell me," she said, wanting to understand.

Thomas shook his head and chuckled. "Maybe if you find out what I'm really like, you'll get scared and run away."

Mallory saw beyond his humorous facade. She took his hand, saying, "I'm not going anywhere. Give me an example."

Thomas sighed as he began. "I was assigned to home teach an older couple, and they refused to let me in the door. The woman told me to my face that the color of my skin was the mark of a curse, and she wanted nothing to do with me. So," he drawled, "I told her that it was evident she disregarded our latter-day prophets. She protested strongly, insisting that she was a righteous woman in every respect. I calmly told her that a prophet of the Lord had officially removed that *curse,* making it clear that all men were equal. She got even angrier, and my partner and I hurried away. I was assigned to another family, and I didn't live in that ward for long. I was glad I'd said what I did to her, but I was angry over it for days. It took a lot of willpower to keep my emotions from getting the best of me."

Thomas added firmly, "As I said, I've learned to handle it—most of the time." He focused his attention fully on her. "My concern right now is for you."

"Me? Why?"

"If I go to church with you tomorrow, *you* might be stared at and judged; perhaps not vocally, but judged just the same. I can almost guarantee that there will be at least one person in this ward who will strongly object to your marrying a black man. Sometimes they keep their opinions to themselves, or they whisper discreetly to their friends. But there are those who consider it their moral obligation to let everyone know that this is wrong."

"How can you be so sure?" Mallory asked, not quite believing that such feelings could occur in her ward.

"Mallory, I've been in many different wards in the years I've been a member of this church. I've been acquainted with several different black people who have married someone white. They all have similar stories."

"Okay, but . . . if we're going to live here, then you have to go to church here eventually. It's not like our getting married is some great secret or—"

"I'm not implying that it is," Thomas said. "I'd say that the sooner I start going to church here, the better. I'm just trying to prepare you for the possibility that it might not be easy. We just have to keep the perspective that we love each other, we know this is right for *us,* and we know that we have the Lord's blessing." He touched his nose to hers. "When you feel confident within yourself that everything's right, then you have nothing to get defensive about. It's just like . . . well, if I know beyond any doubt that God loves me unconditionally, then what anyone else thinks or says doesn't matter."

Mallory thought a great deal about the things Thomas had said. By the time he picked her up for church on Sunday, she still found it difficult to believe that the people in her ward would be anything but perfectly kind and accepting of this man she'd chosen to marry.

"Wow," she said when she opened the door, "you look great."

Thomas grinned. "Yeah, you too," he said.

Mallory's eyes were continually drawn to him as he helped her get Bethany into the car, and through the brief drive to the chapel. At work he was always dressed up, but he usually wore slacks with dark shirts and ties. Today he was wearing a gray double-breasted suit with a white shirt and a burgundy paisley tie. She thought he'd never looked more handsome.

Since auxiliary meetings were first, Mallory had to leave Thomas and go teach her Young Women's class. She was grateful to have her brother in the ward and be able to entrust her fiancé to him. "Don't worry," Matthew said adamantly as they both left their little girls in Primary, "I'll take good care of him."

Matthew visited casually with Thomas, appreciating the comfortable relationship they'd developed. He liked this man and instinctively felt good about his marrying Mallory. He didn't think much about the glances they got as they slipped into priesthood meeting during the opening song, until Thomas leaned over and whispered, "Is it my imagination, or are people staring at you?"

Matthew chuckled and glanced around discreetly. "I think you're right. We might just stir up a little scandal."

"You think you can handle it?"

"Me? Oh, yeah. I like scandal. These people could use a little adventure."

"Well, I hope it's not too much adventure for your sister," Thomas said with a concerned glance. Matthew thought about that for a minute, wondering if prejudice was something they would actually come up against. He had no problem with it, so he'd just assumed that no one else would either.

After the opening prayer some announcements were given, then they did the standard introduction of visitors. The man at the podium pointed to Matthew, saying, "Brother Trevor, could you introduce your guest?"

Matthew stood, nudging Thomas until he did the same. "This is Thomas Buchanan," he said. "Since he's engaged to my sister, that makes us practically brothers."

Matthew was actually stunned as he sat down and realized that everyone in the room was shocked. The tension was brief, but unmistakable. The brother conducting finally said, "It's a pleasure to have you with us, Brother Buchanan."

Following the spirit of Thomas's comment a few minutes earlier, Matthew leaned over and whispered, "Is it my imagination, or did a small earthquake just rumble through the room?"

"Oh, yeah," Thomas said easily. "That was one of those *he's got to be kidding* shock waves."

The elders quorum class was a little more relaxed. Several men introduced themselves to Thomas and made him feel welcome. Congratulations were offered, and a few commented that it was nice to know Mallory had found someone, since she'd had a rough time losing her first husband the way she did.

As they went into the gospel doctrine class, Mallory was waiting with two chairs saved. Thomas sat between her and Matthew, putting his arm around Mallory as he whispered, "How you doing?"

"Fine. And you?"

"Not too bad. So far so good." He winked at her then glanced around, not surprised by the second glances they were getting.

Matthew leaned over, whispering, "I think we just had another shock wave."

"Hmmm-mmm." Thomas forced a comfortable smile.

"Why don't you just kiss her right here and now, and we'll see how high it goes on the Richter scale."

Thomas chuckled softly. "The kiss or the shock?"

Matthew laughed, then bit his lip as the class began.

This time Mallory introduced Thomas, saying with pride that he was her fiancé. Matthew and Thomas exchanged a discreet glance as a subtle rumble of gasps and whisperings went through the room. But the teacher eased the tension with his enthusiastic response. "That's great. We're getting you on a permanent basis then, Brother Buchanan."

"That's right," Thomas said.

"Well, we're glad to have you."

"It's a pleasure to be here," Thomas said, holding Mallory's hand tightly.

"Mallory Buchanan," the teacher said. "I like the sound of that."

"Yes, me too," Mallory said, grateful when he moved on to introduce the other visitors.

During sacrament meeting, Mallory was aware of the stares and glances that Thomas had spoken of. But she felt nothing but pride and contentment to have Thomas at her side. Observing him with Bethany warmed her through, and she couldn't help thinking how cute they looked together as he got up more than once to take her out to the foyer.

Following church, they barbecued with Matthew's family. Overall, Mallory thoroughly enjoyed the day. She appreciated the way they were able to talk comfortably about the reactions they'd gotten at church. Thomas repeated his theories on prejudice to Matthew and Melody in a way that deepened her admiration of him. Then he commented, "It's interesting, in the LDS culture, that people with dark skin are practically revered—if they have anything to do with Lamanite ancestry. The Polynesians, Native Americans, Eskimos— you get the idea. They are all descended from the people in the Book of Mormon, so members of the Church understand the situation clearly. But with blacks, and perhaps orientals, there is so much that people *don't* understand. Prejudice usually comes from ignorance."

"Or example," Matthew said. "In our family, we were raised to believe that all men are equal. It was never a problem."

Thomas chuckled and took Mallory's hand. "I am more grateful for that than you can possibly imagine." He glanced at Mallory. "I'm not sure it would be the other way around."

"What do you mean?" Mallory asked.

"Most of my relatives will be appalled when they realize I'm marrying a white woman."

"Really?" she said, wondering why it bothered her.

"Really," he stated. "I'm telling you that there is a great deal of prejudice in *my* family." He slapped Matthew playfully on the shoulder. "So, I'll just have to stick to *your* family."

Mallory truly appreciated his attitude, which made the minor incidents at church seem insignificant. But through the following week, word filtered back to her that people were surprised and concerned about her choice of a husband. Two well-meaning sisters in the ward called to implore her to think of how difficult this would make life for her children. Mallory simply thanked them for their concern and assured them that she knew Thomas was the right man for her. Melody and Matthew received even more casual advice, perhaps because they were an indirect source to Mallory, and it was apparently up to them to keep her from ruining her life.

The following Sunday, Thomas had to teach his class and wasn't able to come with her. As soon as they found someone to replace him, he would begin coming to church with her every week. With Thomas absent, Mallory was amazed at the well-meant advice she received through the course of the meetings. As she sat in fast and testimony meeting, contemplating the entire situation, she decided she'd get no better opportunity to let everyone know exactly where she stood.

With a prayer in her heart, Mallory went up to the podium to bear her testimony. Instinctively she believed that she could accomplish more by projecting a positive attitude than by expressing any criticism.

Mallory sincerely expressed her gratitude for all she'd been blessed with since her husband's death, most specifically this wonderful man who had done so much to help her heal and find love again. She bore testimony to her undeniable knowledge that he was the right man for her, and she expressed her sincere gratitude to those who had made him feel welcome. She mentioned that since he was the only member of the Church in his family, having a good ward family meant a great deal to him, and that he was making a sacrifice to leave the ward where he was comfortable and appreciated to come here and allow her to stay in her home.

Mallory finished by bearing her testimony of the gospel, then she returned to where she'd been sitting with Matthew's family. Bethany climbed onto her lap and Matthew leaned over to whisper, "Very good. That ought to get some consciences stirring."

"I hope so," she said, then her thoughts turned to Thomas. She just never felt quite the same when he wasn't around.

On a rainy morning in September, Thomas called Mallory to tell her he had a flu bug that had overtaken him in the night. "Could you cover for me?" he asked. "I know there was a lot that needed to be done today, but I can't remember what. I left a list on my desk in the office. When you get there, call me if you have questions."

"I'm sure I'll manage," she said. "But what about you?"

"I'll be fine. I just need some rest."

She questioned him on his symptoms and said she'd stop by later, after everything was under control at the restaurant.

Mallory found Thomas's list and began making phone calls to place orders. She inspected some deliveries that arrived, checked through food supplies, and wrote out next week's employee schedule, only calling Thomas once for help. She was talking with the hostess at the front desk when a middle-aged woman came in alone. She didn't look at all like the type who ate here, and most people didn't come to a fine restaurant to eat alone. Mallory was surprised when she approached and asked for Thomas Buchanan.

"He's not in today. May I help you?"

"Oh," she looked distressed, "did I get the time wrong? I'm Lana Baum. I had an interview with him for a job, and—"

"Oh, of course," Mallory said as she recalled seeing the interview on Thomas's list. "You didn't get it wrong. He's at home with the flu. I can help you."

Mallory led the way up the stairs, already feeling like this woman just wasn't right for the job. Thomas had talked to her more than once about his methods for hiring. He tried to be open-minded, but he didn't hire someone because he felt sorry for them. He had to have a certain caliber of employees to keep the business functioning. However, he said the most important thing was to trust his instincts. "Instincts can override every other rule," he'd said.

As Mallory motioned Lana toward a chair, she had a hard time envisioning her as a server at Buchanan's. She was dressed sloppily and had obviously taken no care with her appearance, even though she was here for a job interview.

Mallory asked her the usual questions and had to admit that Lana seemed responsible and level-headed. She was somehow drawn to Lana, and felt compelled to give her a job. But at the same time, she couldn't help feeling uncomfortable about it. When she ran out of things to say, she took a few minutes to look over the application left on Thomas's desk. She wished she had done it earlier, because she felt an immense relief to see that Lana was applying for a job as kitchen help. She didn't know why she had just assumed the interview was for a server; perhaps because that's what *she* had applied for herself.

Feeling more informed, Mallory asked Lana more specific questions about her abilities and experience. Then she maneuvered in some more personal questions, as Thomas had done with her. He'd said it was important to know a little bit about what was going on in an employee's life, for many reasons.

"It says here you have four children. That must keep you awfully busy."

"Yes, it does. They're all in school now. At the motel where I've been working, I get most of my hours in during school time. They told me at the employment office that this job was daytime. I hope that's the case, so I could be with my kids."

"I don't think that's a problem," Mallory said. She was impressed to see that Lana had a priority of being there for her children.

"It says here that you're married," Mallory said. "Is your husband—"

"He's not able to work right now," Lana interrupted with a defensive tone that made it evident something was wrong.

Mallory just moved on to the next question. When she'd finished the interview, she felt good about saying, "I need to talk to Mr. Buchanan for the final okay, but I'll put in a good word for you. I believe you'll do just fine."

Mallory didn't quite know how to react when the woman began to cry. "Are you okay?" she asked, quickly handing her a tissue. "I'm sorry. Did I say something to—"

"Oh, no," the woman insisted. "Forgive me. I'm just so . . . relieved. I prayed so hard that I could get this job. I hope it's okay for me to say that."

"Of course it is."

"I've been working at a motel, cleaning rooms. I told you that already. But those people have been so difficult to work with. There's so much bad language and contention there. I just couldn't take it anymore. Since my husband's been in the hospital, I *have* to work. And, well . . ." Lana looked suddenly embarrassed, as if she'd realized that she was rambling to someone who was practically a stranger. "Oh, I'm so sorry." She stood up. "I didn't mean to go on and on. You've been so kind. When you talk to Mr. Buchanan, you let me know. And I would understand if for some reason he doesn't want me to—"

"Don't you worry about it," Mallory interrupted. "I'm sure you'll work out just fine. I've got some pull with Mr. Buchanan." She winked and added, "I'm almost Mrs. Buchanan."

"Oh, I see," she smiled, seeming briefly drawn away from her troubles. "That's nice. I wish you the best."

As soon as Lana Baum left, Mallory called Thomas and described the interview to him. "I hired her," she said. "I hope that's okay with you."

"It sounds like you handled it perfectly. With you around," he chuckled, "I don't even need to show up at work."

"Oh, yes you do," she said, "because I'm going to be home taking care of your babies."

"Hmmm," he made a noise of pleasure, "that sounds heavenly."

When Mallory had everything under control at the restaurant, she went home to get Bethany and pick up a few things. She got into Thomas's condo with the key he'd given her, and peeked in to find him sleeping with the radio playing softly by his bed. She put in a video tape to occupy Bethany in the front room, then she quietly got to work in the kitchen. She was startled when Thomas said behind her, "What are you doing?"

"Oh, you scared me to death," she said, then she laughed. "What are you doing out of bed?"

He stuck his hands into the pockets of his bathrobe. "I'm doing a little better . . . I think. All the same," he sat down a little unsteadily, "I believe I'll take it easy for the time being."

"Good idea," she said. "And as long as you're sitting there, you'll save me bringing you dinner in bed. Your stomach's okay, isn't it?"

"Oh, yeah. It's just this fever and achy stuff." He inhaled dramatically. "It smells wonderful. What is it?"

Mallory set a bowl in front of him and announced, "It's chicken soup. What else?"

Thomas stirred it around with a spoon. "With homemade noodles?"

"That's right. I'm not so bad in the kitchen."

He blessed it then took a bite, complimenting her profusely. "Maybe we should add this to the menu."

"Only if you change the name to Mallory's Down-Home Diner," she said.

He laughed. "We could branch out."

"I think we're doing just fine. We'll keep the chicken soup at home."

Thomas nodded and took another bite. "I like that idea, and if I weren't sick I'd give you a big kiss to prove it."

"I'll have something to look forward to," she said, then she laughed for no apparent reason. She simply loved life.

CHAPTER TWELVE

While Thomas was recovering from the flu, he left Mallory to oversee training Lana Baum. The kitchen supervisor did most of the specific training, but Mallory had the opportunity to spend some time with Lana, discussing policies and scheduling.

On Lana's third day on the job, Mallory noticed her taking a break in the little employees' lounge. She stepped into the room and asked, "Do you mind if I join you?"

"That would be fine," Lana said with enthusiasm.

"So, how are you liking it so far?"

"I really like it here. It's a fine place, and good people to work with."

"Thomas tries to be selective with his employees. He wants to have a good atmosphere for those who work here, as well as for the customers."

"You must mean Mr. Buchanan."

"That's right. We're all on a first-name basis here. You may call me Mallory."

"How long have you been working here?"

"Oh, more than a year," she said. "I started soon after my husband was killed. I was made an assistant manager last . . . well, I honestly don't remember. Oh, well. He tells me I got the promotion because I'm a good worker. Personally, I think he had ulterior motives." Mallory chuckled and was relieved when Lana picked up on the humor.

"Your husband was killed, you say? Why, you're too young to be a widow."

"Yes." Mallory glanced at her hands briefly, glad to note that the pain evoked by her comment was minimal. "But some things are simply out of our control."

"Boy, I know that," Lana said.

"Is your husband still in the hospital?" Mallory asked.

"Yes, and he will be for a long time—if he ever gets out." Lana shook her head, and Mallory noticed that she was actually quite pretty. She simply looked worn out. "It might sound awful for me to say, but honestly, there are things worse than death."

Mallory hoped she wasn't prying, but Lana seemed to want to talk. "He must be suffering, then," she guessed with a gentle voice.

Lana made a disgruntled noise. "Not nearly as much as the rest of us."

Mallory didn't quite know what to say, and she was relieved when Lana went on.

"Now, don't think I don't love my husband. I do—or at least I did. The man I loved was gone a long time ago. What's left of him down at the hospital is just enough to keep me and the kids upset and not knowing how to feel. It was after he had a surgery a few years back, and he started taking too many of those painkillers the doctor gave him. Then when he couldn't get them anymore, he started getting something from a friend at work. I knew whatever he was taking wasn't legal, but he wouldn't listen to me. He just kept taking them. He changed. We could hardly live with him. He lost his job. He just kept getting worse and worse off. And then one day, he just up and shot himself in the head."

Mallory clapped a hand over her mouth to keep from gasping.

"Are you okay?" Lana asked. "I'm sorry. I tend to get rambling. I didn't mean to upset you."

Mallory swallowed hard. "No, I'm fine. Please, I want to hear," she said, and she meant it. In spite of the emotion hovering inside her, there was an unexplainable warmth connected with it. She understood now why she'd felt drawn to Lana Baum, and she could feel the Spirit close, as if God wanted her to know that this was an answer to her prayers. It was one more piece in the puzzle of putting her life back together.

Lana talked briefly of how her husband hadn't succeeded in his attempt to kill himself. He'd been in the hospital for several weeks now, struggling through many physical repercussions, including permanent brain damage. She admitted praying that he would just die and be free of his misery, at the same time feeling guilty for wanting to be free of him.

"But it's as you said," Mallory attempted to console her, "the man you loved isn't there anymore. I don't see any need for you to feel guilty."

Lana wiped at a few stray tears, then she glanced at the clock and shot out of her seat. "Oh, my goodness. I've certainly abused my break time. I'm so sorry."

"Don't you worry about it," Mallory said. "You tell them you were helping me."

"But I was—"

"You were helping me," she repeated.

"Thank you," Lana said. "You've been so kind."

"You hang in there, Lana. And keep me posted, okay?"

Lana nodded and hurried to the kitchen. Mallory lost track of the time as she sat where she was with Lana's words catapulting through her mind. *There are things worse than death.*

As thoughts and memories churned, Mallory grabbed her jacket and stepped out the back entrance, surprised to find the rain turning to snow. Since it was fall, she doubted the snow would last long, and she quickly became oblivious to the weather, walking aimlessly away from the restaurant. She avoided the street, sticking more to the parking lots behind the long row of motels and businesses.

As she wandered, Mallory felt the reality of Brad's death strike her all over again. Then she tried to imagine how it might have been if he'd survived. She'd resented his death and ached just to have him live. But what if he had? Would she be dealing with physical and emotional problems beyond her wildest imagination? Would he ever have fully faced up to his problems and gotten the help he'd needed? She'd like to think that he would. But he'd chosen suicide over facing her openly with the problem. And again, Mallory heard Lana's words in her head. *There are things worse than death.*

Mallory had been able to see a long time ago that if Brad had lived, their problems would have been tremendous. The thought had helped console her many times. And of course, she had Thomas now; if Brad had lived, she would never have had the opportunity to share such happiness with him. Still, a part of her had continued to wish that Brad had lived, and that they could have worked it out. She would have gladly done every-thing in her power to help him through his struggles, as long as he'd been willing to help himself. But the bishop had said that he'd refused repeated advice to see a counselor, and she wondered what his attitude might have been toward working through his addiction. She now understood that some things just couldn't be fixed in this life, and perhaps Brad's problem fell into that category. In her heart, she knew that Brad was where he needed to be. Oh, she'd believed it before; but now she truly *knew*. He'd gone home to a merciful Father who would see that he got the help he needed. The world was full of many horrors, and at least Brad was free from that.

Yes, Mallory couldn't question Lana's wisdom; there really were things worse than death. Brad had left her. He'd broken her heart. But in a sad, poignant kind of way, his death had freed both of them from a great deal of pain and heartache. Depending on Brad's attitude and choices concerning his problem, their relationship could have eventually ended in divorce. It was difficult to compare what she hadn't personally experienced, but somehow she knew that the struggles she would have gone through with Brad's problems would have been every bit as difficult as it had been to lose him. And she would have done it. She loved Brad, and she would have gladly done whatever she could to help him, as long as he had been willing to repent and work it out. But that was irrelevant now. He was gone. She had a future worth looking forward to. Yes, there were things worse than death.

* * * * *

In spite of feeling weak, Thomas got ready to go to the restaurant, if only to get out of the house. It had been two days since he'd had any fever, and he felt sick to death of being sick. He arrived and felt a quiver of excitement to see Mallory's car in the parking lot. He went inside expecting to be assaulted with problems that needed solving, but everything was in perfect order. And he knew Mallory was greatly responsible for that. He went into the kitchen and nearly bumped into a woman he'd never seen before.

"Hello," he said. "You must be Mrs. Baum."

"That's right," she replied, looking a little baffled.

"I'm Thomas Buchanan," he said, holding out a hand in greeting.

"Oh." Her eyes widened. She didn't have to say anything more for him to know that she was surprised by the color of his skin. He wondered if it bothered her to be working for someone from a minority race, but she smiled and said, "You're the one engaged to Mallory." He realized then that her surprise was likely more to do with her assumption that Mallory would be marrying a white man.

"That's right," he said, feeling better at just hearing her name. "Where is Mallory, by the way?" he asked more loudly.

Several voices responded with varying degrees of ignorance. Lana said, "I was talking to her in the break room, but that was over an hour ago."

"Hey," the head chef called to Thomas, "I thought you were sick."

"Do I look sick?" Thomas retorted lightly.

"You do look a little pale," he said.

Thomas laughed, along with everyone else. "You ought to talk," he said, and everyone laughed again—since the chef was Polynesian.

Thomas scoured the entire place for Mallory, realizing he was exhausted. The place was a lot bigger than he'd ever noticed before. He actually began to feel worried, wondering how she could just disappear without a word to anyone. Her car was here, and she was scheduled to be working. But she was nowhere to be found.

Thomas uttered a quick prayer, then tried to think where she might have gone. Perhaps he'd just missed her in his search. Maybe she'd been in the ladies' room. He went to the kitchen to talk to Lana, recalling that she'd been the last to see her.

"You say she was in the break room?"

"That's right, Mr. Buchanan. We got talking. In fact, I overstayed my break, but she said it was okay because I was helping her. Of course, she was just being nice, but—"

"What were you talking about?" Thomas asked, feeling uneasy for reasons he couldn't discern.

Lana motioned him away from listening ears and whispered, "She was asking about my husband. He's in the hospital. I tend to get rambling. She seemed a little upset, but—"

"Why is your husband in the hospital?" Thomas asked, trying to sound compassionate, when he was feeling panicked instead.

"He tried to kill himself," she said in a whisper.

Thomas knew he must have looked upset by the way Lana's eyes widened fearfully.

"Did I say something wrong? I'm so sorry, Mr. Buchanan, if I—"

"No, don't you worry about it," he said. "You've been very helpful."

He hurried away, certain now that Mallory had gone somewhere to be alone. He considered scouring the restaurant again, then he noticed that there wasn't a coat or jacket hanging near the back entrance that belonged to her. He grabbed his coat and stepped outside to find that it was still snowing. And her car was still there.

"Help me," he prayed, wondering which direction to go. He'd only walked twenty paces when he saw her walking slowly back toward the restaurant. She stopped when she saw him, and he could see that she'd been crying—a lot. For a moment he feared she would revert to her fear and anguish, and everything would be set back again. The thought brought on a tangible ache as he stepped toward her.

"What are you doing out here?" he asked, noticing that her jacket wasn't nearly sufficient for this kind of weather, and her hair was wet and covered with snow.

Mallory looked into his eyes, then she clung to him as if he'd just saved her life. "Hold me, Thomas," she murmured. "Just hold me, and never let me go. Hold me and tell me everything's going to be all right."

"Everything's going to be all right," he said, holding her as tightly as he could manage.

"I know," she said softly, nuzzling closer. "I just needed to hear you say it."

Thomas insisted that she go inside, but when she began to shiver, he realized there was no place for her to warm up sufficiently.

"I'm taking you home," he said, pausing only long enough to tell somebody they were leaving.

Mallory shivered all the way home. Her teeth chattered so much that it was impossible for her to tell him anything. Thomas helped her into the house and ordered her to put on some warm, dry clothes.

"Are you decent?" he called when he heard the bedroom door open.

"Yes," she called. He found her curled up in her bed, still shivering. He spread her clothes out in the bathroom, then he plugged the hair dryer in next to the bed and worked on drying her hair.

When one side was dry, he ordered her to turn over so he could do the other side.

"There, that's better," he said, taking the dryer into the bathroom. He returned to find her still freezing, but at least the shivering had stopped. He sat on the bed and leaned against the headboard, easing his arms around her. "Are you going to be okay?"

"Yes," she said.

"Do you want to tell me what happened?"

"I don't know if there's much to tell."

"I know you were talking to Lana about her husband. I'm assuming she said something to upset you."

"Initially, but . . . actually, she taught me something."

"And what is that?"

Mallory snuggled closer to Thomas and with emotion told him, "I learned there are things worse than death."

They talked through the things Mallory had been feeling, then she fell asleep in his arms. He eased carefully away and went downstairs to fix something to eat. She woke up with a fever, and he realized that she likely had the flu he'd just recovered from. Her chill had obviously helped it along.

Thomas called Matthew to tell him Mallory was sick, and they were more than happy to keep Bethany for the night. Thomas made certain Mallory had everything she needed, then he went back to the restaurant for a while. He went to bed early and slept hard, waking up much stronger. He went straight to Mallory's house and checked on her, then he got Bethany from Melody and decided this was a good time to work on being her father.

Through the next few days, he kept track of the restaurant by phone and slept in Mallory's spare bedroom. He gained a great deal of confidence with little Bethany, and anxiously looked forward to the wedding date, which was less than a month away.

When the weekend came and he needed to spend more time at the restaurant, Mallory was past the worst of her illness. He was in his office early Friday evening when Lana Baum came in, saying timidly, "Could I talk to you for just a minute, Mr. Buchanan?"

"Sure. Come in. And call me Thomas, please."

"Okay, Thomas. Forgive me, but . . . I know that Mallory left here upset after I'd been talking to her." The woman actually got tears in her eyes. "And then I heard she was sick. I've just been so worried that I said something to upset her, and—"

"Lana," Thomas said gently, "Mallory is doing just fine. And the things you said to her actually helped her come to terms with something that's been bothering her for a long time. She told me you were an answer to her prayers."

"Me?" she mouthed more than said.

"That's right," Thomas said.

"But . . . how?"

"Well, you see, her husband killed himself."

"Oh, my," Lana said, seeming enlightened but concerned.

"So you see, the things you told her helped put her own feelings in perspective. And we both hope that everything works out for you."

"Thank you," Lana said and turned to leave the room.

"Oh, and Lana . . ."

"Yes?" She stopped and turned.

"I'm hearing good things about you. Keep up the good work."

"I will, thank you," she said again and left the office.

* * * * *

As Mallory began to recover, she couldn't help feeling the antici-pation of her wedding day approaching. She looked around the house and imagined Thomas moving his things in and becoming a part of her household. The thought warmed her through. He'd already sold his condo, and the transaction would be completed by the end of next month. She felt frustrated, wanting to go through the house and make certain everything was in order. But she felt too weak to do much of anything.

Searching for something to keep herself busy that wouldn't take a lot of energy, she recalled that there was still a dresser drawer filled with things that belonged to Brad. Taking a deep breath, she pulled the drawer all the way out and dumped its contents on the floor, leaving the drawer upside down on the floor, which made a little table for Bethany to color on while Mallory worked. The numerous items scat-tered about were mostly junk, or things that had no value to her whatsoever. She found nothing that stirred any sentiment at all. She set aside some things to put in a box in the basement that regularly went to Deseret Industries for charity, and the rest went into the garbage.

She left the drawer as it was while Bethany played there, and she went on to other things. Later, after Bethany had gone elsewhere to play, Mallory returned to the bedroom and found the drawer still lying there. She grabbed a rag to dust it out and turned it over, feeling suddenly upset.

Mallory's hand trembled as she reached out to touch the envelope taped to the bottom of the drawer. Her name was scrawled there in Brad's handwriting, and she tried to comprehend that it had been hiding beneath a drawer full of junk all this time. Carefully she pulled up the tape that held the envelope in place, and took a deep breath before she opened it. Was this what she thought it was? Could it be what she had longed for all along—some kind of personal explanation of his death? She hardly dared hope as she pulled out a single sheet of paper, her heart pounding at the sight of his familiar handwriting. The date was the day he'd died. Taking another deep breath, she began to read.

Dear Mallory,

If you are reading this, then I know you've reached a point where you felt strong enough to go through my personal things. I can't even imagine how you will respond when you discover that I've left you this way. I hope you can one day forgive me. If you haven't already discovered what kind of man I really am, I'm sure you will eventually. It's impossible for me to explain or defend myself, so I'm not even going to try. I can't live with the deception anymore. Although, I always thought of it more as protecting you, rather than deceiving you. But I want you to know that in spite of how things might appear, I truly do love you, Mallory. And I love little Bethany. Take good care of her, and I hope you will find a man who can be strong enough to love you the way you deserve.

Brad.

Mallory wasn't surprised at the heartache she felt in reading his final words to her. And she wasn't surprised at how clearly she could imagine him writing it. She couldn't comprehend the pain he must have been in; the desperation he must have felt. She wasn't surprised at the way his letter felt so brief, and she ached to have more. She was surprised, however, at the sense of relief she felt as she folded it up and put it back into the envelope. She felt as if he'd finally come back to tell her good-bye. And now she could let him go and move on to a new life, knowing that Brad really did love her.

Thomas came by a short while later. She was sitting on the bed with the letter still in her hands when she heard him come in and start to play with Bethany. The baby giggled as he tickled her, and Mallory could hear his laughter. He appeared in the bedroom doorway with Bethany in his arms.

"There you are," he said. "Is something wrong?"

Mallory shook her head and held out the letter.

"Run along, baby girl," Thomas said, setting Bethany down. He took the letter and asked, "What is it?"

"Read it. You'll understand."

Thomas opened the envelope and quickly read the page. She was right. He understood. But he wasn't sure how it had affected her. "Where did you find this?" he asked, sitting close beside her.

She pointed to the empty drawer, still sitting on the floor. "It was taped inside, underneath a bunch of his junk that I'd put off going through."

"And how are you?"

"I'm fine," she said firmly. "Really. It actually made me feel better. I can't say why exactly. I just feel better."

"Good," he said. "I'm glad."

They sat for a minute in silence until Bethany came running in, throwing herself into Thomas's lap.

"Hey there, baby girl," he said, "are you ready for the big day?"

"Gotta new dress," Bethany said. "Mama get married. Bethie gotta new dress."

"Ooh," Thomas said, "what color is it?"

"What color is everything at this wedding?" Mallory asked.

"It must be green," Thomas said. Then he put his arm around Mallory and asked, "What color are you wearing, gorgeous?"

"I don't know," she said facetiously. "How about if I wear orange?"

"Nah."

"Pink," she said. "Pastel pink like that ugly dress Darrell gave me."

"Never!" Thomas said with drama. "I have an idea. I'll wear black, and you wear white. Then we'll match ourselves."

Mallory laughed. "That's the stupidest thing I've ever heard."

"Well, my tux *is* black, and your dress *is* white."

"Yes, but . . ."

"While we're in the temple, however, I'll wear white, too."

"That would be a good idea."

Thomas kissed her and whispered, "It's going to be the best day of my life."

"Oh, no," Mallory said, "there will be many best days beyond that. *I promise.*"

"I'll hold you to it," he said and kissed her again.

Thomas's kiss had become familiar to Mallory, but it never ceased to set fire to something inside her. She looked into his eyes as he drew slowly away. It was obvious that he felt the same fire. "Ooh," he said, "it's been a while."

"We've both been sick," she said, and he kissed her again. And again. Mallory quickly became caught up in the way he made her feel, which was somehow different from Brad's effect on her. She didn't stop to analyze it. She only knew that Thomas's display of affection stirred something deep in her; something that she'd hardly known existed.

Thomas finally pulled back, then came to his feet. "Oh, boy," he said with that little chuckle he was famous for. "I think we should eat. I brought Chinese food."

"Really? That sounds divine. I hope you brought chopsticks."

"Of course," he said. They went to the kitchen, where they found Bethany kneeling in the middle of the kitchen table, looking into the little white cartons of food.

"What are you doing?" Thomas said, startling her. She tried to back off the table, and he grabbed her before she fell. "You're a silly girl," he added, and hugged her tightly before putting her into the high chair.

After dinner was eaten and cleaned up, Thomas said, "I rented a couple of videos. You want to watch one?"

"Sure," she said. "You put it in. I'll get Bethie's pajamas."

Mallory got Bethany ready for bed and let her play as the movie got underway.

"I hope it's good," Thomas said. "I heard them talking about it at work."

Mallory attempted to concentrate on the movie, but her thoughts kept wandering to that letter. The reality of finding it made Brad's death suddenly feel close. But she snuggled up next to Thomas on the couch and did her best to get lost in the movie. They paused it long enough to say prayers with Bethany and put her to bed, then they turned out the lights and went back to the TV. The movie actually ended up being quite good, but Mallory felt distracted with thoughts of Brad.

Thomas turned on the lights and turned off the TV. Then he sat back down next to Mallory, startling her as he did. "Where were you?" he asked, taking her hand.

Mallory gave a tense laugh. "I don't know," she admitted. "I keep thinking about . . . Well, I guess finding the letter and all, I just . . ." She couldn't put words to her thoughts.

"Hey," he put his arms around her, "it's okay. I can understand why those feelings would come back up once in a while. But you're going to be fine."

Mallory wanted to believe him, but she had to admit, "I felt this way so much after he died. It's like . . . I was afraid to be alone with my thoughts; they were almost like ghosts, haunting me."

Thomas felt concerned for her, but he wasn't certain how to approach it. "Do you want to talk about it?"

"Not really," Mallory said, certain that putting her thoughts to words would only make them all the more real.

"Well, maybe I should just leave and let you get some sleep. Why don't you put some good music on in your room and try to rest."

Mallory doubted she could rest, but it was getting late and she knew Bethany would be up early. "I suppose I should," she said.

Mallory kissed Thomas good night at the door, not willing to admit that she was afraid to be without him. She locked the door after he left, then she took his advice and put in a CD that played relaxing music, setting it on continuous play. She was surprised at how quickly she fell asleep, but she woke up somewhere in the night and heard the music still playing. She took a quick trip to the bathroom, then attempted to settle back down. Her mind returned to the letter she'd found and the way it had made her feel. While there had been a definite peace in having it, and she felt more of a closure with his death, the memories it stirred were disturbing. She imagined him writing it, and the trouble he'd gone to in order to move the contents of the drawer and tape the letter in the bottom. She could almost see every step he took beyond that. She remembered where he'd kept the gun. She tried to concentrate on the music, but she couldn't force away the image of Brad loading that gun and putting it to his head. She wondered what went through his mind at the very end. And that's when she started to cry.

Finally, Mallory forced her thoughts away from the horror of Brad firing that gun. But not far enough away for comfort. Instead, her mind filed through the events leading up to his death. She cried harder as she remembered the details of their interaction. She wondered, as she often had, if she had somehow contributed to his death. In her heart, she believed there was nothing she could have done to make any difference. But her mind relentlessly asked the questions over and over, evoking an internal battle between guilt and resignation.

Mallory had heard many times that grief could catch you off guard. But she never would have dreamed that there was still so much of it bottled inside her after all this time. She cried like she hadn't since she'd lost her baby. And thoughts of that only intensified her emotion. She felt as if she'd drown in her own tears, if her heartache didn't strangle her first.

CHAPTER THIRTEEN

*W*ith practically no sleep behind her, Mallory called Thomas a little after six-thirty the next morning.

"Yeah," he said groggily into the phone.

"It's me," Mallory said. "I'm sorry to wake you, but . . ."

"What's wrong?" he demanded, immediately sounding more alert.

"It's difficult to explain," Mallory said, unable to keep from sounding emotional.

"Maybe you should have called me a long time ago," he said. "Do you want me to come over?"

"Yes," she said, more relieved by his offer than she was willing to admit.

Knowing that Thomas was on his way over, Mallory quickly made her bed, showered, and got dressed, grateful to feel busy, which distracted her from her thoughts. When Thomas arrived, she was breaking eggs into a bowl to mix up an omelet.

"What are you doing?" he asked, coming into the kitchen.

Mallory glanced up to see that he was wearing jeans and a sweat-shirt. She rarely saw him dressed so casually, and his appearance spurred a tingle somewhere inside her that was already beginning to calm her scourged emotions.

"I'm fixing breakfast," she said.

"Is that why you called me over here? To share breakfast?"

"No, but . . . I'm starving and . . . I need to . . . stay busy." Her voice cracked as the emotion she was fighting forced its way to the surface. As Thomas's arms came around her, she couldn't deny feeling better already. But she wondered how he'd react if he knew the truth of her feelings. The thought frightened her, but she couldn't go on with something like this left unspoken between them. She only prayed he would understand.

"Come on," he said, taking hold of her shoulders. "I'll help with breakfast, then we can talk."

Mallory nodded and returned to mixing the omelet. While it cooked, Thomas fixed some toast and got the juice out of the fridge. After the meal had been blessed, he said, "Okay, talk."

Mallory nodded again, grateful that Bethie was still asleep. When she didn't say anything, Thomas said, "You're not talking."

"I don't know where to start."

"Is this about Brad?" he asked, and she nodded. "Okay. I'm assuming that your finding that letter yesterday has stirred up some old feelings."

"I guess that's it," she admitted, then went on to tell him how her thoughts had hovered with the memories of his death and the days leading up to it. They finished eating but remained at the table while Mallory told him that she knew in her heart she'd forgiven Brad for the problems he'd had that had hurt her, but she couldn't help feeling a great deal of heartache over his death. Thomas listened quietly, saying little. She was about to get to the heart of the problem when Bethie came running down the stairs. Thomas laughed and picked her up, then he fixed her a scrambled egg while Mallory put some dishes in the dishwasher.

When Bethie was busy eating, Thomas took Mallory's hand and made her sit back down. "I think you were getting to a point," he said.

"What makes you think so?"

"I can tell. Just keep talking."

Mallory took a deep breath and fidgeted with her hands. "Thomas, I . . . I love Brad. I believe I always will."

When she said nothing more, he leaned toward her, saying, "Is this supposed to be a revelation to me, Mallory? Did you think I believed his absence from your life magically erased your feelings for him?"

"I don't know. I guess I just . . ."

"What?" he asked when she hesitated too long.

"We're about to be married, Thomas. And I feel somehow . . . guilty for admitting that I still have feelings for Brad when . . ." Again she didn't finish. They exchanged a long, hard glance while her heart beat painfully fast. The determination in his eyes made her certain he had an opinion on the subject, but Bethie began fussing and he stood up to help her.

"Wait," she said, taking hold of his arm. "Don't you have anything to say?"

"I certainly do," he said. "And as soon as Bethie's cleaned up, we will finish this conversation."

Mallory sighed and willed her heart to calm down. After Thomas washed the scrambled eggs off Bethie's hands and face, Mallory took her upstairs to get her dressed. She left her to play and returned to the kitchen to find it all cleaned up and the dishwasher running. Thomas dried his hands and hung up the towel, then he motioned elaborately toward the chairs where they'd been sitting. As he sat across from her and looked into her eyes, Mallory feared she would die of heart failure. She realized then that the issue she'd brought up had been bothering her far more than she'd admitted, even to herself. And there were points to the situation that hadn't even been brought up yet. She prayed inwardly that they could get everything into the open, hoping the reality wouldn't end up coming between them.

"Mallory," Thomas said in a gentle voice that helped calm her, "I love you with all my heart." He took both her hands across the table. "I'm guessing from the way you're acting that there's much more to this than you're saying." Mallory held her breath, feeling as if he'd read her mind. "If I'm wrong, feel free to correct me, but I'm also guessing that this has something to do with the fact that you cannot be sealed to me, because you are already sealed to Brad."

She felt the guilt rise into her eyes and glanced down quickly. Again, he'd hit the nail right on the head.

"Mallory," he said, tightening his grip on her hands, "look at me." She lifted her eyes and met his penetrating gaze. "We have both been well aware, since we made arrangements with the temple, that our marriage will be for time only. This is no surprise to me."

"Are you telling me you don't have a problem with it?"

"I didn't say that," he replied with a subtle edge to his voice. "The reality is hard for me, Mallory. I want to be with you forever. But there's nothing I can do about it. I have to do my best to live right-eously, believing that God will bless me with the happiness in the next life that I earn in this one. But the fact is, you *are* sealed to Brad. And even though he hurt you, you've told me enough that I'm well aware your love for him was deep and strong. And it still is, I know. If we believe that he is progressing and overcoming his struggles on the other side—which we do—then he may very well have the right to be with you forever. Neither of us knows what his choices will be, or how he will be judged for the mistakes he made. Would we feel differently about each other if he had died of cancer, or in an accident? You love him; you've forgiven him. And we have to accept the reality that our marriage may be for this life only. It's a matter of faith; of trusting in God to work it all out the way it's meant to be."

"I know, but . . ." A surge of emotion made her falter.

"What?" he urged gently.

"It's just . . . hard. I love you, Thomas. I cannot fathom being without you. But then, if I'm completely honest, I felt the same way for Brad. I married him with the belief that we would be together forever, and I can't imagine backing down on that just because he made some mistakes and . . ." She couldn't go on.

"Hey," he said, wiping at her tears, "there is no good in stewing over this, Mallory. There's nothing we can do beyond making the most of what we have. We'll have a good life together. That's no small thing. I love you; you love me. If we do our best to live righteously and trust in the Lord, everything will work out the way it's meant to."

Thomas watched Mallory crying silent tears, and found it took all his strength to keep from crying himself. How could he tell her that the reality of their situation tore him apart inside? He couldn't. It was as simple as that. What he'd told her was true; there was nothing they could do to change it. She was sealed to Brad, which made the prospect of eternity something they wouldn't completely understand until they passed through the veil. He'd told her it was a matter of faith; he only wished he could truly find peace over it in his own heart. But there was no good to be found in troubling her with his concerns. He knew marrying her was the right thing to do, and if a lifetime was all he would have with her, he would do everything in his power to make it a good one.

The subject was dropped when Bethie crawled onto Thomas's lap with a storybook. He read it to her, then slipped away to get to the restaurant before it opened. Mallory left a short while later to work the lunch shift. Thomas beamed when he saw her come in, and she couldn't help but anticipate being his wife. There was no tangible reason not to be completely happy, so she pushed her anxiety away, praying that one day she would be able to find peace over the fact that she couldn't possibly choose between the two men she loved in the eternal perspective. She reminded herself that, as Thomas had said, it was a matter of faith. Through the following days she did her best to put it into the Lord's hands and let go of it, concentrating on the wedding as it drew closer.

Two weeks before the big day, Mallory invited her family over for dinner, using it as bribery to get their help with the announcements. Her mother had graciously done the address labels on her computer, updating the list since she'd done announcements for Caitlin's wedding. Janna had sent those going out of state a few days earlier, but they had yet to get the remainder of them ready to mail.

Matthew stopped by on his way home from work to see how she was doing, and it was nice to have some time alone with her brother before everyone else arrived. She felt certain he'd been inspired to be there when she answered the phone to hear Brad's mother, who was angry over the wedding announcement she'd just received. "I don't see that it is any of your business," Mallory said assertively. When Mrs. Taylor rambled on, Mallory said good-bye and hung up.

"What was that all about?" Matthew asked.

"Brad's parents are upset because I'm marrying a black man," she snarled. "They don't want their granddaughter raised with *such an influence*." She mimicked her mother-in-law rather unkindly. "Can you believe that? She's got a lot of nerve. They haven't shown the least bit of concern for Bethie since Brad died; not so much as a birthday card."

"Well, what they think simply doesn't matter."

"I know," Mallory said, but she felt emotional anyway.

"Thomas is a good man, and you're going to be very happy together."

"I know," she said again, then forced herself to finish cooking dinner.

Matthew went home to change his clothes. He returned with Melody and the children just a few minutes after Janna and Colin arrived. While Melody and Mallory worked in the kitchen, Janna, Colin, and Matthew stuffed announcements and pictures into envelopes. Mallory kept her eye on the clock, wondering what was keeping Thomas. When he finally came through the door, she felt butterflies just to see him. Everything felt better when his arms came around her. Then she looked into his eyes and noticed obvious distress. "What's wrong?" she asked quietly.

"I was late because I had to make some calls to get some extra shifts covered. Do you think you can put in some extra time tomorrow?"

"Of course, but . . . is somebody sick?"

"Janice has the flu," he said, then his voice lowered. "And Lana's husband died. The funeral is the day after tomorrow. I think we should go."

"Yes, of course," she agreed. Then she took a deep breath, as if she could literally feel Lana's relief, which ingrained the perspective of her own struggles a little deeper. "Now she's free to get on with her life."

Thomas nodded, perceiving a deeper meaning to her words. His countenance brightened as he told her he'd made arrangements at the restaurant so she wouldn't have to work much the week before the wedding. They were both taking a week off afterward.

The family ate dinner and worked together to clean up the kitchen, then they got the announcements all ready to mail except for the stack Thomas set aside to take home, where he had address labels ready and waiting.

Attending the funeral for Lana's husband was more difficult than Mallory expected it to be. Memories of Brad's death hovered in her mind, but she prayed silently to be free of regret. And with Thomas's hand in hers, she couldn't help but be reminded of how far she'd come since Brad's funeral. She had a bright hope for the future with this man she'd come to love. It was unsettling to have difficult memories lingering so closely, but she was able to talk freely about them with Thomas during the drive home. His compassion and understanding made her feel one step closer to finding complete peace over the events of the past, and filled her with hope at the prospect of a bright future.

The following days went smoothly, with the exception of a few phone calls from well-meaning relatives who had received announcements and felt it necessary to warn Mallory against the hazards of interracial marriage. Mallory listened to what they had to say, then politely told them that she had no doubt that she was doing the right thing. If anything, their comments only increased her certainty that marrying Thomas was the best thing she could do with the rest of her life.

Two days before the wedding, Janna and Colin came over so Colin could play with Bethie while the women went over some last-minute details. Mallory was continually assaulted with butterflies, and she couldn't deny that she was thoroughly happy. The phone rang, and her tingling increased as she checked the caller ID. It was Thomas.

"Hello, my love," she said as she answered the phone and he chuckled warmly.

"Hello," he said, and the happiness in his voice was evident. "Guess what? My family is here. I want you to meet them. Is it all right if we come over?"

"That would be great. Actually, I just put some brownies in the oven."

"Ooh, aren't you ambitious."

"Not really; I just had to have some chocolate to soothe my nerves."

"Are you nervous?" he asked lightly.

"More . . . anxious," she said, and he chuckled.

"Yeah, I know what you mean."

"So," she said, "remind me of who is coming, and their names. I don't want to embarrass myself."

"I wouldn't worry about that," he said. "They'll love you."

"Okay, but . . ."

"Well, my two aunts are here."

"Emerald and Pearl."

"That's right."

"And they are your father's sisters."

"Yes, and Pearl's brought her daughters, Julia and Lucille. And Emerald's daughter is Beverly."

"Don't you have any male cousins?"

"Pearl has three sons, but they're scattered all over the country, and I wasn't terribly close to any of them. Emerald had a son who was killed several years ago. But it's like I told you, most of my relatives didn't appreciate it when I became a Mormon. These are the only ones who really care about *me.*"

Mallory smiled. His happiness at their coming was evident. She wondered what it might have been like if his parents were alive. And of course he would never invite his brother, under the circumstances.

With so little family left to him, she was grateful these people had made the effort to come.

Twenty minutes later, Thomas arrived with his aunts and cousins. And Mallory immediately loved them. Pearl was as thin as Emerald was heavy. But both his aunts were equally vibrant, full of hugs and laughter as they came into her home.

"Well, if she just isn't the sweetest thing ever," Emerald said as Thomas introduced her to Mallory. Then she engulfed Mallory in a hug so comfortable that it was tempting to never let go.

Pearl then took her turn at hugging Mallory, saying with a laugh, "Well, if you had to marry a white woman, you certainly found a pretty one."

"I did indeed," Thomas said. Then he introduced his cousins. Beverly was a bit tomboyish, with very short hair and a deep, hearty laugh. She showed Mallory pictures of her three little sons and talked about how much fun they were. Julia and Lucille were a contrast to Beverly, and yet the three of them were obviously as close as their mothers. Mallory was almost stunned by their beauty and elegance. She noticed the color of their lipstick and nails, as well as their clothes; colors that would make Mallory look clownish. But with their dark skin and black hair, the effect was remarkable. They each in turn hugged Mallory in greeting, expressing their delight in knowing that Thomas had found someone to make him happy.

"Where's Bethie?" Thomas asked, as if he'd just noticed her absence.

"Oh, Mom and Dad went to the grocery store and took her along. They should be back soon."

Mallory was serving warm brownies when her parents returned. Thomas made the introductions and everyone fussed over Bethany, especially Emerald. Bethie clung to Thomas, wary of so many strangers. But Emerald chuckled and said, "She's never seen anyone like me before."

Thomas chuckled with her. "I daresay she hasn't."

They all moved to the family room and sat down, where the conversation was comfortable and easy. Eruptions of delightful laughter only increased Mallory's happiness as she sat with Thomas's hand in hers, listening to the exchange of stories and small talk. Bethany gradually warmed to their visitors and was soon sitting on

Emerald's lap, playing with some odds and ends that Emerald had pulled out of her purse.

While Mallory was digesting the reality that she and Thomas would be married the day after tomorrow, she enjoyed watching his family interact with hers. She'd rarely heard so much laughter as they got along marvelously. And each time she caught Thomas's eye, she felt the reality settle a little deeper. She felt truly grateful to see evidence of the Lord's blessings in her life.

Melody and Matthew came by after their children were put to bed, with instructions to call if they needed anything. The evening wore on and Bethany was put to bed, but the adults continued to talk and laugh, as if they were *all* family. After a while, Matthew put on some music and started to dance with his mother. Mallory had grown up watching her parents dance occasionally for no apparent reason, and the children had often joined in. But she laughed to observe them now. Thomas took Mallory's hand and joined them. Colin started dancing with Emerald, and in a few minutes *everyone* was dancing, while no one seemed concerned about whether or not they had a partner.

It was nearly midnight before everyone finally filtered out of the house, except for Pearl and her daughters, who would be using Mallory's guest room and the sofa sleeper in the family room. She made certain they had what they needed, then they visited another little while before she went up to bed, filled with perfect contentment. Her anticipation was sweet, knowing in her heart that nothing was so right for her as being Mrs. Thomas Buchanan.

* * * * *

Returning to his condo with Emerald and Beverly, it only took a few minutes for Thomas to see that they had what they needed. He pulled out the sofa bed and Beverly went right to sleep, but Emerald fixed herself a cup of cocoa and insisted that she needed to wind down a little before she could sleep. Thomas sat across the table from her, grateful for the opportunity to be alone with Emerald. She'd been a prominent part of his life; the closest thing to a mother that he had.

They exchanged small talk for a few minutes before her eyes deepened on him. "So," she said, "you certainly seem happy."

"I am," he admitted readily. "And I do believe you like her."

"I do," Emerald said with a warm chuckle. "And I like her parents, too. It's evident they're good people."

"Yes. They've been wonderful; her whole family. You know, Emmey, not one of them has even blinked sideways at me. Not once have they given me anything but complete love and acceptance."

Emmey shook her head. "You're real lucky there, child. Yes, sir."

"Not lucky, Emmey—blessed. I am very blessed."

"Yes, indeed, you are. And how do people around here feel about your sweet Mallory marrying a black man?"

"Oh, it's what you'd expect. But it's nothing we can't handle. Most people have been fine with it."

"That's good, then. I was afraid your Mormon church leaders might have a problem with marrying you and a white girl."

"No, that's not a problem, I can assure you."

"Well, I'm glad of that. 'Cause I've certainly heard of it happening."

"Yes, I'm certain it does," he said. Emmey made a noise of disgust, and Thomas felt the need to make a point. "Now, if I tried to marry a white woman back home, do you think the minister would have been willing to do it without having a whole lot to say about it?"

Emmey sighed. "I guess you're right there. Some things just never stop being hard; some things."

"You're right, Emmey. But we are very blessed." He kissed his aunt's cheek and hugged her tightly.

"You're a good boy, Thomas. You've always been such a good boy. You deserve to be blessed; yes you do."

Emerald went on to bring him up to date on his relatives, most of whom he hadn't seen in years, and probably never would again. Then they finally went to bed a little before two. But Thomas still had trouble sleeping. He was so excited about getting married that he felt like a child on Christmas Eve. It was just as he'd told Emmey—he was truly blessed.

Mallory was amazingly calm the day prior to the wedding, and astounded to realize that everything was under control. She hardly saw Thomas a minute, but when they talked on the phone at bedtime, she was seized by a wave of childish excitement. She wondered if she'd ever been so happy in her life.

Mallory's happiness only deepened the following morning as she knelt across the altar from Thomas and exchanged vows. She felt a twinge of sadness in realizing that their marriage was for time only, but it passed quickly as she reminded herself that however things might turn out in eternity, she had a full life ahead with this incredible man. The doubts and fears she'd once felt in turning her heart over to him were completely absent.

Thomas's family was waiting outside the temple, along with Mallory's brother, Dustin, who had been put in charge of Bethany. They went together to the east side of the temple where they took pictures, and Mallory found herself laughing often for no apparent reason. Each time she did, Thomas laughed with her, as if they shared some great secret. It seemed no words were needed to express their mutual happiness.

The reception was pulled off without a glitch. Mallory didn't feel the least bit nervous or uptight, even when she was well aware of some people's being quite stunned at the evidence of this marriage. She could almost imagine some of their guests coming just to be certain the photograph enclosed with the wedding announcement hadn't deceived them. One of her mother's friends actually said to Mallory, "He really is black."

"Yes," Mallory said, beaming with pride as she looked up at Thomas, "and I really do love him."

She laughed with pure bliss as Thomas scooped her into his arms and carried her into the finest hotel room she'd ever seen. He laughed with her, taking her straight to the bed. And the next thing she knew, she was looking up into his face. His laughter stopped abruptly as the reality descended over them both in the same moment. She read a thousand thoughts in his eyes, but they all came together with the same message. His love for her shone through brilliantly.

"Mallory," he murmured, and his hand trembled as he lifted it to touch her face. Pressing his fingers into her hair, he kissed her in a way he never had before. A once-familiar sensation quivered inside of Mallory as his kiss deepened and he eased closer. Then, in a heartbeat, she found herself in the middle of something she'd never known existed. Treading further into unfamiliar territory, she felt helpless to capture something that she had no experience with. *Passion.* How could she have been married to a man for four years, and never once felt this way? She only contemplated the question briefly before she turned her attention fully to the moment. She was with Thomas. She was his wife. And nothing else mattered.

After feeling caught in the center of some kind of exquisite cyclone, Mallory was almost startled to feel herself suddenly surrounded by complete calm. Thoroughly content, she nearly drifted to sleep, at the same time feeling as if she'd just emerged from a dream. The dream merged into a perfect reality as Thomas spoke close to her ear. "I love you, Mallory Buchanan."

Mallory opened her eyes to look at him while her mind attempted to grasp all she had experienced with him. "And I love you," she murmured, pressing a hand down the length of his arm and back up again. She found the contrast of their skin color somehow magnificent and beautiful, in a way she'd never considered before.

Thomas drifted to sleep with his arms wrapped around her. But Mallory lay awake for more than two hours, attempting to understand why her experience with Thomas made particular memories of her relationship with Brad suddenly feel very unsettled. She prayed fervently to be able to understand what she was feeling. A level of comprehension finally filtered into her mind, then she tucked it away, reminding herself that she was on her honeymoon. She snuggled closer to Thomas and drifted to sleep, content and perfectly happy.

The following day they drove south, heading into southern Utah where they explored Arches National Monument, Bryce Canyon, and even the Grand Canyon. After returning home, it only took a few days for Thomas to move the remainder of his things from his condo and settle in. Mallory liked the way the house took on a different flavor as his belongings mingled with her own, including the unique decor she had once admired in his front room.

A few weeks after the honeymoon they invited Colin and Janna over for dinner, and Thomas did most of the cooking. "I've never tasted anything so exquisite in my life," Janna declared.

"It's no wonder you can make a good living with food," Colin added. "I think we'll put you to work at the next family barbecue, and show off your talents."

Thomas chuckled. "It would be a pleasure," he said.

When the kitchen was cleaned up, Thomas showed Janna and Colin some of his family history work, which provoked a poignant conversation. When it was time to put Bethany to bed, Janna followed Mallory up the stairs to visit with her while she bathed the toddler and put her into pajamas.

"You seem happy," Janna said to her daughter.

"I am," Mallory said with no hesitation. She told her mother some of the highlights of their honeymoon, and when Bethie was put to bed, Mallory sat with Janna in her bedroom, where they chatted aimlessly until a lull came in the conversation.

"Mother," Mallory said tentatively, "can I talk to you about something that's . . . sensitive?"

"Of course. You're not going to embarrass me."

"I might embarrass myself. But maybe if I had talked to you about this years ago, my life might have gone differently."

"There's no good in speculating over such things. Just tell me what's on your mind."

Mallory pushed a hand through her hair. "I learned something on my honeymoon, Mother. It took me a while to piece it all together in my head, but . . . I've figured some things out about Brad."

"Okay," Janna said when Mallory was quiet.

"I don't know how to say it exactly. I mean . . . I've heard you say that intimacy in a relationship can somehow mirror the other aspects of a relationship. But I don't think I fully understood that . . . until now. What I'm trying to say is . . . well, I think that my intimate relationship with Brad was completely dysfunctional. And I just didn't know any better. I had nothing to compare it to."

Janna leaned back and sighed as Mallory's purpose became evident.

"I realize now that a part of me knew something wasn't right, but he convinced me that my lack of fulfillment was *my* problem. I remember him actually telling me that no man could keep me satisfied; that my desire to be intimate more than once a month was somehow perverse."

Janna closed her eyes for a moment and shook her head. Her expression alone assuaged Mallory's need for validation.

"As I thought all of this through, I also learned something else." Mallory sighed. "I always thought that Brad was sweet and sensitive.

And I suppose in many ways he was, but . . . well, I always looked at
our lack of arguing as a sign that our marriage was good. I can see
now that Brad was passive; it was as if he'd do or say anything to
cover up the fact that he had a problem. The only problem I didn't
stand up to him on was the intimacy issue—and he truly had me
convinced that there was something wrong with *me.*" She started to
cry as years of hurting over that very thing rushed forward.

Mallory had rarely seen her mother angry, which made the vehe-
mence in Janna's voice all the more startling. "It's evil, Mallory, when
a person covers their problems by destroying the self-worth or char-
acter of another person. It's *evil.* Do you hear what I'm saying?"

Mallory nodded. "Yes, Mother, I know, but . . . I have to
remember that I'm not in a position to judge Brad for what he did or
didn't do. I'm grateful for the understanding I have of what was
happening, and I can see there is still a great deal I need to work
through. But I have to forgive him and move on. I have to appreciate
all that's good in my life."

"You've come a long way," Janna said in a gentler voice.

"I suppose I have." Mallory sighed deeply. "As horrible as life has
been for me since I lost Brad, I can't help feeling grateful for what
I've learned. I hate the thought of being back in that relationship,
lost in ignorance; hurting without being able to recognize why. Even
though I never consciously admitted it, I think part of my fear in
marrying Thomas was my belief that I had problems in that respect.
And now, what I've learned gives me more peace than I could ever
put into words."

Janna took her daughter's hand and squeezed it gently. "Do you
ever wonder what might have happened if Brad had lived, and you'd
discovered his problem some other way?"

"I've thought about it a great deal, actually. Of course, now that I
have Thomas, I can't help but be grateful that everything worked out
the way it did. But I truly believe that Brad and I would have been
able to work things out . . . the way you and Dad did. I'm certain it
wouldn't have been easy. And of course it would have depended
upon his desire and commitment to getting beyond the problem, but
. . . I'd like to think he would have loved me enough to do whatever
it took."

Janna nodded in agreement, then she hugged Mallory tightly. "I love you, Mom," she said, grateful beyond words for having a mother with so much strength and wisdom. She truly was blessed.

CHAPTER FOURTEEN

*L*ittle more than a month beyond the honeymoon, Mallory began to feel familiar symptoms. She said nothing to Thomas until she took the opportunity to have a test done. Then she went to the restaurant to meet him for lunch. He was standing at the front desk discussing something with the hostess when she walked in.

"Well, good morning, Mrs. Buchanan," Thomas said with a smile that warmed her through.

She glanced at her watch. "It's morning for a few more minutes." She kissed him in greeting, and they left together to go to lunch. When he had parked the car outside a Chinese restaurant, she took his hand. "Before we go in, there's something I need to tell you."

"Okay," he said, turning toward her.

Mallory glanced down and took a deep breath. "I'm pregnant, Thomas."

"Really?" He grinned. Then he laughed. Then he hugged her tightly.

Halfway through lunch he said, "A baby. Wow. That is incredible." He took Mallory's hand over the table. "Are you happy about it? Do you feel ready?"

"I do," she said firmly. "It fills something in me that's felt a little empty ever since I lost that last baby. I mean it when I say that I've never been happier." Thomas smiled, and she couldn't deny that the evidence of his happiness deepened her own.

As time passed, Mallory's happiness in being married to Thomas was so complete that she almost felt guilty. In comparison, she could see now that her relationship with Brad had been incomplete. His dysfunction had seemed too subtle to grasp at the time, but now that she could look at it from a distance, it was very clear. Still, she found peace in knowing that he was where he needed to be. He was getting the help he needed, and all was well with him now.

It took little time for Thomas to feel completely comfortable in the ward. He was asked to be a counselor in the elders quorum presidency, and he quickly immersed himself in the calling, enjoying the opportunity it gave him to get to know people and be involved.

The business continued to go well. They opened the restaurant in Orem, and within weeks it was bringing in good crowds. Mallory worked less now that she didn't need the income, but she enjoyed being involved and still put in some hours each week.

There were occasional moments when Mallory sensed prejudice from others because of their unusual marriage. But she felt confidence in the love they shared, and she knew Thomas felt the same way. There was nothing anyone could say or do to make them wonder if being together was the right thing. They both knew it in their hearts.

Bethany thrived on Thomas's presence in the home. She quickly took to calling him Daddy, and Mallory loved to watch them together. If not for the stark contrast in their coloring, no one would ever guess she wasn't his child. No father had ever cared for a daughter so completely.

Matthew and Melody had a baby girl about five months before Spencer Thomas Buchanan was born with little difficulty, weighing in at nine pounds even. He was a beautiful baby who got a lot of attention from family and ward members. According to tradition in the Trevor family, many friends and relatives attended the sacrament meeting where Spencer was blessed and given a name by his father. Even though Janna had no blood relatives, and Colin's family was too spread out across the country to attend, they both had many good friends they had accumulated through the years, and some had become like family. At times it was difficult for Mallory to recall that some of these people weren't actually related. They had been around so much through her growing-up years that she knew them better than most of her father's siblings and their families.

Hilary Hayden had been her mother's best friend for as long as Mallory could remember, and her husband Jack, who was a paraplegic, had actually stayed in their home when Mallory was a child.

Ammon and Allison Mitchell had come into their lives by way of Jack and Hilary, since Jack and Ammon were well acquainted. But they too had become good friends of the family. In fact, Jack and Ammon were in business together; it was Mitchell-Hayden Construction that had built Mallory's home, and Matthew's as well.

Sean and Tara O'Hara had also been around as long as Mallory could remember. Sean was a psychologist, and Mallory had been well versed on the immense help he'd given her parents through the crises in their past. And ironically, Sean had known Ammon's wife, Allison, from way back, since he'd practically lived with her family while he was in college.

Along with all these people came a mass of children, and they all gathered at Thomas and Mallory's home for the traditional potluck dinner following the meeting where Spencer had been blessed. Thomas enjoyed the laughter and conversation going on around him, while his little son was passed around and admired. He felt immensely blessed to be part of such an incredible family, and all the good people that came along with them. His life was rich and full, and he couldn't think of one reason he shouldn't be perfectly happy— except for that one little nagging doubt that hovered relentlessly in the back of his mind.

The opportunity to bless his son had touched him deeply, and he still felt his emotion hovering close to the surface. He felt joy and contentment unlike anything he'd ever known. So, why did he have to be plagued by that one bothersome question? It was a question that couldn't be answered.

He was startled from his thoughts when Colin put a firm hand on his shoulder, saying, "That was a beautiful blessing you gave your son."

Thomas nodded and managed a smile, suddenly too overcome with emotion to speak. He was dismayed when Colin picked up on it. "Is something wrong?" he asked quietly.

Thomas swallowed hard and shook his head, hurrying into the kitchen, which was presently devoid of people. He took hold of the counter with both hands and hung his head, squeezing his eyes shut as the tears refused to be held back any longer. He thought he was alone until Colin's hand grasped his shoulder once again.

"What is it, Thomas?" he asked gently.

Thomas shook his head, unable to speak. Colin put a fatherly arm around him and waited patiently. Thomas finally got hold of his emotions and wiped his tears. He chuckled tensely. "Forgive me," he said. "I've felt emotional since the blessing, but . . . it just got hold of me."

"So, what's bothering you?" Colin asked. "Or is it none of my business?"

"I'm just . . . having a tough time with the fact that . . . well, I'm not sealed to Mallory. And my children are automatically born under the covenant of her sealing. I know I'm supposed to have the faith that everything will work out in the next life, but . . . I guess it's just easier said than done. And sometimes it just . . . gets to me."

Colin blew out a long breath. "That's a tough one, Thomas. I wish I knew what to say."

"I know Mallory loves me. But she loves Brad, as well. I know he made some mistakes. But that doesn't necessarily mean that . . ." Thomas shook his head, unable to finish.

"Yeah, I hear what you're saying," Colin said.

At that moment Sean O'Hara walked into the kitchen, heading toward the fridge with a large bowl of salad.

"Oh, forgive me," he said, obviously noticing the tension. He put the bowl away and moved toward the door. "I'll just leave the two of you to—"

"No, wait," Colin said, and Sean turned around. "Maybe we could use a little psychological input."

Thomas knew that Sean O'Hara had been a psychologist for many years, but he didn't know him well enough to feel completely comfortable with having his concerns shared. Colin explained the situation briefly, then Sean sighed and folded his arms. "That's a tough one," he said.

Colin chuckled. "How profound, Sean. I already said that. And I'm no psychologist."

Sean laughed and hit Colin playfully on the shoulder. "That's rather a judgmental thing to say," he added with mock indignation.

"Well, I *am* a judge," Colin retorted.

Thomas laughed at their ridiculous banter, but at least the tension had been alleviated.

"You know, Thomas," Sean said more seriously, "in my profession I've seen some interesting things come up that are very . . . shall we say, unique, to Mormonism. Your situation is one of them. As a people, we are focused on eternity. We try to see things in the eternal perspective; we live for eternal blessings. And most of the time, that outlook is truly a blessing in our lives. But in cases like yours, I can see where focusing on certain aspects of the next life could actually make life more difficult. You're caught in a technicality that can't be worked out from our mortal perspective. And you're not alone; there are a lot of good men out there who have married widows who are sealed to another husband."

"And how have they coped?" Thomas asked, wishing this man could give him an easy answer. But he knew there wasn't one.

"I don't know," Sean said with a little laugh. "Maybe I should take a poll or something."

"Oh, you're a lot of help," Colin said with light sarcasm.

"Hey, I'm just a psychologist. Not a prophet," Sean said with a sparkle in his eyes. Then he became serious again, turning his focus fully to Thomas. "But I *do* know that God is just and fair, and he's not going to leave any righteous man to live through eternity in misery. The important thing is to hold tight to what you believe in, and not let discouragement or a lack of understanding on this issue pull you away from what's important. And I believe, that with time and some effort, you can find peace in your heart."

Over the next several weeks, Thomas's mind often returned to the things Sean had said. And he did feel a little better. Life was good, and he was determined to enjoy it. He found it took a conscious effort to ward off negative feelings about the issue, and occasionally he found himself feeling angry toward Mallory because she actually loved Brad. Of course, it only took a minute for him to consciously realize that it was good and right for her to love Brad. If the situation was reversed, if he had died with weaknesses to work out on the other side, he certainly would like to believe that his wife would continue to love him.

Having Spencer around made it easy to relegate his concerns to the back of his mind. Being a father brought more joy into his life than he could ever have imagined. When Spencer was two months old, Jake returned from his mission and the family met to celebrate, discussing the fact that it wouldn't be long before Dustin would be sending in his papers.

Mallory was well aware that Thomas continued to feel nagging doubts about the sealing issue. And she couldn't blame him. For herself, she actually felt grateful to know that it didn't have to be dealt with in this life. And when it came time to deal with it, she believed that God would know what was best for all of them. But then, the children were sealed to *her,* which made it impossible for her to fully understand what Thomas was feeling. She only prayed that he would find some peace over it and not let it dampen his happiness.

Beyond that one concern, Mallory wondered why she had ever doubted that Thomas Buchanan could make her happy. Stopping to take account of her life, she was continually amazed at her happiness. Then fate twisted her feelings so quickly that it left her head spinning.

When an employee quit the restaurant unexpectedly, Mallory gladly filled in a few hours here and there, enjoying being out of the house a little while Melody took the children. Thomas left early in the afternoon to take care of some business at the Orem location, while Mallory covered the phones and front desk in the restaurant where she was most comfortable. She was surprised to answer the phone and hear a woman's voice speak tersely, "I need Mr. Buchanan, please."

"I'm afraid he's not in. May I take a message?"

"No, I need to talk to Thomas."

The shift to familiar terms in this woman unsettled Mallory. "I'm sorry. He should be back within a couple of hours. I'd be glad to help you with anything you might need."

"Who exactly is this?" the woman asked.

"This is *Mrs.* Buchanan," Mallory stated firmly, not liking this woman's attitude in the slightest.

There was a long moment of silence preceding a snide, "I don't believe it. He's *married?* Nice of him to let his family know. I'll call back, *Mrs.* Buchanan. Thank you very much." She hung up before Mallory could get in another syllable. She stared at the phone for a full minute, wondering if that was who she thought it might be. Would Thomas's ex-wife—who was now married to his brother— suddenly turn up wanting to . . . what? Mallory couldn't fathom what she might want. But she didn't like it.

When Thomas returned, he greeted her with a kiss and asked for an update. She told him the pertinent messages, figuring she'd save the mysterious woman for last.

"Anything else?" he asked, holding her hand in his across the desk.

"A woman called for you, and she wasn't very polite. No," Mallory corrected, "she wasn't even a little bit polite."

"What did she want?"

"To talk to you. That's it. No message."

Thomas looked briefly unsettled, but his expression quickly warmed and he leaned close to her ear, whispering familiar phrases of love and adoration. He eased back when the door opened, then his eyes shifted in that direction and Mallory saw them change. It was difficult to tell if he was upset or just stunned. Mallory turned to see a woman standing just inside the door, as if she'd been frozen by the same means that had suddenly made Thomas immobile. She was one of the most beautiful women Mallory had ever seen. The fact that she was black intimidated Mallory somehow.

"Hello, Thomas," she said in a tone that didn't remotely resemble the voice she'd used on the phone.

"What are you doing here?" Thomas asked with no tone at all.

"I called to let you know I was in town, but you weren't here. Some woman claiming to be your wife answered the phone. I almost accused her of lying. I can't believe you would get married without letting us know."

"No, Sandi," Thomas stated without apology, "I didn't send you a wedding announcement. And I didn't send a birth announcement, either. I didn't figure my happiness was of any consequence to you, or your husband, under the circumstances."

Sandi glanced discreetly toward Mallory, as if she'd just realized they weren't alone. "Can we talk privately?" she asked.

Thomas looked at Mallory, then at Sandi. "You can say anything you want right here."

Sandi sighed in disgust. "You think you need an employee to act as a witness or something? You think I'm going to say something to—"

"This is my wife, Sandi." With mock gallantry he added, "May I present Mallory Buchanan."

Sandi looked Mallory up and down as if she'd come from Mars or something. "You've got to be kidding," she said. Then she gave a quick, sardonic laugh, staring at Thomas in the same way. "I can't believe that you, of all people, would lower yourself to . . ." She glanced again at Mallory. "Oh, really, Thomas. Your father would turn over in his grave."

"You have no idea what my father would and wouldn't do. Is there a reason you've come here, or did you just want to harass me for old times' sake? If you . . ." Thomas stopped abruptly when the door opened and a couple walked in.

Mallory forced back the tears stinging her eyes and showed them to a table. When she returned to the lobby, Thomas and Sandi were both gone. She only had to go to the bottom of the stairs to realize they were in his office with the door closed. Resisting the urge to eavesdrop, Mallory returned to the front desk, wishing Sandi Buchanan had just stayed away.

Janice, one of the servers, came to the front desk in search of Thomas. Mallory was tempted to tell her he was busy and handle whatever she needed. But she told Janice that Thomas was in his office—with his ex-wife—perhaps hoping she might interrupt whatever might be going on up there. Janice smirked subtly and headed that direction. She came back just a moment later, looking as if she'd seen a ghost. She glanced almost guiltily toward Mallory and hurried past. Mallory felt a sick knot form in the deepest part of her, wondering what Janice might have overheard that she didn't want to tell Mallory. Then, with no warning, thoughts of Brad's betrayal hurled into her mind. And marching right after them came memories of Darrell's deceit. Would Thomas betray her trust as well? Did his love for his first wife still exist? Would he succumb to old feelings in spite of all the hurt he'd endured? Perhaps the hurt would make it more difficult for him to be strong. After all this time, while Mallory had believed that Thomas was everything she'd ever dreamed of, would he prove to be just like the men gone by in her life? Logic told her he wouldn't, but something deeper and more powerful was afraid. And she hated it.

* * * * *

Thomas sat on the edge of his desk, watching Sandi slowly pace the office while she poured out the details of her breakup with Robert.

When she finally ran down he said, "So what do you want me to do, Sandi? Do you want me to act surprised to discover that he's a manipulative cheat? I've known that since I was twelve. He cheated me out of everything. *Everything.*" He couldn't help sounding angry.

"I know that now," she said. "And I'm . . . truly sorry . . . for the hurt I've caused you, but . . ." She dabbed at her eyes and laughed softly. "I must say I was surprised to find you married. Quite honestly, I was hoping that . . ."

"You're kidding, right?" Thomas said when she didn't finish. "You come back here after all this time and think I'm just going to fall into your lap like a lovesick puppy?"

"I don't know what I expected, Thomas. But I know I still care for you. I made a mistake."

"What do you want me to say?" Thomas raised his voice in mocking sarcasm. "'Oh, Sandi, I love you. What could I have been thinking to let him take you away from me? I'd give up everything just to have you back.'" Following a long silence he gave a bitter chuckle. "You're dreaming, Sandi. I've never been happier in my life. Whatever we had once is *long* gone. If you came all the way to Utah to seduce me, I'm afraid you've wasted the trip."

Thomas said nothing as her tears turned to anger. He'd wounded her pride, and she was obviously determined to wound him back. But he just let her rant for a few minutes before he opened the door, saying, "Enough already. I've got work to do."

Sandi walked through the door ahead of Thomas. She went down a couple of steps, then turned back. "I love you, Thomas," she said, and reached up to kiss him before he even knew what was happening.

Mallory stood partway up the stairs, trying to convince herself that this woman hadn't just kissed her husband and told him she loved him. She'd headed up the stairs determined to prove to herself that nothing was amiss. But the sickness smoldering inside her increased tenfold as Sandi walked past her, looking positively smug, as if she knew something that would deeply hurt Mallory. Was it the same something that had upset Janice?

When Sandi was gone, she looked up at Thomas, wishing she could read his mind, wishing she could be absolutely certain his love for her was stronger than anything that might come between them.

But her past fears and hurts were already too close to the surface. She wanted to ask him what had happened, but she almost wondered if she could believe him. She knew it wasn't fair. She knew her assumptions were based more on her fears than on reality. He'd never done anything to warrant her mistrust—as far as she knew. Not knowing what to feel or how to face him, she turned and walked away, hoping that time would ease her fears.

Thomas found her a short while later at the front desk. He whispered discreetly, "Are you all right?"

"I'm not sure," she admitted. "But I don't want to talk about it right now."

Thomas looked concerned, but he said nothing more except, "Let me take over here. I think you could use a break."

Mallory left without saying anything. She didn't even look at him. She sat in the employees' lounge for only a few minutes before she realized that she'd never find peace if she didn't confront this head-on. She found Janice killing time with a book, since the place was practically empty, as it usually was this time of day.

"Could I talk to you for a minute?" Mallory asked. Something fearful rose into Janice's eyes so quickly that Mallory had to quell the urge to scream at her and demand to know what she'd overheard. Instead, she calmly urged her to a quiet corner where she whispered, "I need to know . . . whatever you heard up there. I need to know."

"Really, Mallory, I don't think it's my place to—"

"I need to know," Mallory interrupted.

"Maybe I misunderstood," Janice said. "Maybe I heard something out of context that . . . really isn't significant. It's just not like Thomas to say something like that, and . . ." Janice's eyes widened, as if she feared she'd already said too much.

"Tell me," Mallory said. "I have to know what I'm dealing with."

Janice took a deep breath. "I'll tell you if you promise me you'll talk to Thomas about it, and not go assuming something without having the whole story."

"Okay, fine. Tell me."

Janice hesitated, apparently urged on by the insistence in Mallory's eyes. "I heard him say that . . . he loved her . . . and he'd give up everything to have her back."

Mallory felt a shock rip through her, not unlike the moment she'd found out that Brad had a pornography problem. Not unlike the moment she'd discovered her husband had shot himself in the head. Not unlike the moment she'd discovered that Darrell was controlling and manipulative, and she'd almost given him everything. Perhaps it was being so comfortable with that kind of shock that made it difficult to discern reality in the face of it.

"Mallory," Janice nudged her back to the moment, "are you all right?" Mallory didn't respond. "There has to be some logical explanation. He's too good a man to just . . . fall at his ex-wife's feet like that."

Mallory forced herself to swallow enough to say, "Thank you, Janice. I'll talk to him."

"You'd better," Janice said, "or I will."

Janice left Mallory in her dazed stupor, while memories whirled around in her head, only to mix with her present fears. Losing Thomas would devastate her; she felt certain she could never survive it. But discovering that he was not what he appeared to be would be far worse. She doubted that she could ever trust again, let alone cope.

"What are you doing?" Thomas's voice startled Mallory from thoughts so deep that she'd forgotten where she was. "Are you ready to go home? Everything's covered now." Mallory didn't respond. "Are you okay?" he asked.

Mallory couldn't bring herself to lie. Her emotions were too intense to try and hide them. She shook her head and pushed past him. "I'll get my things out of the office, and . . ." She didn't finish as her voice broke, threatening to spill the enormity of fears that she hardly dared look at, let alone voice.

On her way to the office, Mallory willed herself to remain calm. If she acted on the emotions bubbling inside of her she would explode, and she couldn't do that here. She reminded herself that she loved Thomas—and he loved her. But stronger voices in her mind quickly drowned out anything simple and logical. Once she got to the office, she became lost in thought all over again, wondering how she was going to handle this. She had to talk to Thomas. But how? How could she approach this without sounding trite and mistrusting?

"All right," he said, closing the door as he entered the room. "We're not going anywhere until you tell me what's going on. I haven't seen you this upset since before I married you. What is it?"

Mallory said nothing. Her heart was pounding. Her throat was dry.

"Mallory," Thomas said, reaching to take her hands into his. Instinctively she recoiled and moved away. He looked stunned. "Are you trying to tell me that Sandi's visit upset you this badly?"

Mallory managed to nod.

"Why?" he demanded. "Did she say something to you? Did she—"

"No, but . . ." Mallory forced the truth out, knowing she had to say it. "But . . . Janice overheard you, and . . ."

Thomas's brow furrowed. His eyes narrowed. "Overheard *what?*" he insisted, wondering what he was being accused of.

"You . . ." Mallory's emotion began to bubble out. "You . . . told her you still love her . . . that you would give up everything . . . to have her back . . . and . . ."

"I did not!" he almost shouted. "Mallory, it's . . ." The determination in her expression forced him to recount his conversation with Sandi, then he squeezed his eyes shut. "Oh, for heaven's sake, Mallory. I said it sarcastically. I told her she was a fool for coming back here, believing that I *would* say something like that. Do you hear what I'm saying?"

Mallory nodded, but the emotions rumbling around inside of her had built up so much momentum that they wouldn't relent.

Thomas looked into his wife's eyes and felt something die inside of him. He stated with confidence, "But you don't believe me."

"I . . . don't know what . . . to believe," Mallory sputtered.

"You can believe that I am nothing more or less than what I have always been. You can believe that my love for you and our children is greater than anything else in this world. That's what you can believe!"

"I know, but . . ."

Thomas sighed. "You *don't* know, or you wouldn't be standing there looking as if your world had ended." Defensiveness merged into his own fears of the past, and it was impossible to keep his anger from taking hold. "You know, Mallory, I've done everything in my power to prove to you that my love is real, that you can trust me. But maybe it's just not possible. I understand that my brother is available. Maybe you could trust *him* without question. Everyone else did."

"Don't be ridiculous," she snapped.

"I don't see that as being any more ridiculous than you standing there insinuating that I would do or say *anything* to betray your trust. If that's the way you see me, then it's apparent you don't know me at all. You should *know* I love you. You shouldn't even have to question it. And if that's not prejudice, I don't know what is."

Mallory put all her concentration into controlling her emotions while Thomas angrily gathered his things. He moved toward the door, saying, "I'm going home. If you want a ride, I'm leaving now."

Neither of them said a word during the drive. Mallory told herself that he was right; her assumptions had been petty and ridiculous. But she couldn't find her way out of these emotions, and she didn't know how to explain it to him without sounding like a fool. All she had suffered rushed to her head in torrents, making her wonder how life could be so utterly cruel.

Thomas kept his attention purely on the road, wishing he could find his way past this anger and let her know that his love for her was pure and strong. But at the moment, every past hurt in his life hovered right between his head and his heart. All the prejudice and deception. All the losses and heartache. All the misunderstanding and unfairness. They were all wrapped up now in Mallory—because if she couldn't love him for who he was, and give him the trust he'd earned, he couldn't see much purpose in his life.

Thomas was startled when he saw a deer cross the highway some distance ahead. He breathed a sigh of relief to see that the animal had made it safely across four lanes of traffic, then he realized that all of the cars ahead of him had come to a complete stop. Everything suddenly turned to slow motion as it became evident that a collision was inevitable. He felt Mallory's hand on his leg, gripping so hard that it hurt. He heard her gasp, then hold her breath. Instinctively he twisted the wheel, taking the car into the turning lane in an effort to avoid rear-ending the car in front of him. For a split second he felt certain he'd avoided disaster, then he saw the truck move none too slowly into the turning lane from the other direction. Thomas had no idea what he did with the steering wheel or the brakes. He was only aware of the car sliding sideways, while thoughts and memories tumbled through his mind that at any other time would have taken hours to digest. Mallory screamed and turned toward him as if he could save her. He felt a jolt. Heard metal tearing. And glass breaking. Then everything came to a dead stop.

The ensuing silence was paralyzing. Then, the time that had stopped suddenly seemed racing to catch up with itself. He first recognized the pounding of his heart, and determined that it was a good indication that he was alive and conscious. He then heard Mallory gasp as if she'd been holding her breath. *She* was alive and conscious. He turned to look at her. Their eyes met. And nothing else in the world mattered. They clung to each other and cried, oblivious to anything going on outside their nucleus of safety. "I love you," she murmured, touching his face to assure herself he was all right. "I love you so much. I'm so sorry, Thomas. I love you."

"I love you, too," he whispered, and just held her until those who had stopped to help came to check on them.

It wasn't until they arrived home in their car, which was still drive-able, that the full reality began to sink in. They were both shaking as they sat together on the couch, recounting the miracle. Neither of them had so much as a scratch or a bruise. The police had been aston-ished to hear many eyewitness reports that the car had been sliding sideways, moving neatly between the lanes of traffic as if it was deter-mined to defy the laws of motion. The truck that had narrowly escaped a head-on collision had skidded past Thomas's car, with only their bumpers connecting as they passed each other. The bumper had been torn from Thomas's car, and the taillights had shattered. The truck's damage was only a broken headlight and a minuscule dent.

Thomas and Mallory both agreed that angels had been with them, protecting them from death or injury. But even more miracu-lous to them was the perspective they'd found in their brush with death. The pettiness of past hurts and fears were insignificant and meaningless. Only the love they shared mattered, and the perspective of that love now came clearly into view.

"Do you know what's most frightening of all?" Mallory asked, grateful for the feel of Thomas's strong arms around her, and for the evidence of her children in the room.

"What?" he whispered, pressing his lips into her hair.

"If one or both of us would have died with feelings like that between us." She sniffled and wiped away a seemingly endless stream of tears. "Forgive me, Thomas. I know my own perspective was the problem. You pledged your honesty to me the first time you took me out. I will never doubt you again."

Thomas just held her closer, murmuring his own apologies. He knew his own pain had made him defensive. But none of that mattered now. They were together. They were alive. And their love grew deeper as it emerged whole and strong.

Later in the week, Mallory answered the phone to hear a voice that sounded so much like Thomas that if it weren't for the formality of the conversation, she'd have believed it was. "Do you know when I can reach him?" he asked when Mallory indicated Thomas wasn't home.

"He should be home around six. Can I give him a message?"

After a moment's hesitation, she wasn't at all surprised to hear him say, "This is his brother. Just tell him I called."

Mallory felt nervous and uptight, wondering what Robert Buchanan might want after all this time. Could it just be coincidence that Sandi had shown up, declaring she'd left Robert, only days before Robert himself called? She was hesitant to tell Thomas when he came home. Fearing it would upset him, she approached it through a back door. "Did you get any unusual calls at the restaurant this afternoon?" she inquired casually.

"No, why?" He looked mildly alarmed. But then, after the scene with Sandi, she couldn't blame him.

Mallory took a deep breath. "Your brother called here, asking for you."

Thomas sat down a bit unsteadily. "What did he want?"

"He didn't say. Do you think it has something to do with Sandi leaving him?"

"I don't know, but . . . I don't want to talk to him. If he calls again, just tell him that—"

"I'm not going to lie to him, Thomas. Isn't it better that you at least find out what he wants?"

"It probably is," he had to admit. "But I don't trust him."

Twenty minutes later, Robert called again. Mallory answered the phone and eyed Thomas warily as she said, "He's right here. Just a minute."

Thomas took the phone reluctantly and Mallory whispered, "Do you want me to leave you alone?"

Thomas shook his head firmly and took hold of her hand. He cleared his throat and took a deep breath, saying as naturally as he could manage, "Hello."

"Hello, Thomas. It's Robert."

Thomas swallowed carefully. "Hello, Robert. I wish I could say this is a surprise."

"I'm assuming you've seen Sandi recently."

"I have," he stated, determined to stick to the facts and not give in to his emotions.

"I'm also assuming, since a woman answered the phone when I called earlier, that Sandi didn't meet with much success in trying to get you back."

Thomas chose his response carefully. "Did you think she would?"

"No."

"Well, *she* certainly seemed to think she would."

"Between the two of us, I would bet her ego is pretty bruised by now."

"I could care less about her ego."

"Or mine?" Robert asked tentatively.

"Or yours," Thomas admitted with honesty. Then there was silence. "Is that why you called? To discuss Sandi's ego?"

He heard Robert clear his throat. He seemed nervous, which was extremely uncharacteristic of his brother. "I called because I wanted to tell you myself that it's over between the two of us. And . . . even though I don't expect it to make any difference, I want to . . . apologize for the things I did that came between us. I was hoping I could see you and—"

"That won't be possible," Thomas interrupted.

"Why not?" Robert sounded genuinely hurt, but Thomas couldn't fathom that it might be genuine.

"It's just not. I appreciate the call, but . . . what's done is done."

"Thomas, we're brothers. I just want to—"

"Yes, we're brothers, Robert. And you cheated me out of . . ." Thomas stopped himself as he felt the anger rising. "It doesn't matter anymore."

"It *does* matter. I've done a lot of soul-searching, and I want to make things right between us. I've—"

"Like I said, that won't be possible."

"I find it difficult to believe that you, of all people, would be so mistrusting and—"

"Stop and look what trusting you got me, Robert." His anger took hold again and he quickly added, "I have to go. Take care of yourself. It's what you're best at."

Thomas hung up the phone, honestly forgetting he wasn't alone until Mallory tugged on his hand. Her expression was so stunned that it startled him. "I take it there's a reason you were so terse with him," she said.

"A reason?" he echoed, thoroughly appalled. "He had the nerve to ask if he could see me. He wants to make things *right* between us."

"And?"

"Do I have to repeat what he's done to me?"

"No."

"That man took *everything* from me."

"He didn't take your spirit, your integrity, your testimony. He didn't take away your will to achieve your dreams and make a good life."

Thomas disregarded her consolations. "He took the business, my wife, my father's love and respect, my—"

"That's right," Mallory agreed. "But now there's nothing he can take from you. You have a good life. You have your own business. You are in control of those things, and you're not stupid enough to allow your brother to manipulate you out of even a degree of that control. You don't have to put yourself into a position where he can hurt you in order to forgive him."

Thomas glared at her as the raw truth came to the surface. "I'm not sure it's in me to forgive him."

"And who is that going to hurt?"

"Me. Only me."

"No, not only you. Don't think you can carry around this festering wound for the rest of your life and believe it won't affect the kind of person you are, which in turn affects me and the children."

Thomas focused his gaze on her as he said, "Are you trying to tell me that you've completely forgiven Brad for what he did to you?"

He was stunned into humbly taking account of himself when she answered firmly, "Yes, I have. It's taken a long time, and a lot of prayer and soul-searching, but I know in my heart that I *have* forgiven him. I also know in my heart that you need to forgive Robert—and Sandi. You'll probably never see Sandi again—at least I hope not." She laughed softly, then her expression became even more severe. "But Robert is your brother. He's the only immediate family you have left. Whether or not he has changed is irrelevant. *You* are a man with enough strength and integrity to do what's right, even if it's not easy."

Thomas sighed, hating the reality that she was right. "I don't trust him, Mallory."

Mallory looked into his eyes and said firmly, "The only way to learn to trust is to take a risk. It's like I said, you don't have to open yourself up to more hurt in order to admit that he's your brother, and you have come to terms with the ill feelings between you. I'm not suggesting you let him move in, or that you give him a job." She softened her voice. "Of course, it's up to you. I know it's difficult. I'll stand behind you whatever you choose to do, but I believe in my heart you would feel better about yourself if you came to terms with it."

Thomas only sighed and walked into the other room.

CHAPTER FIFTEEN

*M*allory said nothing more about Robert. But even the passing of days didn't dispel the way he plagued Thomas's thoughts. In his heart he knew Mallory was right; it was just so difficult. He prayed to find peace, and to find the method and motivation to let Robert know that he was willing to hear what he had to say. He finally got up the nerve to call him on Saturday, but it soon became evident he'd gone out of town and couldn't be reached. The following day, Thomas got up from the dinner table to answer the door—and found Robert standing on his porch.

Following a moment of stunned silence while they each absorbed the other's presence, Robert muttered quickly, "I know you don't want to see me, and I don't blame you. But I've come a long way. All I ask is ten minutes. Okay?"

Thomas said nothing. He just recalled all of the effort and prayer that had gone into finding peace with his brother. And now Robert was standing here. He stepped aside and motioned him into the house.

Thomas had barely closed the door when Bethany came running to investigate. Robert's eyes were drawn to the child. "If you have company, then I can come back or—"

"I don't have company," Thomas stated, picking Bethany up. He smiled at her, if only to keep from feeling the unfamiliar reality of his brother's presence. "This is my daughter."

"But she's . . . white."

"Very good," Thomas drawled, but his sarcasm was facetious. "Actually, she's my stepdaughter. But I don't look at it that way."

Robert looked a bit stunned. "Forgive me, but . . . you married a white woman?" Thomas nodded. "I always thought you were more conventional than that."

With pride in his voice, Thomas stated, "Love isn't always conventional. But when it's true, it's color-blind."

"You're happy," Robert stated.

"Very much so, actually."

"I take it, then, that . . ." Robert was interrupted as Mallory came to see what was taking so long.

"Hello," she said, well aware of Thomas's nervousness. She extended a hand. "You must be Robert."

"That's right." He shook it firmly. "You must be the new Mrs. Buchanan."

"Call me Mallory," she said.

"You have good taste in women," Robert said lightly to Thomas. But Thomas's expression only became more intent.

"This one has far too much integrity to stray. Don't waste the effort."

Mallory swallowed hard. She could almost feel Robert recoiling from the bitterness of Thomas's tone. She prayed this wouldn't turn into a disaster. A moment later, Robert said, "I think I deserved that."

"Yes, you did," Thomas said.

When silence ensued, Mallory motioned them toward the couch. "Why don't you sit down? Can I get you some lemonade or—"

"No, thank you," Robert said. "I'm fine."

"I'll just . . . leave the two of you to . . ." She left the sentence hanging as she ushered Bethany from the room.

Thomas took a long, hard look at his brother and reminded himself of his desire to be free of the burden that hung between them. He sat down, and a moment later, Robert sat across from him.

"So, you're here," Thomas said. "You can say whatever you like. Beyond that, I can't make any promises."

Robert fidgeted with his hands and chuckled tensely. "I've been trying to memorize this for days, but now that I'm here . . ."

"Just say what you need to say," Thomas said.

"I . . . want to ask your forgiveness, Thomas. It's as simple as that. I don't even expect you to believe me, or accept it. I just had to see you face to face, and let you know of my regret. I could spend a long time trying to justify my actions. But the fact is, I was selfish and foolish. I don't expect us to become best friends or anything. It's just that . . . I'm at a point in my life where I've either got to give up or make a new beginning. Giving up just isn't in me, so . . . if I'm going to start over, I have to start with you. It's as simple as that."

Thomas absorbed his brother's words. He liked what he was hearing, but habit made him hesitant to accept it. He decided that getting more information would be good. "So, what made Sandi leave you? Did she get tired of you the way she got tired of me, or—"

"Actually, I think that's part of it." He chuckled tensely again, seeming more nervous than when he'd come in. He glanced around as if to take account of Thomas's present life. "Perhaps we're both better off without her; you especially."

"I am, actually," Thomas said. "I'd go through it all again to have what I have now."

"Maybe that puts some perspective on what happened between us," Robert said. Thomas wasn't certain he liked how deeply that penetrated him. If he was so grateful for having Mallory in his life, could he continue regretting the losses that had made his present circumstances possible? Hadn't Mallory found peace in Brad's death as a result of all the compensating blessings she'd received? "Maybe it takes a jerk, doing something stupid, to help put good things into place," Robert said.

Thomas thought about that for a minute, too. He felt the evidence of prayers being answered as peace began to settle over him. Mallory had been right; he didn't have to trust Robert in order to forgive him. But perhaps, with time, he could *learn* to trust him again—if he demonstrated a desire to be trusted through his actions. And maybe they'd never see each other again. Maybe trust was irrelevant.

"So," Thomas said, when the silence became heavy again, "why this sudden turnaround? Did Sandi leaving hurt you so deeply that—"

"Actually," Robert interrupted, seeming a little more relaxed, "I think the turnaround is the *reason* Sandi left. You see, I started going to church with her. Then I suggested that maybe we should make some lifestyle changes that might make our lives better. Apparently she's very comfortable with her lifestyle. But I realized I was very uncomfortable with mine. I guess that makes us incompatible."

Thomas listened and acknowledged what his brother had told him. But he said nothing until a particular statement jumped out at him: *going to church* with *her*. Sandi was a Mormon. And in spite of all her indiscretions, and her passiveness about religion, she was still a Mormon. He saw his brother smile subtly. "Are you trying to tell me something, Robert?"

The genuine glow in Robert's eyes managed to get past all of Thomas's hurt and fear just before Robert admitted, "I've been taking the missionary discussions, Thomas." He took a deep breath, then the sincerity of Robert's confession trickled down his face as he added, "I want to be baptized. And I want you to be the one to do it."

It took Thomas a full minute to grasp what his brother had said. And then he had to ask himself if this was genuine. But a warmth rushed over his shoulders, spreading out to every nerve of his body, as if to verify that his brother's change of heart was real. It was easy to come to his feet, and even easier to extend his hand. Robert stood to meet him, gripping Thomas's forearm firmly. And then they embraced. Thomas felt hesitant to let go as tears of joy and forgiveness coursed down his face.

They were interrupted by a cooing sound. Thomas stepped back and turned to see Mallory holding the baby. He and Robert both wiped at their tears simultaneously. But only Thomas noticed the glisten of moisture in Mallory's eyes as she observed them.

"I thought you might want to meet our son," Mallory said to Robert. She handed the baby to him, ignoring his hesitance. He laughed as he glanced from Thomas, to the baby, to Mallory, then back to the baby. "His name is Spencer," Mallory said.

"He's a good-looking kid." Robert made a funny face at the baby, who smiled in response.

"He has a beautiful mother," Thomas said, and put his arm around Mallory. He'd never comprehended such happiness.

Thomas invited Robert to join them for dinner, since they'd barely begun eating before his arrival. It only took a few minutes to reheat the food, then they sat at the table visiting long after they'd finished eating. Tears were shed again as Robert recounted the experiences that had led him to accepting the gospel. When he bore sincere testimony of its truthfulness, Thomas just squeezed Mallory's hand and wept.

When they finally got up from the dinner table, Thomas asked Robert to come with him to the den. Mallory found them there long after the children had been put to bed, perusing genealogical records and reminiscing about their childhood. She just let them alone, in awe of how good life could be.

The following day Robert returned to California, and arrangements were made for Thomas and Mallory to go the next week for his baptism. A few days before they were supposed to leave, Mallory was surprised to get a call from Sean O'Hara.

"How are you doing?" he asked.

"I'm good," she replied. "How are you?"

"Great," he said. And then he got to the point. "Hey, we were wondering if you and Thomas could come over for dinner tomorrow evening. There's someone I'd like you to meet."

Mallory was taken off guard. She knew Sean and his family well, but their contact had always been through her parents. She couldn't recall ever having dealt with him directly on anything.

"Will my parents be there?" she asked, wondering if it was a stupid question.

"Did you want them to be?" he countered with a little laugh.

"No, I mean . . . it doesn't matter. I was just . . . wondering."

Sean chuckled again. "There's no reason to be nervous, Mallory. It's just a dinner invitation. Why don't you talk with Thomas and call me back."

"All right," she said and got off the phone.

Mallory immediately called her mother, but Janna knew nothing about it. "Sean and Tara are wonderful people, Mallory. You should feel flattered to get such an invitation. Just go and enjoy yourself."

She then called Thomas, who seemed eager to accept Sean's offer. She called Sean back, and he sounded truly excited when she said they would be coming.

The following evening, after Bethany and Spencer had been deposited at Matthew's home, Thomas drove toward Sean O'Hara's. "Why are you so nervous?" he asked Mallory.

"It's just . . . weird. Nothing like this has ever happened before. They are my parents' peers. Why would they be inviting *us* to dinner?"

"He said there was someone he wanted us to meet. I'm certain we'll figure it out soon enough."

"But he's a psychologist, for crying out loud. Maybe he figures there's something wrong with me, and—"

"Don't be ridiculous. He's a family friend." Thomas glanced at Mallory, chuckling at her obvious distress as he took her hand. "Relax," he said, and she smiled meekly.

Through the remainder of the drive, Mallory managed to *appear* relaxed. But she was decidedly nervous. When they arrived, Thomas opened the car door for her and rang the doorbell, chuckling softly as he noticed the way she was wringing her hands.

Mallory told herself that as soon as she was with Sean and Tara, she would probably feel completely at home. She was anticipating having one of them answer the door and put her at ease. But when the door opened, they stood facing a man she'd never seen before. He was about the same height as Thomas, but he appeared a little older than her father—although she decided it would be impossible to guess his age. In spite of graying temples and deep lines at the corners of his eyes, he had a virile, rugged look to him which was enhanced by the jeans he wore with a white button-up shirt and a tweed jacket.

"Hello," he said, breaking into a boyish smile. "You must be Mallory and Thomas."

Mallory was taken aback again by his accent; he spoke with a thick Australian brogue.

"Yes," Thomas said, discreetly nudging Mallory to her senses.

"Come in," the man said. "I think Sean's upstairs for a minute."

"Thank you," Thomas said as they stepped inside and the door was closed.

The man was about to introduce himself as Sean came down the stairs, saying, "Did I hear the doorbell?" He smiled. "Oh, you got it. Come in. Make yourselves at home. I see you've met Michael."

"We were just getting to that," the man said.

"Thomas and Mallory, this is Michael Hamilton, a very dear friend of mine."

"It's a pleasure to meet you," Thomas said, extending a hand.

Mallory shook Michael Hamilton's hand, feeling a little in awe without understanding why.

"The pleasure's all mine," Michael said as Sean ushered them to the kitchen, where Tara was putting the finishing touches on a salad and visiting with a woman who was obviously Michael's wife. Again, Mallory found it impossible to guess this woman's age. She was beautiful, with a subtle, refined air about her.

Sean introduced her as Emily Hamilton, then she spoke in a voice traced with an accent. "I've heard so much about you," she said, taking Mallory's hand. "You're Colin and Janna's daughter."

"That's right."

"It's truly a pleasure," Emily added.

"You know Allison," Sean said to Mallory.

"Ammon's wife. Of course."

"Michael and Emily are her parents."

"Really?" Mallory laughed, already feeling more relaxed.

It quickly became evident that Emily was American, but she'd lived in Australia since she'd married Michael, and it showed in her voice.

During the meal, Mallory found she was completely enthralled with the conversation going on around them. She couldn't help but like Michael and Emily, but she was completely baffled as to why Sean would have made such a point of bringing them together. Why her? Why not Matthew? Or Caitlin? And why *only* her? Why wasn't the rest of her family involved?

When dinner was over, they moved to the front room to visit. They'd only been seated a few minutes when Sean said, "There's a reason I wanted the two of you to get to know Michael and Emily."

"We suspected there was," Thomas said easily. "Although spending the evening with good company is reason enough."

"The thing is," Sean said, "the two of you have a lot in common with Michael and Emily."

Thomas smirked and said, "He doesn't *look* black."

Michael laughed boisterously. "No, I'm just a *foreigner*."

"While we're in America you are," Emily protested. "I'm the foreigner most of the time."

"That's what I like about you," Michael said to his wife, and she smiled endearingly.

While Mallory was expecting Sean to explain his purpose, Emily turned directly to Mallory, saying gently, "We understand your first husband was killed."

Mallory was taken so off guard that all she could do was nod.

"You see," Emily leaned forward, "my first husband was killed as well."

Thomas took Mallory's hand. He felt warmed by Sean's insight in bringing Mallory together with this woman who could give her some empathy concerning their common experiences. He was surprised to hear Michael say, "And Emily is sealed to him."

Suddenly everything changed. The puzzle pieces fell perfectly into place. Sean had been aware of Thomas's concern over not being sealed to Mallory. He knew now why they had been invited here. But he wasn't prepared for the sudden rush of emotion that overtook him as he looked into Michael Hamilton's eyes and read something deeply compassionate. Thomas managed to blink back the tears before they fell, but he felt drawn to this man, whose expression alone seemed to say that this issue was something deeply difficult for him—or at least it had been. Without a word spoken, Thomas could feel an underlying peace surrounding Michael. He ached to feel that kind of peace, and prayed in his heart that this man might have something to say that might soothe his troubled heart.

"You see, Thomas," Michael leaned his forearms on his thighs, and it almost felt as if the two of them were alone, "I did pretty well at handling the circumstances for a long time. In fact, I hardly gave it a second thought for years. And then Emily nearly died, and I had to face the reality that if I lost her, I could very well be losing her forever. The children she had before we were married weren't mine at all, and even my blood children were technically sealed to another man."

Thomas felt his heart racing as this man expressed his own thoughts so perfectly—thoughts he'd hardly dared say aloud.

"Emily's first husband had had some problems, but I couldn't possibly judge where he might stand in the eternal perspective. He was not necessarily any less entitled to be with Emily forever than I was."

"But you seem to have come to terms with it," Thomas said.

"I have," Michael said with confidence.

"How?" Thomas asked with a breathy voice.

Michael laughed and rubbed a hand briefly over his face. "Trust me, Thomas. You don't want to use the same methods. But perhaps I can tell you what I learned once I got past floundering around in my fears and doubts."

Thomas leaned forward, keeping Mallory's hand tightly in his. He noticed Emily taking Michael's hand as well, and a deep gaze passed briefly between them before Michael turned his attention back to Thomas.

"That's one of the main points, actually," Michael continued. "If you entertain doubt and fear, then you're giving Satan access to your weaknesses, and he's more than willing to play upon them. For me, I spent years fearing I would lose Emily, and I refused to talk about it or try to work it through. My fears ended up causing a deep rift in our relationship, and the adversity just kept getting worse. So, if I had it to do over again, I would have talked openly with Emily about my feelings right from the beginning. And I would have turned to the Lord to ask for help in overcoming my doubts and fears. When I came to my senses and did those things, I eventually got the answer I was looking for."

Thomas said, "And what was that, if I may ask?"

"My fears were replaced with peace. But," he added, lifting a finger, "through the years I have discovered something that I hadn't expected. I *want* to be with Emily forever, and I believe that I will be. But as the peace over that issue has settled in more deeply, I've come to realize that it really doesn't matter. If I trust in God, and I know that he will bless me for my righteousness, then I know that whatever happens, I will find happiness and be at peace. It's as simple as that. When it came right down to it, the problem was inside of me. And there were other things going on that contributed to what I was feeling."

Michael hesitated a moment, glancing at Emily as if to give her a silent warning. Her expression remained serene and supportive. Michael faced Thomas again, saying, "I had a rough time with the way Emily's first husband treated her. At the time, I wouldn't have thought that harboring such feelings had anything to do with my desire to be with Emily forever. But eventually I came to see that I had to forgive him for the things he'd done to hurt Emily. And I had to stop comparing myself to him, as if I could somehow justify in my mind that I was a better man than he was. Such judgments and decisions are not up to me. And once I came to terms with those things, it was easier for me to feel the Spirit, and to find peace."

Michael leaned back and smiled at his wife. Thomas sighed and did the same before Michael added, "You know, Thomas, eternity is a wonderful thing, as long as we don't lose sight of the reasons we're really here. Even if a lifetime is all you get with someone, it's still a lifetime. If I lost Emily now, it would break my heart. But I still wouldn't change a thing. The years we've shared have been more incredible than words could describe. I'm grateful for every minute we've had together. And I look forward to many years of life ahead . . . together."

Michael put his arm around Emily and hugged her close to him. When a minute passed in silence, Sean asked Thomas, "Does that help any?"

Thomas couldn't keep his voice from cracking as he said, "Yes, actually, it does . . . very much." He turned to look at Mallory. "I've never been happier. Mallory is the best thing that's ever happened to me."

"I can relate to that," Michael said, looking at Emily.

"Yeah, me too," Sean said, giving Tara a long gaze. Then he turned to Michael and said, "We've come a long way, eh?"

"Yes, I believe we have."

"Remember when I first came to your home for dinner, and I couldn't even cut my steak because my hands were practically useless?"

"I remember," Emily said, then she turned to Thomas and Mallory and briefly explained how Sean had been in a car accident that he shouldn't have survived. He'd completely recovered except for the damage done to his hands, which had been over his face when it had gone through the windshield. Michael went on to say that Sean had joined the Church against his father's wishes, and had been disowned. He'd come to Utah with practically nothing, and his hands had been useless. Sean added to the story that Michael and Emily had helped him through the necessary surgeries, and had become a second family to him.

The conversation shifted to Sean's wife, Tara, when it came up that she'd not been dating Sean for long when she'd been raped and ended up pregnant. Sean and Tara had actually gotten married, and they'd been together when she gave birth to that baby and gave it away to a couple who couldn't have children of their own.

Mallory felt Thomas's hand tighten around hers as they listened to the struggles these people had been through. Quite naturally,

Michael began talking of how he'd fallen in love with Emily before she'd married her first husband. And he'd spent more than a decade with a broken heart and a lot of bitterness. The story of how they'd come back together following her husband's death was deeply poignant. They talked about the miscarriages Emily had had, and how she'd nearly died during one of them. And then of the twins she'd given birth to following a severe car accident, and how one of them hadn't lived long.

When the conversation finally settled into a peaceful quiet, Michael said, "Yeah, I'd say we've all come a long way."

"And if my parents were here," Mallory said, "they could certainly add their two cents' worth."

Sean shook his head. "Mallory's parents have a story that could top us all. They've had more than their fair share of difficulties."

"Which reminds me," Emily said to Sean. "I've meant to ask you how Melissa is doing. Do you still keep in touch?"

"We do," Sean said, then he briefly explained to Thomas and Mallory that Melissa was a woman he had nearly married in college. She had ended up marrying a man who had lost his wife to cancer; the irony being that his wife was Melissa's sister. Eventually Melissa had also gotten cancer, but she'd beaten it.

"They're doing well," Sean finished. "Bryson and Melissa are a shining example of finding silver linings in the clouds of adversity that we come up against in this life."

"Well," Thomas admitted, looking at his wife, "I don't know about you, but all of this makes me feel very grateful. In spite of all we've been through, life is good."

"What *have* you been through?" Michael asked lightly. "Come on, it's not even midnight yet."

Thomas laughed softly. "All right. See if you can beat this." He briefly told the story of Mallory losing her husband to suicide, then discovering that it was likely tied into his pornography problem. And then how she'd lost the baby. Then Mallory told a brief version of the circumstances with Thomas and his brother.

"But," Mallory said, "like all of our stories, this one too has a happy ending. We're going to California the day after tomorrow. Thomas is going to baptize his brother."

They all expressed their pleasure, and Sean said, "That *is* a happy ending."

"Speaking of happy endings," Emily said, nudging her husband, "you didn't tell them about Jess and Alexa."

"Who?" Sean asked.

"My great-grandparents," Michael said. Then he turned more toward Thomas and Mallory, as if what he had to say applied to them somehow. "My great-grandmother, Alexa, was married to a man named Richard Wilhite. She kept fairly detailed journals, and the story of her life is quite fascinating. They weren't married terribly long when Richard was killed, and some time later she married my great-grandfather, Jess Davies. They had twins, Tyson and Emma. Emma is my grandmother. Of course, they weren't members of the Church, since I was the first to join in my family. So, when we did their temple work, we had Alexa sealed to both men."

"Can you do that?" Mallory asked.

"When it's done by proxy for the dead, yes," Michael said. "We have no way of knowing which husband Alexa is meant to be with eternally. From her point of view, she readily admits that Jess was the love of her life, and he was the father of her children. But in many cases, there aren't journals or personal records available in doing work for the dead. If she is sealed to both men, then it can be worked out properly on the other side. We have already requested that our children do the same for us once we're gone."

As Michael was apparently finished, Thomas drew in a deep breath in an effort to absorb this one more piece of information that helped assuage his own doubts and fears.

The things Michael Hamilton had said stayed with Thomas through the following days. He prayed to fully grasp what he'd been told, and to find his own peace related to the issue. And he was surprised at how quickly he found it. He couldn't say for certain how everything would turn out in the next life, but he knew it would be okay. And he felt an immeasurable gratitude for having had the opportunity to hear first-hand of this good man's experiences.

Somewhere between Utah and California, Mallory took hold of Thomas's hand, saying, "You're feeling better, aren't you, about the sealing." It wasn't a question.

"Yes," he said firmly, "I am. Somehow I just know that everything will be all right. We have a good life ahead of us, Mallory, and I intend to live it to its fullest." He kissed her hand and smiled warmly. "We are truly blessed."

"Yes, we are," she said. Then she grinned. "It's like Sean told us: this *is* a happy ending."

"Oh, no," Thomas said with that little chuckle he was famous for. "This is only the beginning."

AUTHOR'S NOTE

I began writing more than twenty years ago, with the hope that one day my books might actually be read. For many years I wrote one book after another, historical romantic stories that I believed could make a mark in the world. I had written several of these books before I ever considered writing an LDS novel. Through the years, as I've written for members of the Church, these historical novels have kept a special place in my heart. Now, with eleven books in print, I am still amazed at the avenues where my creativity has led me. Of course, there are still dozens of topics I could approach that would explore how, through the gospel, we can heal and find peace. But I am only one writer, and therefore I'm excited to see other writers exploring some challenging topics in the LDS market.

As for me, I am now going back in time. For those of you who have followed my stories since Michael Hamilton first left Australia to go to BYU, you'll recall him mentioning certain tidbits about his grandparents and great-grandparents. In truth, I created those characters long before I created Michael. Of course, they're not Mormons. (If they were, Michael wouldn't have been a nonmember.) My hope is that these books will branch out to a broader audience, giving the world an opportunity to read good stories with characters who believe in God, and actually suffer consequences when they sin.

Now the time has come to embark on a whole new journey. I can't find words to express my excitement at the prospect of sharing this part of my world with you. My next book will be set in Australia in the late eighteen-eighties, and after that I hope you'll travel with me to several other parts of the world. The adventure has just begun!

Enjoy and God bless,
Anita

P.S. And you should know that this year, Allison *will* be going home for Christmas.

ABOUT THE AUTHOR

Anita Stansfield is the #1 best-selling romance writer in the LDS market. Her first novel, *First Love and Forever*, was published in the fall of 1994, and the book was winner of the 1994-95 Best Fiction Award from the Independent LDS Booksellers. Since then, her best-selling novels have captivated and moved hundreds of thousands of readers with their deeply romantic stories and focus on important contemporary issues. *For Love Alone* is her eleventh novel to be published by Covenant. Anita has been writing since she was in high school, and her work has appeared in *Cosmopolitan* and other publications.

An active member of the League of Utah Writers, Anita lives with her husband, Vince, and their four children and two cats in Alpine, Utah. She currently serves as the Achievement Days leader in her ward.

The author enjoys hearing from her readers. You can write to her at:
P.O. Box 50795
Provo, UT 84605-0795

PLT

𝒫